I0688757

HIS FROZEN DREAMS
A ROCKY POINT WEDDING BOOK TWO

VANIA RHEAULT

 Created with Vellum

ABOUT THE BOOK

Jared didn't want to fall in love . . .

Then he picks Leah up from the airport, and he knows he has no choice.

When his wife left him to move to New York to work for popular fashion magazine, Jared swore he'd find a woman who loved living in Rocky Point as much as he did.

Leah is not that woman. He just has to make his heart believe it.

Leah hates living in New York . . . but she can't leave the big-city stress for small-town love.

Or can she?

With responsibilities she can't ignore, Leah will have to choose between the safe life she's been living in the city or risking it all for Jared's love and the wide-open spaces that will heal her heart.

CHAPTER ONE

"You want me to do what?"

Jared Hollister pushed a Louis Vuitton suitcase into the storage space of his red and white four-seater Cessna 172. He knew what the gold LVs scattered all over the brown case stood for—and what they represented.

"Get in?" he asked, slamming the hatch closed.

"I'm not flying in that. I saw *The Mountain Between Us*. If we crash, I'll die on a mountainside and wild mountain lions will eat my remains."

He shoved his hands on his hips. "He saves her. I read the book. Besides, we don't have mountains in Minnesota. If the plane goes down, I can land in a field and the worst that could happen is a cow would lick you. Disgusting, but not lethal."

She stood frozen in place, wearing black flats without socks, jeans that hugged her legs so tightly he was surprised she could bend her knees, and a thin bluish-grey coat that made her grey eyes shimmer like brand new quarters. But her brown hair lacked any luster, and an unhappy frown pulled at the corners of her mouth.

"What did you say your name was again?"

Marnie said she didn't want one of her bridesmaids driving to Rocky Point from Marengo, and she asked him to pick her up at the airport. The woman told him her name when he'd greeted her inside, but he'd forgotten it the minute he heard it. He wasn't much good with names, but this woman was a quivering ball of anxiety and he wanted to calm her down.

"Leah. Leah Bristow. Marnie asked me to be a bridesmaid, and I was stupid and said yes."

A gust of wind blew against her, and she shivered, pressing her hands to her stomach.

"Why? Don't you like her?"

"I don't have time for this."

"Lady, you look like a vacation will do you some good."

She glared. "Thanks a lot. I'm going to rent a car. I saw a rental agency inside the airport."

He shook his head. "I can't let you do that." Didn't want her to do that. As skittish as she was, she had no business being behind the wheel of anything. She'd end up in a ditch in ten seconds flat. "I promised Marnie I'd fly you to town. I'm Jared Hollister," he repeated in case she'd forgotten his name, too. "We're going to be seeing a lot of each other for the next little while. I'm a friend of James's, and a groomsman."

Thinking they should have had this conversation inside, he pulled off a glove and held out his hand.

She gripped it, her fingers as cold as ice without mittens.

A shock traveled up his arm when their hands connected, her soft skin rubbing against his callouses.

Static electricity.

That's all it could be in this cold, dry air.

"Come on. I'll get you there in one piece, I promise. I

have thousands of flight hours. But we need to hurry up. I told Marnie I'd have you at the resort in time for check-in, and I have stuff to do later."

He opened the passenger door of the Cessna his grandmother left him when she passed away. He used the plane often to fly between Rocky Point and the surrounding larger cities. This trip wasn't all about giving Leah a ride. He'd dropped off a few care packages as well as picked up a couple of boxes to bring back with him.

Looking a little green, she climbed in, and he helped strap her in, her warm breath grazing his cheek as he leaned over her.

He settled into his own seat, secured a headset onto his head, and started flipping switches.

The Marengo airport was on the small side and had light flight traffic, but today he needed to wait a few minutes for two planes to take off before the runway cleared.

"Here, you can put these on if you want to talk while we're in the air." He handed her another headset, and she looked at it like she'd never seen one before.

He concentrated on his pre-flight check, asking the tower for clearance to take off. An easy flight, they'd be in the air for less than an hour. The weather was good for it—blue skies, the sun sparkling against the snow. He patted Leah's thigh as they taxied down the runway. "It'll be okay. Maybe some slight turbulence because of the wind," he said, hoping she wouldn't throw up in his plane.

Relaxing into the seat after one of the easiest ascents he'd ever had, he flicked his gaze to his passenger. She adjusted the headset and white-knuckled the armrests.

"That wasn't so bad, was it?"

"No, I guess not," she yelled, and he flinched.

"You can speak normally. That's what the microphone is for," he said, tapping his.

"Sorry."

"No problem."

He enjoyed the flight, though he'd done the trip many times. He hadn't lied when he told her if they ran into any problems he'd land them in a field. There wasn't much between Marengo and Rocky Point. In every direction, farmland buried under a thick layer of snow stretched into the horizon.

"How do you know Marnie?" he asked.

"We work together. Kind of."

He didn't know how someone "kind of" worked with someone else, but he didn't ask.

"Did you really read the book?"

He huffed a laugh. Out of anything she could have asked him. "Yeah, I did, but I heard the movie was better."

For the first time since they met, she smiled, and it lit up her face.

And for the first time since he met his wife twenty years ago, his heart did a little skitter.

That was bad.

Very, very, bad.

Leah gradually relaxed and loosened her grip on the armrests. "There's nothing down there."

"I told you," he said, but pointed. "There's a big farm. Old Pete owns a lot of cows. We're about twenty minutes from town."

The tiny plane buzzed, and her seat vibrated with it.

When Marnie said she would have someone pick her up, this was the last thing she expected. He was cute, though. Light brown hair. The olive green work jacket he wore brought out the murky green shades in his hazel eyes. Scruff covered his jaw. Slim build. Strong hands.

Competent.

Married his high school sweetheart, she bet. Had a passel of kids at home. A couple of dogs.

Her stomach lurched. Her antacids were in her carry-on Jared stowed with her other luggage. She'd have to sit through the burn until she could unpack.

"Is this what you do?" she asked, gazing down to the ground. A tree here and there broke up all the white.

"Do you mean for work? I have a full-time job," he said. "Delivering packages is a side business."

"Is Rocky Point road-accessible?" Maybe that's why Marnie sent Jared to pick her up.

"Lady, this isn't Alaska, and I'm no bush pilot. Rocky Point's on a lake, yeah, but we have roads. Settle down, city girl. We have running water and electricity. We even go to the bathroom inside."

She blushed and looked away. A hard edge had found its way into his voice. He didn't like women who were from the city. That was okay. She wasn't here to stay and the last thing she wanted was another man.

Her bare ring finger on her left hand still felt strange, and she wasn't in any hurry to date. In fact, she may never want to again.

They sat in silence for the remainder of the flight. After landing—she had to admit he handled the plane like he'd been flying forever—and passing the plane off to a young man dressed in blue coveralls, he walked with her over the icy tarmac. The Rocky Point airport consisted of several large buildings that looked like they were used to store airplanes, hangars, she remembered they were called, one small building, and a traffic tower.

Jared loaded her suitcases into the extended cab of a gigantic white pickup truck that had a bright red snowplow attached to the front.

He opened the passenger side door and she tried to climb in, her flats searching for purchase on the running board. Her foot slipped, and he caught her around the waist, his solid chest pressing against her back. He didn't let go until she was sitting in the seat.

"Sorry," she murmured.

"No problem," he muttered in reply.

He let her fasten the seatbelt this time and slammed the door shut. Lifting a hand at the person who was driving his plane across the tarmac, Jared trotted around the hood of the truck. He climbed inside, started the engine, and turned on the heater, blasting cold air.

She tightened her thin coat around her.

"You're going to need warmer clothes unless you packed something," he said frowning, looking at her out of the corners of his eyes.

"This is all I have," she said, burrowing into the seat, shivering. "New York is apparently warmer than Minnesota."

"Marnie has some activities planned, and I would check with her. I don't think your definition of winter gear is going to cut it."

"I will." She'd have to. She couldn't be this cold for two weeks.

The outskirts of Rocky Point flew by her window as he drove them to the resort. The rustic building didn't sit on a mountain, but it offered a slope steep enough to allow for ample skiing. A gigantic lake stretched out in front of her. From this far away, people on the ice were black specks dotting the expanse of white.

"It's pretty."

"It's a nice spot," he agreed, stopping under the canopy and shifting into Park. "I'll help you unload, then I need to get going."

He pulled her four suitcases—two large ones, a smaller one, and her carry-on—out of the extended cab and set them just inside the sliding glass doors. His movements were confident and efficient. Almost rigid. She could read his body language . . . he didn't want to be here.

She thought she should thank him for the ride and his time, airplane fuel couldn't be cheap and he might have taken time off work to pick her up, and she dug in her purse and slid a fifty out of her wallet.

He scowled and pushed the money back at her. "I did it for Marnie. You can keep it."

Dropping her arm by her side, she said, "Okay, I'm sorry. Thank you."

"You're welcome. I'll see you tonight."

She blinked. "You will?"

"Marnie planned a small dinner. She wants us to get to know each other. I think she put a schedule in everyone's rooms. I gotta go. Nice to meet you, Leah Bristow."

She watched him drive away, his white truck disappearing down the hill.

Nice to meet you, he said. His tone implied it was anything but.

The first thing Leah did after the porter—actually, a kid wearing dress pants, a white dress shirt, and a purple and gold tie—brought her suitcases to her room was find her antacid and guzzle a few ounces. The stress of traveling made her ulcer flare up. Not a surprise since *everything* made her ulcer flare up, and her entire abdomen burned.

The second thing she did was call her grandmother.

"She's resting now, Miss Bristow."

"That's okay. Please tell her I arrived safely, and I'll try calling her tomorrow."

"I will. Enjoy your vacation," the aide said. "You needed one, I think."

She took a breath to respond—retort?—but the busy nurse already hung up.

She couldn't look that bad, she thought, studying herself in the full-body mirror attached to the wall near the bathroom door.

What had Jared seen when he looked at her? What would Marnie see? The rest of the bridal party?

She could blame the lines on her face and the exhausted shadows in her eyes on the day spent traveling, but that would be a cop-out.

Things had gotten bad, pure and simple. She didn't have anyone to talk to, and she wouldn't demean herself by paying someone to listen to her troubles.

Strong women could handle it.

Just because she didn't look the part didn't mean she wasn't capable.

A gift basket sat on a table near a large window that overlooked the slopes. She leaned against the cool glass and blew out a breath. She would enjoy the two weeks here. The resort featured all the amenities a five-star hotel in any city would offer their guests. Hot tub. Sauna. Fitness center.

Swimming pool. A dining room, a salon and spa, the ball-room where Marnie and James were holding their reception. The skiing, of course. A lounge boasting a full bar. She could sip on wine. It didn't aggravate her stomach too much if she kept an eye on how much she drank.

Marnie hadn't listed many activities on their schedule, though there were a few that gave her pause. Ice fishing? And there was no way in hell she was participating in the polar plunge, whatever the hell that was, even if it supported a local charity. The get-to-know-you dinner tonight sounded safe. A pool party she could handle, though she doubted she would actually swim. Sitting in the hot tub would be nice. Other things closer to the wedding like an evening putting together table centerpieces for the reception and an hour here and there to make sure the dresses fit would be okay. Otherwise, she was on her own to do as she pleased.

Catch up on her sleep.

Poke around town.

See Jared.

Whoa. Where did that come from? She definitely wasn't going to be spending any time with him. He'd taken a dislike to her and she didn't blame him.

Is Rocky Point road-accessible? She thumped her head against the window. Could she have sounded any more stupid?

People never get a second chance to make a first impression, but maybe she could smooth over what he thought of her. If she cared.

She didn't want to, but she did.

She hung up her clothes to let the wrinkles fall out of the dresses she packed. She needed to take a shower and rinse off the travel stink. Sip some more antacid.

Make the best of these two weeks and go back to New York with her head on straight.

Exhausted, she laid on the king bed, a fluffy pillow under her tired head.

Two hours later, after a collage of horrid dreams, she stumbled to the bathroom feeling like she hadn't slept at all.

At a table near the wall, Jared sat with James watching the Vikings game on James's phone. They were having a good year, the Vikings that was, but they would drop the ball, literally and figuratively, by the New Year and blow their chances at the Super Bowl like they always did. Their string of luck so far gave everyone hope, and James slapped his back after another touchdown.

Marnie slipped into the seat next to her fiancé, looked at the screen, then sipped his beer. "What do you think of her?"

He ignored her, thinking she was speaking to James. This would be James's first time meeting a couple of Marnie's friends.

"Jared?"

"What?"

"What did you think of her?"

"Of who?"

Her smile fell. "If you have to ask, then I guess she didn't make a very good impression."

"You mean Leah?"

She brightened. "You remembered her name, that's a start."

"Don't do this, Marnie."

"Don't do what?"

"James? A little help here?"

"The Vikes are still up."

Jared rubbed his hand over his eyes.

"I'm not doing anything." She poked her bottom lip out in a slight pout. "I was wondering if you two got along, that's all."

"We got along as well as two strangers who have never met each other before can get along."

"Then you won't mind if I ask you to take her into town tomorrow?"

"She can't catch the shuttle and go by herself?"

"I can take her, babe," James said, not moving his eyes off the little screen but giving Marnie's knee a quick rub.

"No, you can't. We're having breakfast with your parents in the dining room at ten. Your mom's freaking out because Auntie Ruth is threatening to fly in for the wedding after she said she couldn't come. All the rooms here are booked."

He sighed. "No, don't worry about it. I can do it. I have to work most of the day, but I'll have a couple of hours in the afternoon before going back for the game. The Polar Bears play tomorrow night."

Marnie nudged James's shoulder. "Maybe we can go. Remember some of the good old days."

James tore his gaze away from the game, smiled, and kissed her. "I remember you in that cute little cheerleading skirt."

"And I remember what you did to me after you got me out of it." She giggled.

"I need another drink," he said, standing. While he adored Marnie and James, their happiness bit at him. They'd waited to get married. Went to college, dated other people, settled into their careers. Found each other again when they were ready to make a commitment.

He hadn't done it that way.

"Can you tell her that you'll bring her into town? She's sitting in the corner with Autumn."

"Yeah. Don't worry about it. Whatever you need me to do, just ask." He didn't want Marnie to worry about anything. Doing the odd job was part of being in the wedding party.

"Thanks, Jared."

"Don't mention it," he mumbled as he headed toward the bar.

Leah sipped on a glass of red wine. When she'd stepped into the event room, Marnie screeched, excited to finally meet her in person, and for the first time since she accepted Marnie's invitation to be in the wedding party, she relaxed.

The seared steak served at dinner had been delicious and just standing in front of the decadent dessert buffet added ten pounds to her hips. Jared steered clear of her, but that wasn't anything less than what she expected. She knew no one besides Marnie and Jared, and when a woman who had a blonde, wavy bob sat next to her, she welcomed the chance to make friends.

"Hi, I'm Autumn Bennett," the blonde said, holding a tablet that had a detachable keyboard.

She reached out her hand to shake Autumn's. "It's nice to meet you," she said, hoping to put all her human resources training to work. If there was anything she could do and do well, even if it stressed her out, was chat up people she didn't know. Except Jared. She'd put her foot into that one, and he didn't seem willing to forgive her for it. "I'm Leah Bristow. Are you a bridesmaid?"

"Yeah. I grew up with Marnie here in town. How do you know her?"

"From work."

"Do you work in Decatur, then?"

"No. Technically speaking, I'm Marnie's manager, and I'm based in New York where her store's headquarters are located."

Autumn laughed. "That's right. I remember her saying something about that. Rocky Point must be a change for you."

"It is," she allowed, "but I think I'll like the change of pace. For a little while. What do you do?"

"I'm a reporter for the *Rocky Point Daily Journal.* I'm covering Marnie's wedding for our Lifestyles blog. To say not much goes on around here is an understatement. The paper tries to get as much mileage as it can from activities that take place around town. We get a couple hundred hits a day, nothing crazy. Can I interview you for that? Kind of a 'get to know you' feature for the wedding series I'm doing?"

"I'm not sure what there is to know, but sure. Part of being in the wedding and all that, right?"

Turning on her tablet, Autumn said, "Thanks. Weddings can go either way, you know? Some people stress out about having to miss work, or they can't afford the ugly dresses. Others say to hell with it and decide to have a good time. I'm thinking you've done the latter."

"I'm stressed out, but not about missing work. I had the vacation time coming and I haven't been out of the city in years. I'm not a good traveler though, and Jared, I forgot his last name, put up with me, flying me here from Marengo this morning. After a nap and a shower I'm feeling better, and I'm looking forward to relaxing these next two weeks."

"You look great! And that dress is lovely. You can't find clothes like that around here, even in Decatur."

While she answered questions about herself, she poured a little more wine into her glass. To her surprise, Autumn didn't seem to be in a hurry to talk to anyone else, storing her tablet and keyboard in a bag and settling in with her own glass of Prosecco and a piece of cheesecake after she finished the interview.

"What do you ladies got going on?"

A man dressed in black slacks, a black shirt, and a black and pink striped tie who had a camera hanging from around his neck sat next to them, and if she wasn't mistaken, Autumn straightened. Just a little.

She leaned her elbow against the back of her chair. "I'm entertaining Autumn with details about my boring life," she said, noting how he turned his body toward Autumn's.

"This is Cole. He runs a camera for the WDAZ nightly news, and he's a part-time photographer at the paper. Remind me to have him take a shot of you for the blog. This is Leah. She flew in from New York today," Autumn said, rounding out the introduction.

"Are you a groomsman?" she asked, shaking Cole's hand.

"Nope. Grew up here, but James and I didn't hang out in the same circles. Then he took off to go to school and never came back, like a lot of us."

"Oh. Who else is in the wedding party? I'm doing a terrible job circulating." She wasn't in a hurry to remedy the situation. Despite Autumn's compliment, she was bone-tired and knew she looked it.

Autumn sipped her wine. "Don't worry about it. You'll

have plenty of time to meet everyone. Well, you know me, now. Jared. Logan's a groomsman." She gestured to a tall blond man laughing with James and an older man Leah hadn't met yet, then to a brunette who had highlights streaking her hair sitting next to Marnie. "That's Callista Carter, but she likes to be called Callie."

"I'm the only one not from Rocky Point." Somehow that made her feel like even more of an outsider.

"No, Callie's from Decatur. She and Marnie are neighbors, that's how they know each other. Speaking of mingling, I suppose I better. I have more mini interviews to do for the blog. It was nice meeting you, Leah. We'll chat again."

"It was nice meeting you, too, and I'm looking forward to it," she said, sorry to see her go. She enjoyed talking to her. Autumn was a sweet woman, and she wondered about the slight pull of tension around her eyes and what would cause it.

She pasted a stiff smile onto her lips and Cole took a few quick snaps with his camera. She hoped he knew photo manipulation and would erase the dark circles under her eyes. Maybe add a little color to her cheeks. God knew she could use some.

Sitting the corner, she people-watched. Everyone looked happy, festive, the Christmas holiday three weeks away.

She sipped her wine, a dark red she hoped wouldn't bother her too much. Her stomach had calmed a bit, and she rubbed her belly. If she could get her stress and blood pressure under control during this trip, it would all be worth it.

"Don't you know nobody puts Baby in a corner?" Jared asked, sitting next to Leah at an empty table crowded with wineglasses and empty dessert plates. Half a piece of chocolate cake was left on her plate, and he wanted to tell her to eat it and put some meat on her bones.

He'd been able to avoid talking to her for most of the evening. Dinner had given him an hour reprieve, but he was getting tired of Marnie's "look," and he thought it best to make transportation arrangements with Leah before she went back to her room.

"Baby wanted to be in the corner. She was miserable without Johnny. Did you read that book, too?" Her eyes crinkled with amusement.

"No. My daughter's friend slept over and they watched it last night."

"My grandmother didn't allow it, and I watched it in secret. It took me a couple of times to realize she didn't let me because Penny had an illegal abortion. My grandmother's very conservative."

"I used it as a lesson in safe sex," he said.

Dammit. He didn't want to be talking sex with Leah. He barely knew the woman but he chuckled to himself when she blushed.

"You sound like a good dad."

"I try. Marnie sent me over to tell you I'll pick you up tomorrow and take you into town."

"You don't have to. The resort has a shuttle. One of the brochures in my room said it runs every two hours. I can take that. But I looked at the activities schedule and Marnie doesn't have anything going on I can't skip. Everything that's outside is voluntary. I'm not one for a polar plunge with or without clothes."

"That one would be without, and it would be interesting to watch you jump naked into the lake."

She sputtered. "That's what it is?"

He laughed and forked up a bite of her cake. "There are ways to warm up afterward. But you need a heavier jacket for the events that do need clothing. If you decide not to participate, you'll miss out on some fun things." He nudged the cake plate toward her and handed her the fork. "Eat some more cake. You're on vacation. You look like you're having a good time."

Her hair shimmered under the fluorescent lights, and her eyes didn't look so tired. He'd seen her laughing while she talked to Autumn, and it put roses on the apples of her cheeks. Or she could still be thinking about being naked, but either way, the color suited her.

Her dress was a plain black, letting her glowing complexion steal the show, but she wore a couple pieces of silver jewelry.

Understated but classy.

"Fun things?" she asked, lifting the fork to her lips. She smoothed the bite off the tines, and he shifted in his seat.

"Fun things?" he echoed. He looked away and gulped his beer.

"You said I don't want to miss the fun things." She took another bite.

"Yeah, you know. Ice fishing. Building snowmen. Skiing. Sleigh rides." He pictured her cuddled up with someone under a blanket singing Christmas carols as the horses pulled them through the woods. He must really be lonely if he was jealous of an imaginary man. It wasn't any of his damned business what she did. She could have a husband at home, and the way she kept rubbing at her belly, she was probably knocked up, too. Well, he could find out the first easy enough. "Are you married?"

Sadness crept into her eyes, and she slowly lowered her fork to the plate. "I was, but I'm not anymore."

He jerked his head in a nod. Fine. She wasn't married. At least he wouldn't feel like a slimeball for being attracted to her.

But that's all it would be. A simple attraction. He didn't have to do anything about it.

Pissed Marnie put him in the middle of this, he lurched to his feet. "I need work most of the day, but I can pick you up about four, if that isn't too late?"

"Okay," she murmured.

"Okay. See you tomorrow."

Jared kissed Marnie's cheek and shook James's hand, and he looked back at Leah before he left. She stared down at her empty plate, her shoulders trembling.

He made her cry.

Great.

Just great.

"What'd you make her cry for?"

"I didn't mean to." Guilt ate at him on the drive home, and when Briar asked how the meet and greet went, he confessed all.

"You'll have to make it up to her."

"Like hell I will."

"No, seriously, Dad. She doesn't know anybody here

except Marnie, and she's going to be busy doing bride stuff. You have to get her to do something or she'll sit in her room for two weeks. Come on."

"Why did I think talking to you about this would be a good idea?" He idly straightened the kitchen but Briar already did most of it while he was at the resort.

"Everyone always says we're two peas in a pod. You wanted me to tell you what you already knew. You don't need my permission to spend time with her. I've told you before it would be nice if you found someone."

"I don't need my daughter playing matchmaker."

Marnie would be doing enough of that over the next two weeks.

"I'm not. There hasn't been anyone around I'd want you to be with." She sat at the kitchen table and opened a can of soda. "But fresh blood, I can work with that." She wiggled her eyebrows.

"Don't get it into your head. She's from New York, and she acts like it. I don't need that, Briar. I really don't."

"I'm sorry. Mom—"

"Is off limits. I've told you that, too. Don't you have homework?"

"Yeah. Will you be at the game tomorrow night?"

"I'm at every game. Why?"

"Just wondering if you have wedding stuff to do."

"No. My job comes first, even if I did. Bills don't stop because you're a groomsman. In fact, they increase. Tux rental, a gift for the bride and groom, bachelor party—"

"All right, all right." She stood up and took her soda can with her. "I'm going over with Tiff and her mom. And don't forget, the SnowBall's a couple of days after Marnie's wedding. You said you'd fly me to Marengo to go shopping." She kissed him on the cheek. "I love you, Daddy."

"Ah-huh. I bet you do."

He knew she did, and he loved her more than anything too, but sometimes raising a teenaged daughter alone was a big pain in his ass.

Leah smoothed her hair and pushed her arms through the sleeves of the jacket she ignorantly thought would suffice. She'd never been to Minnesota before. How was she supposed to know that in the winter the high rose to maybe twenty degrees Fahrenheit, if they were lucky?

She stood outside the resort and waited for Jared, her breath coming out in white puffs, and she pushed her hands deeper into her pockets, trying to keep them warm. Shopping for warmer clothes wasn't a bad idea, and the "fun stuff" Jared said she didn't want to miss piqued her interest. Maybe he'd join her.

He stopped his massive truck under the stone canopy, and remembering his hands on her yesterday, she waved him off when he opened his door to help her inside. She threw her purse into the seat and climbed in, successfully, though ungracefully, after it. "I really could have taken the shuttle," she said, pulling the heavy door shut.

"That wouldn't have been very hospitable," he said, driving down the steep hill.

"You're not doing it to be hospitable," she said as she buckled her seatbelt. "Marnie's making you."

He laughed. "Guilty. But it's fine. Game days are always hectic, and it's nice to take a short break."

"What do you do? You never said." She liked the lines around his mouth when he smiled.

"I manage the sports arena."

"I have absolutely no idea what that means."

"I keep the skating rink maintained, the schedule for the ice on track. I do the employees' scheduling and keep the snack bars stocked up for the public when there're games and whatnot."

"What do you do in the summer?"

"The same. We have ice all year round."

"Oh, wow."

"On a much smaller scale, but yeah. Figure skaters have summer practice so they don't get rusty, hockey players practice for the next school year's tryouts, there're adult hockey leagues, and the curling club shares the rink, too. It's the coolest place to go in the summer when it hits ninety, and on odd calendar days, the public can walk around the arena."

"What made you decide to do that? Do you like it?"

"In a small town like this, it's because I got lucky. If I didn't like it, I'd be screwed, but it's okay. Comes with challenges like most jobs do."

He drove down Main Street, and she peered out her window at the Christmas lights and storefronts decorated for the holiday. "This is a cute little town. What keeps it going?"

He parked in front of a store called the Rocky Point Supply Company and said, "The resort mostly, now that the paper mill closed down. That was a sad day, and we lost a lot of good people to Marengo and Decatur. The mill provided hundreds of jobs, and the town's economy took a huge hit. Now we have to focus on tourism, and the resort's a big part of that. The slopes aren't open in the summer, obviously, but there's swimming and boating. Lots of fishing. There are a few smaller resorts in the area, too, and maybe I can show you around later. For now, let's get you a few things."

Shivering, Leah gratefully followed him inside the warmth of the store, but she groaned in disappointment. How would she find anything here? The lights blinked above her, dim and foreboding, the clothing fixtures looked like they were hundreds of years old, and worn brown carpet covered the floor.

A curvy older woman approached them wearing a Rocky Point Supply Company sweatshirt. "Hey there, Jared! What brings you away from the arena?"

"Hi, Helen. This is Leah. She's a bridesmaid in Marnie's wedding. She didn't think she'd need snow gear, but Marnie has a few things planned and she wants to join in. Leah Bristow, this is Helen Brunswick. She owns the Supply Company."

"Nice to meet you," she said, shaking the woman's hand, several large and gaudy rings decorating her fingers. "Do you run this place by yourself?"

"Since my Glen died, I keep one or two on staff, you know, to pitch in, but I don't get many shoppers anymore. They drive, or fly," she said, side-eyeing Jared, "to Marengo, or to one of the other smaller towns that has a mall. Rocky Point shrinks every year."

"I'm sorry to hear that. About your husband, I mean."

Helen patted her shoulder. "Thanks. I'm thinking about selling this place. It's not the same going it alone, is it?"

She rubbed at her stomach. "No, it's not." She didn't miss her ex-husband, but living alone took some getting used to. Even if it was calmer, more peaceful. There was a hint of loneliness under the quiet.

"Well, anyway, we don't want to keep Jared. Big game tonight."

"Yes, ma'am," he agreed, hooking his thumbs into the front pockets of his jeans. "Polar Bears versus the Marengo Jets. Biggest game of the year."

"They can handle it. They always do. What are you going to need, dear?" Helen asked, leading them toward the back of the store.

Jared answered for her. "A better jacket. Choppers, pacs, hat, scarf. Maybe some snow pants. Do you think you'll want snow pants? She should probably have snow pants."

She stopped in the aisle as he threw the strange words at her. "Wait. What are pacs? And choppers? I thought a chopper was a helicopter."

Helen laughed. "Choppers are mittens, at least, they are this far north. Pacs are boots. Here, we'll show you. What size are you?"

She sat on a bench and toed off her flats. "I'm a seven."

Kneeling at her feet, Jared set a large cardboard box Helen handed him on the floor and pulled out the cutest pair of boots Leah had ever seen. Made of creamy white leather, black laces zig-zagged through silver hooks, and white fur peeked out the tops. A thick black rubber sole made the boots waterproof. She couldn't wait to put them on. "Those are adorable."

He held one of her feet, and she froze, his warm hand molding to the arch of her foot. She met his eyes and yanked her foot out of his grasp. "I can do that." Her cheeks burning, she shoved her feet into the boots and stood.

"Make sure you have room for thick socks," he said, sitting back on his haunches.

Helen looked between them, but Leah stared at her boots. She didn't want to know what the woman was thinking.

"Then maybe I should go up a half size, or a size," she said, wiggling her bare toes.

"I'll grab you a seven and a half, and that should be perfect. Let's go look at jackets and snow pants. The choppers are up front, since they sell so fast this time of year. Kids are always losing them." Helen pushed her into the fitting room area, her arms full of a white parka, matching snow pants, and a white and silver hat that had a pompom attached to the top.

The stalls were tiny, and they all had cheap, streaky mirrors attached to the walls. She smiled when she read, "Sawyer loves Evie" scratched into a flimsy door. The whole store needed a good coat of fresh paint. An Outdoor Wonders store would never look like this.

She skipped using a stall and put everything on in front of a larger mirror in the hallway. There was a lot more room, and she needed it, shimmying and stumbling, shoving her legs into the snow pants. They'd definitely keep her warm, and she loved the parka, the fur trim of the hood brushing her cheek. She walked onto the selling floor sweating under all the layers. "I can barely move."

Jared glanced up from a display of wool socks. "You look . . ."

"Cuter than a bug in a rug," Helen finished. "You look like you're ready to build a snow fort or start a snowball fight."

"I feel warm enough to do it."

"Hon, when the wind is whipping in your face and you've been outside for longer than two minutes, it won't feel like enough, I can tell you that. But it's better than what you had. Choppers and a scarf. I have one that matches that hat."

Jared waited while Helen rang her up. The boots ended

up costing as much as the jacket, but the purchase was worth it. She wore the boots, jacket, choppers—glorified mittens in her opinion, but they were warm and soft on the inside—and hat out to the truck, and she did feel considerably warmer than before.

The sun had gone down while they were shopping, and the dark sky made it feel like the clock had already struck midnight.

"I'll drive you back to the resort," he said, easing away from the curb.

"Are you going to the arena now?"

"Yeah. We need to get ready for the game. Why? Did you want to go?" he asked, stopping for a red light.

"I've never been to a hockey game before."

"All right, but you'll need to find a way back. I stay pretty late on game nights to lock up."

"That's okay. I can take care of myself. I always have," she said softly. She could order an Uber, or, if they didn't have drivers in this little town, she could call a taxi. The shuttle might even be running, bringing guests to and from the game. "Thanks for taking me shopping. I feel bad for Helen. Her store needs some attention." She tried to be polite because she liked Helen and didn't want to insult her. It would have been rude to say the Supply Company was in utter shambles and it was no wonder why no one wanted to shop there.

"She's been talking about retiring for a while now. It's hard to give something your time and energy when you don't want to be there."

"You sound like you know that from experience," she said as he turned into a parking spot in the back of a gigantic two-story brick building.

"Sometimes you're not enough for someone," he said,

killing the engine and pushing the truck's door open. "Come on, I'll give you a quick tour before I get roped into the million things I have to do before the game starts."

She followed him into the building and wondered whom he hadn't been enough for. He mentioned a daughter, but he never brought up a wife.

He'd asked her if she was married. Maybe he wasn't, either.

He should have made her go shopping by herself, but how was he to know how adorable she'd look in her winter clothes? And how turned on he'd be? She looked like the Pillsbury Doughboy dressed in white, and it took everything he had not to scoop her up, kiss her senseless, and peel off all those layers. Slowly. One by one.

Which didn't bode well for him, since she didn't act like she'd give him the time of day if he asked. Maybe she didn't feel the sizzle he did. Or tried not to feel.

He was done with city women. He needed a woman who would be content here, making a home in a small, dying town. If she didn't want that, then he didn't want her.

"I'll show you around." He led her upstairs first, where the concession stands were located. The smell of popcorn, or rather, burnt popcorn, and hot dogs permeated the air. The popcorn machine was broken again, and he'd need to tinker with it before the crowds started showing up for the seven o'clock game. A hockey game wasn't a hockey game without popcorn.

"What's burning?" she asked, wrinkling her nose.

"The popcorn machine's busted. I'm going to have to

beg the school board to buy a new one. Do you want a hotdog?" he asked, just to make her squirm. Women like her didn't eat hotdogs. She proved his point when she grimaced.

"No, I'm good, thanks."

"This is where everyone comes between periods. We sell a lot of food up here."

She looked over the ice through the large viewing windows. "This is a nice place. The rink's huge. I like the polar bear."

He smiled at the enormous growling polar bear wearing a green and black parka—the school colors—encased in the ice. "That's the high school mascot. Rocky Point's all about hockey, like every other small, northern Minnesota town. Let's go downstairs."

He brought her down to the ice, waving to a few people the arena employed. The arena wasn't like Helen's store, and he had a lot of help.

"What's all this black stuff," she said, bouncing on the rubber.

"That keeps the skaters from having to wear guards on their skates to walk around. It's important to keep their blades sharp."

"Why?" she asked, pressing her nose against the plastic barrier to peer at the ice. It had kept a puck from hitting him in the face a time or two.

"They skate better. You don't cut steak with a dull knife, right? You don't shave with a dull razor. You'd cut your legs up." He cleared this throat. Better not think about her legs. "Sharp blades grip the ice. We have a skate sharpener here, two bucks a pair. We charge a minimum to keep the machine maintained. Did you want to try skating while you're here? In town, I mean? The rink has open skate on Wednesday and Thursday mornings. It's five dollars for two hours, but I know someone who could get you in for free."

"I would maybe try that. Do you skate?"

He shook his head. "Not often. I did when my daughter was small. She loved it and was always begging me to bring her out. She's sixteen and takes figure skating lessons now. She's on the cheerleading squad, and you'll see her skate before the game and between periods. When you live here, the 'fun stuff' loses its appeal and you're stuck in the day to day of normal, monotonous life."

She leaned against the plastic barrier. "Why don't you move then? You said it yourself. The town's dying. Why stay?"

He stepped closer, took off his glove, and traced her lips. They were becoming chapped from the cold. Pain clouded her steely grey eyes. Someone had hurt her.

He couldn't let her do that to him. If he fell, even just a little bit, she'd have the power, and he wouldn't do that again.

"Because my heart's here. In the people. In the way we take care of each other. In the simple way we live. In the way my daughter and I have roots here. Where's *your* heart, Leah Bristow?"

CHAPTER TWO

Jared sat on a low stool and poked around the back of the popcorn machine, his cell phone on speaker while he waited to talk to maintenance support. He should have replaced it before the biggest game of the year, but budget cuts forced him to repair the machine using an ample number of swear words, spare parts, and bubble gum. His luck and his patience were close to running out.

"Hey, boss, there's trouble."

Billy stood behind the counter, shifting on his feet.

"What's up?"

"Mitch Sinclair's sitting in the bleachers."

"Who?" Jared picked up his phone and glared at the screen, like that would make someone answer his call any faster. If the rep could talk him through how to replace the temperature regulator, he could maybe get a few more games out of the stupid thing without burning any more popcorn.

"Mitch Sinclair, the guy . . ."

He rubbed the back of his hand over his forehead. "Billy, I'm on the phone. We're already running low and we're not even done with the first period. People are going to be pissed if they can't get a refill."

"Yeah, I know, but it's getting bad out there."

"What do you mean 'bad?'"

"No one wants him here. He's got a woman with him, but lots of people are talking trash. Ed keeps circling around like a shark, giving him the evil eye."

"Shit."

Things clicked into place and he hung up. He'd have to call back. Known for his short fuse, if something, or someone, made Ed Dunlop unhappy, it wouldn't take much for him to act on it.

He stood in front of the viewing window, and Billy pointed to the left side of the arena, near the top. It wasn't difficult to pick out Mitch and his date. People watching the game were giving him a wide berth as to not be mistakenly associated with the man. Ed paced near the ice while he glared up into the stands.

"He's allowed to be at a game, Billy."

Billy, a high school kid who did odd jobs around the area to help his parents pay for hockey equipment, pursed his lips. "I got nothing to say about Mitch Sinclair, 'cept my dad blames him for what happened."

"Well, I don't, and he's allowed to go to a game that's open to the public." He pulled his phone out of the back pocket of his jeans and brought up Ed's cell number. Through the viewing window, he watched the older man who acted as security at the bigger games answer his phone.

"Ed, it's Jared. I'm at the window."

Ed looked up at him.

"Leave Mitch Sinclair alone. He's got a right to be here, like anyone else."

"He's causing some shit, Jared," Ed said, his beady eyes focused on him.

"I don't care. He's not doing anything except watching the game. He's got a date with him too, doesn't he? She's one of Marnie Zimmerman's bridesmaids, I met her last night. Leave them alone. I mean it."

Ed disconnected without agreeing, jabbing angrily at his phone, and he sighed. "He's not going to listen, but I'm hoping if it's as bad as you say it is, Mitch will leave on his own."

It was cowardly, taking the low road, but he had other things on his mind, like the fucking popcorn machine he'd been told he couldn't replace until the next fiscal year.

"You did what you could," Billy said. "The period's almost over. I'm gonna see if any of the players need anything."

"See you later," he said absently, keeping an eye on Ed who marched in the opposite direction of the viewing window.

Redialing the popcorn machine's manufacturer, he sat on the stool behind the concessions counter and let his thoughts drift to Leah while he listened to the hold music.

Leah sat on a hard, wooden bleacher near the ice. Speakers pumped pop music into the arena, and cheerleaders on skates wearing dark green leg warmers shook their pompoms and butts with equal enthusiasm. The game program listed the cheerleaders in alphabetical order, but it didn't help her identify which girl was Jared's daughter.

People filled the bleachers, and she scooted over when someone plopped next to her.

"No need to move," Autumn said, handing her a disposable cup. "Unless you don't want to sit next to me."

"I suppose I'll risk it, since you were nice to me yesterday. What's this?" The contents smelled sweet, and she sniffed in appreciation and suspicion.

"Hot chocolate. Can't freeze your ass off watching senseless violence, I mean, a hockey game, without a sugar rush."

She laughed. She liked Autumn and hoped they would stay in touch after she went home. "What are you doing here if you don't like hockey?"

"I'm covering it for the Lifestyles page. Sports will get the technical scoop, but I'll blend in the people aspect. Marnie and James are around somewhere, and Callie said she'd be here with Mitch, the resort's maintenance man. She said something about having a plugged drain yesterday. I said I'd try my best to watch out for them, but it's going to be difficult with all these people. You should've met up with them, then you wouldn't have been sitting by yourself."

She sipped the hot chocolate and the rich flavor flooded her mouth. She swallowed. "I came with Jared. Kind of."

"Oh, really?" Autumn sipped her hot chocolate as well, the black plastic cover hiding her smile, but her twinkling eyes gave her away.

"He brought me here after helping me pick out new clothes at the Supply Company." She wiggled her feet in her boots and held out her free hand. "I have pacs. And choppers." She tensed, waiting for Autumn to make fun of her, but she nodded in approval.

"You'll be warm. For tomorrow."

"What's tomorrow?"

"Ice fishing. You're going to go, aren't you? Marnie's and James's parents have ice houses, but it's supposed to be nice. You can sit outside and fish without one."

"Oh." She didn't have any idea what Autumn was talking about, but she was on vacation and she was willing to give anything a try. "Sure, I'll be there."

"Great! Breakfast at the resort, and then we'll spend the day fishing."

"You're going, too?"

"Yeah. I'm covering it for the blog. It's great I can do bridesmaid stuff and get paid for it."

"That's nice. Is Cole here?"

"Yeah. Somewhere. He's filming clips for the news."

"Are you two a couple?" she asked as the cheerleaders skated off the ice. While they'd been talking, people filled the bleachers to capacity and some began chanting, "Pol-ar *Bears!* Pol-ar *Bears!*" and others from the opposing team screamed, "Jets! Jets! Jets!"

The players skated around the ice holding their sticks above their heads, mouth guards dangling from their helmets. The announcer began to introduce the players and who would sing the "Star-Spangled Banner."

Autumn leaned over to shout in her ear. "No, we're not. He used to be married to my sister."

The enthusiastic crowd made it impossible to say anything more. The players were wild, and quite a few times she was afraid for the . . . her first thought was to call him an umpire, but that was baseball. The referee. If she didn't mind feeling stupid, she'd ask Jared after the game to make sure.

In the middle of the third inning—no that was baseball again, Jared called it a period—Autumn picked up her things. "I'm going to head out and beat the rush. The Bears have this locked, anyway. Do you want a ride to the resort? I don't mind dropping you off."

Leah weighed her options. Jared would be busy after the game and she should go while she had a ride, but she wanted to see him. She felt like their conversation wasn't over and her feelings were a muddled mess. She shouldn't have to defend herself because she liked living in a big city. She rubbed her belly, her ulcer burning. Okay, maybe she didn't like living in the city, but she couldn't do anything else.

"No, I'll stay 'til the end, but I appreciate the offer."

"You're welcome. See you tomorrow, then. And check with Marnie. I think she wants everyone to meet for breakfast at ten."

"I will. Thanks for the hot chocolate."

Autumn waggled her fingers as she inched into the aisle. Two fighting hockey players slammed into the plastic barrier, and she bobbled her cup, her heart hammering. Autumn laughed. "Careful."

She watched the rest of the game, clapping and cheering with the others when the Polar Bears won four goals to zero. The crowd thinned quickly, and it wasn't long before she sat by herself, a few people standing around chatting. Feeling stranded, she thought maybe she should have caught that ride with Autumn after all.

She scanned the people who were left, hoping to find someone she knew, though the only place she would have met anyone was Marnie's meet and greet last night. Luckily, Marnie and James were standing in a group on the other side of the arena laughing and talking. Relieved, Leah stood and waved, hoping to catch their attention. Marnie glanced away, noticed her, and waved back. But then one of the people they were speaking to turned around, and Jared met her eyes. He pointed at her, and she took that to mean to stay put. She sat on the bench again and waited as he slid across the empty ice.

"You stayed," he said, opening a door in the side of the rink.

"Yeah. I wanted to see the Polar Bears win," she said.

And you.

"Do you want to catch a ride with Marnie and James? They said they'd take you back to the resort if you were ready to go."

She shoved her hands between her knees. "If I stay, will you take me back?"

He flicked the pompom on her hat. "Sure, if you don't mind waiting. I have to run the Zamboni, then I can drive you."

She tingled, happy he didn't make her leave. "What's a Zam . . . bon . . . i?"

"Come on, city girl, I'll show you."

She didn't know what a Zamboni was. That's the kind of woman he was hanging out with. But despite the glaringly obvious clue they couldn't have less in common, he was pleased she stayed.

If he could convince himself she'd be a fling and nothing more, maybe he'd feel okay talking her into bed because God knew, he needed something. Anything. He sighed. He already knew it would be pointless to try. He wasn't that kind of guy.

"How was your shift?" Leah asked.

She clomped behind him as he led her to the storage

room where they kept the Zamboni. It was his job to clean the ice before locking up for the night. It's why he got home so late—the machine took forever. Usually, he cranked the music in the arena to have something to listen to, but tonight he'd talk to Leah.

"Just a few hiccups. The popcorn machine, mainly. Did you . . . notice anything while you were watching the game?" he asked. Maybe Mitch and the commotion he caused hadn't been as bad as Billy made it out to be. He hadn't heard anything more about Ed, and he hoped the whole thing passed without incident.

"No. Well, what do you mean?"

She watched the game on the opposite side of the arena from where Mitch and his date sat. If she hadn't heard anything, that was a good sign things hadn't gotten out of hand.

"An undercurrent of hostility? Anything like that?"

"No. Was there trouble tonight?"

"I hope not. Forget about it," he said, pulling the doors open wide. He changed the subject. "This is a Zamboni."

"What does it do?" she asked, circling the machine.

"It repairs the ice. Sometimes people call it an ice resurfacer. It sprays water over the ice and fills in the gouges the skaters make. We have figure skating lessons in the morning, and they'll need smooth ice or they could trip and fall. Falling on the ice hurts."

"That's . . . cool, I guess," she said, pushing her hat farther up her forehead.

He laughed. "Nice pun, but no, it's not. It's pretty boring." He paused. "I'll let you drive it, if you want."

She perked up at that. "Yeah?"

"Yeah. Come on."

He opened a wide door in the side of the ice rink to let

the Zamboni through, and he steered them on course before giving her the wheel. There wasn't much standing room, but her boots easily fit near his. They swapped places and he leaned his ass against the dash near the steering wheel. "Did you have fun tonight?"

"This is the best part," she said, staring steadily at the ice, her fingers gripping the wheel. The machine's engine grumbled, but she raised her voice loud enough to be heard. A couple of people standing on the upper deck waved, and he knew he'd be grilled later.

He wasn't seen with a woman very often, and when it happened, it made news. Good thing Cole and Autumn left, or there'd be a picture and blog post about them on the *Rocky Point Daily Journal*'s website in the morning.

"Should I be worried about my job?" he teased.

"No, but . . . I've been thinking about Helen."

"What about her?"

"Do you think she needs help?"

"Doing what?"

"Well . . . She said she was thinking about selling her store, but she won't get much with the condition it's in."

"You want to help her with her store? What did you say you did again?"

"I'm an HR director."

"And that makes you qualified?" he asked through clenched teeth. Her wanting to help Helen made him mad, even if the gesture was sweet. She'd worm her way into the community, into his life, and after she left, the hole would be bigger than before.

Just like last time.

"I'm HR for a large chain of sporting good stores. Outdoor Wonders? Have you heard of them?" She stopped speaking to turn the corner, and he righted the wheel when she bumped into the side of the rink.

"Yeah, I have."

"I hire the stores' management. I hired Marnie. That's why I said I kind of knew her. Meeting her at the meet and greet last night was the first time we've met in person. We got to know each other over email and Zoom. But, anyway, I know how a store like that should look. It would take a few days to get things in order, but it wouldn't be difficult. Marnie walks through her store every day to reach her office. She knows how a store like that should look, too. She could help Helen."

"She's too busy with the wedding."

"True. It's all talk." She shrugged. "Helen wouldn't appreciate me sticking my nose into her business anyway."

He braced his hands against the dash while she finished the wide oblongs that tightened and tightened until all she needed was the final strip down the middle. They reached the opening in the side of the rink, and Jared waved to Billy who usually stayed in case Jared needed anything.

The main lights went out, leaving the security lights glowing around the arena, the orange reflecting in Leah's grey eyes.

"Let's park this, and we can get going, too."

She stood up, and he moved around her, but instead of taking her place behind the wheel, he leaned into her, the subtle scent of her shampoo catching his nose.

"This is a bad idea," he murmured, brushing his thumb over her lips.

"Yeah, it is," she said, but she told him something else when she tilted her head, asking him to kiss her.

Her breath fanned his cheek, sweet, mixing with the cool scent of the water glistening on the rink.

If she stayed, this could be his life. Her, his daughter, and the ice.

But city women were cold, colder than the ice below them, frozen. He'd spent most of his marriage trying to thaw one out. It didn't work.

Goddamned he would do that again.

Setting his jaw, he shoved himself into the seat. "Get down. I'll meet you at the truck. Do you remember where it is?"

"Y-yes. I think so."

He yanked his keys off the bunch hanging from his belt loop. "Start it up, will ya? It's cold out there."

Grasping his keys, she stumbled off the Zamboni, slipping on the thin layer of freezing water under her boots.

He fumed as he parked the machine and turned off the light in the storage room. He was being a dickhead. It wasn't her fault she twisted his thoughts all up.

By the time he closed and locked the door, she was gone, and silence greeted him . . . along with his own guilt.

"Hey, great game!"

The next morning, squinting against the sun as he walked across the frozen lake, Jared held up his hand in acknowledgment. Like he had anything to do with it. But after every home game no matter if they won or lost, everyone always gave him undeserved credit. As if he were some kind of ice god. Keeper of the Ice.

"Coach has a good team this year," he said, his boots crunching over the snow. He searched for James. He knew where James's parents parked their ice house. In theory. In reality, all the houses looked the same and he could be wandering for hours.

"Heard you got caught kissing one of Marnie's bridesmaids," Missy Iverson said, grinning, holding a disposable cup of coffee and standing near her grandson who was cutting into the ice to make a fishing hole. A baker at the larger of the two grocery stores in town, Missy would be making James's groom's cake for the rehearsal dinner and the four-tiered monstrosity for the wedding reception.

He scoffed at the comment. He didn't need to be reminded of how he treated Leah last night, and if people wanted to start rumors that they were a couple, he wouldn't stop them. He'd lived in Rocky Point all his life and knew the harder someone tried to deny something, the truer it became.

He finally found James's dad's fish house and sank into one of the purple and gold canvas Vikings chairs positioned in a semi-circle around a few fishing holes, white and red bobbers floating.

James sat in another, sipping a beer, though it was barely eleven, mumbling about hair of the dog. Sunglasses shielded his eyes against the glare.

The sun blazed against the white, and the dazzle gave him a splitting headache. He'd been up half the night wrestling with a guilty conscience. He needed to find Leah and apologize. The apology would go a lot further if he told her why she made him angry. It wasn't any of her business, but eventually she'd hear the story with or without him. Especially if people thought they were sleeping together, ah, seeing each other.

"Where's everyone else?" he asked, scanning the lake. The sunny weather made the day a popular one for fishing, and people scattered around the ice, some sitting in ice houses, some out in the open. The temperature hovered in the upper twenties, and if he hadn't felt like shit, it would have been a pleasant way to spend the day.

"Probably sleeping," James growled, slouching in his seat. "What I would be doing if Marnie didn't insist we do this."

"Late night last night?"

"We went to the Viking after the game and met up with some friends. Stayed longer than we should have."

"Why didn't you ask me to go?"

"Someone said you went to the resort with Leah, and Marnie said not to bother you. You didn't?" His eyes blood-shot, James looked at him over the rims of his sunglasses.

He scowled. "No. I gave her a ride, that's all."

"Huh. Heard you had hot sex on the Zamboni. That's kinky. Cold, but kinky."

Jesus Christ. He went from kissing to having sex in ten minutes, and his dick stirred at the thought. "No. I got a little short with her and I need to apologize."

James, his good friend since Kindergarten, nodded. He knew the score. "You tell her about Rita?"

"Why would I? After the wedding she's going home."

"You don't want her to?"

"I've only known her for a couple of days. Give it a rest, okay?"

"All right . . . I'm just saying, people said they saw you pretty cozy last night."

"I let her clean the ice, that's all."

"Ah-huh."

He glowered, but sunglasses hid James's eyes and his head was tipped back, resting against the edge of his canvas chair. "Is anyone fishing, or are we gossiping like a bunch of girls?"

"I'm fishing," James mumbled.

"I meant for fish."

"Hey, Jared. Heard the Bears weren't the only ones who scored last night. About time, son."

Greg Larson, the owner of the small, and only, hardware store in Rocky Point, didn't wait for a response and hurried by them.

"Why is my sex life everyone's business all of a sudden?" He wished he had a cup of coffee.

"Nothing else to do," James said.

He scoffed.

"No, seriously. Leah's the first woman you've spent time with since Rita left. They're happy for you."

"Then they need to stop being happy. She's got a life and a career in New York. Why does anyone think she'd stay in this shit town for any longer than necessary?"

"'Shit town?'" James asked. "You don't mean that. You love it here."

"That's what Rita called it, and those two women are exactly the same. I'll do my part as a groomsman, but stop shoving us together. And that goes for Marnie, too."

"You got up on the wrong side of the bed this morning. I guess because you didn't get any," James said. "Marnie hooked a Keurig up to the generator. Go get some coffee. Missy brought out some donuts and I told Marnie to set aside a Boston Cream for you. Maybe the sugar will make you feel better. After you're done groveling, bring me back a cup, will you? Fishing's exhausting."

"Life's exhausting," he said, but because a cup of coffee was too much to resist, he heaved himself out of the chair and did as he was told.

Besides, he'd never turn down a Boston Cream.

Leah sat in her chair, a cup of coffee sitting in the little net cupholder in the chair's arm. It all seemed so primitive. A generator for the coffee machine. Trying to catch fish out of a hole carved into the lake by some weird twisty machine called an auger. Looking into the hole creeped her out, water sloshing over the top. Every once in awhile someone would pull a fish out of the lake, and she'd curl her lip in disgust. They were long, spotted, and ugly. Marnie called them sturgeon, but she didn't care what they were. Though she was far from being a vegetarian, she ate meat all the time, she'd steer clear of the fish people were pulling out of this lake.

"Have fun at the game last night?" Marnie asked, holding a cup of coffee, standing over her fishing pole, and staring at the bobber.

"Yeah, the game was interesting, Autumn explained the rules. Those kids are rough," she said, surprised watching the hockey game hadn't bored her . . . or given her a heart attack.

"We heard you and Jared had a good time, after the game. He let you drive his Zamboni." Marnie dissolved into a fit of giggles.

"We need to cut her off," she told Autumn. "She's had too much caffeine."

"I need it. We went downtown to the bar last night and met up with some old high school friends. I can't believe the people James and I went to school with have real jobs. They're running this town. We've all grown up." Marnie mock sniffled, wiping away an imaginary tear with her mitten.

"Don't change the subject," Autumn said, clutching a pen in her gloved hand. "I want to know what happened last night between Leah and Jared."

"Nothing happened. He let me drive that machine and it was fun. Then he brought me back to the resort. We talked a little bit about nothing, and that was all."

"Oh, that's disappointing." Marnie bent down and gave her fishing pole a wiggle in its bright red holder.

"No, it's not. He's a nice guy, but . . ."

Autumn leaned closer. "But what?"

"I get a feeling he's not available. He acts very closed off."

"He's been hurt," Autumn said. "His ex-wife wasn't very nice."

Marnie frowned. "That's not true. She's one of my best friends. Not everyone's cut out for small-town living."

"Did you ask her to be a bridesmaid?" Autumn asked, Marnie's retort not affecting her.

"As a matter of fact, I did. She said it would be too awkward because Briar told her James asked Jared to be a groomsman."

"Did she grow up here, too?" she asked.

"Yeah, but like I said, small-town life isn't for everyone."

"Maybe he never got over her." That made sense, and now that she knew the story, she'd stay away from him. It's not like she was going to have a happy, cozy life here, either. After the wedding, she'd go back to the city and live the same crappy life she'd been tolerating before.

"It's been a long time, but some people don't," Autumn said softly, smiling in sympathy.

"Then I hope one day he can and finds someone who likes it here." She took a deep breath of the crisp, clean air.

The frozen water spread out for miles, nothing marring the view except dots of people enjoying the day. The sun shined in the cloudless bright blue sky. The clothes she bought at the Supply Company kept her warm. The coffee tasted amazing.

She couldn't stay, but she could understand why people lived in this little town.

"Autumn, you stayed," she said.

"Well, I moved to go to the University of Decatur and worked at the *Herald* for a few years, but then I was stupid and came back after my fiancé and I broke up. A man I was in love with a long time ago moved back here after he graduated, and I thought maybe I had a chance, but I found out he wasn't available. At least, not in the way I needed him to be. And I was even more stupid and bought a house. The housing market here hasn't been the same since the paper mill closed and I probably wouldn't be able to sell it, not for as much as I'd need to. But I'm slowly being given more responsibility at the *Journal* and Rocky Point's within driving distance of some bigger towns. That works for now. It's going to have to."

She patted Autumn's arm. "I'm sorry. That *does* suck."

Shrugging, Autumn said, "It is what it is."

"Yeah."

Autumn started writing in her notebook, and Leah dozed in the sun, let the hum of conversation from people nearby wash over her.

Marnie's dad stopped to talk, and Cole took a couple of pictures of them sitting around. Mugging for the camera, Marnie pretended to pull a big fish out of the water, but when her hook was empty, everyone laughed.

A full bladder roused her to her feet, and she stepped inside the fish house to use the bathroom. Or rather, a bucket that had a toilet seat attached to the top. It was better than going in a hole in the ground, or ice, but not by much. She had to take off her jacket and undo her snow pants in order to pull down her fleece-lined leggings, but the effort was worth it. She used a pump of hand sanitizer someone courteously left near the bucket and made another cup of coffee, adding the chocolate creamer Marnie shoved into a pile of snow to keep cool.

She fastened the lid to the cup, and she peeked her head out and asked if anyone else wanted more coffee.

Jared stood chatting with Marnie, and catching her eye said, "I wouldn't mind, if it's not any trouble."

Jared had to give Leah points for manners.

"Sure. Black? Or we have chocolate creamer."

"Yeah, black's fine. Thanks."

She didn't smile, but she didn't spit at him, either.

"We're all pretty bummed you two didn't get it on last night," Marnie said when Leah closed the fish house's door.

"You and half the town. You asked me to help her out, and I did. She's got her bearings now, and she knows every-one. I don't need to be her chaperone anymore."

Marnie frowned. "Is that how you felt? I'm sorry if you don't like her, but she's really nice."

"Yeah, she is, and I like her fine, but that doesn't mean I'm falling in love."

"You don't have to, dummy," Marnie said, rolling her eyes and slapping his shoulder. "Just be friends with her, for

God's sake. Why does it have to be all or nothing with men?"

"Because women usually expect it to be," he retorted. But he considered. Marnie had a point. Except . . . the tired pull around the corners of her eyes and the way her shoulders shook when he'd made her cry at the meet and greet, they did things to his heart that said more than friends.

Marnie narrowed her eyes. "You're saying Leah wants more than friends? Did she tell you that?"

"No," he muttered.

"Then stop making this complicated. Besides, you're right. She knows everyone now, you don't have to babysit her anymore, and this is the last group activity for a couple of days. I want everyone to have fun, relax, maybe do some skiing. You don't have to be around for that, unless you and James have plans."

"James is hungover."

"I better go check on him."

"Bring him some coffee, will you? He asked me to, but after I say goodbye to a couple of people, I need to head to work."

Marnie reached up on her tiptoes and kissed his cheek. "You're one of my good friends. I care about you, and I'm sorry things didn't work out between you and Rita. She always had stars in her eyes. Even when we were kids. I want to see you happy."

"I am happy."

"Are you, though? Here's Leah with your coffee."

"I need to interview some more people for the blog," Autumn said, standing and gripping her notebook and pen. "I'll catch you guys later."

"I'm going make James some coffee and poke at him like the loving wife I'm going to be," Marnie told Leah, who was approaching them holding two cups of coffee. One wafted a sugary scent that smelled like chocolate, the other a rich blend that made his mouth water.

"Okay," Leah said, eyeing him. "I'll see you later."

"Yep." Marnie slammed into the fish house, and an awkward silence settled between them. He reached out for a cup of coffee and Leah handed him one, their fingers brushing.

"Thanks."

"No problem. Marnie buys a coffee brand I've never heard of before, but it tastes really good."

"That's good." He winced. He sounded like such a moron.

"I'm going to head back to the resort. I didn't get a lot of sleep last night and I could use a nap."

"Yeah. Listen, before you go, can I talk to you for a second?"

"Isn't that what we're doing? Talking?"

He started walking away from Marnie's parents' fish house. They were fishing about a mile from the resort, and it loomed on the hill that gently sloped into a beach in the summertime. In the winter, the angle made an easy passageway for snowmobilers to reach the ice.

"Yeah, but I wanted to apologize for last night. I didn't mean to be . . ."

"An asshole?" she said.

He shot her a look, squinting against the sun. "I don't think I would have put it that harshly, but yeah. I was a jerk, and I'm sorry."

"It's okay. Autumn and Marnie, we weren't gossiping about you or anything, but they told me . . . You haven't gotten over her, your ex-wife, I mean, and that's fine. I mean," she said, fumbling. "I got out of a sticky marriage myself, not long ago, and I'm not looking . . . don't feel like I'm . . ." She met his eyes.

Tears shimmered, and he called himself every kind of stupid. Her lips trembled, and he wanted so badly to kiss her and smooth away the hurt. To hold her and tell her things would be all right. But he didn't have the right to tell her that. He had no idea what was going on in her life to make her any kind of promise.

"Yeah. I understand. Do you want a ride back to the resort? My truck's parked over by where James is fishing."

"Ah, no. I'll walk. It's not that far, and I need the air and time alone. But thanks." Her smile wobbled, and he bit the inside of his cheek. He wouldn't kiss her. He *wouldn't* kiss her. Now that they were on the same page, he wouldn't confuse her. Or himself.

"Okay. I'll ah, see you later then." Without group activities to throw them together, he wouldn't have an excuse—reason, dammit—to see her, and not having a plan had him grasping at straws. Like a high school kid taking the long way to class hoping to bump into his crush.

"Yeah. Can you tell Marnie I'm going back? I don't want her to worry."

"Sure. No problem."

"Thanks."

She turned toward the resort, a dejected slump to her shoulders. Wearing all white, she blended into the snow, and in less than five minutes he'd lose her against the glare of the horizon.

He needed to pick his truck up and put in his hours at the arena. The late start would mean he'd be there for the senior figure skating practice that evening. It would be nice to see Briar, even for a few minutes. At sixteen, she came and went as she pleased. Sometimes they crossed paths, sometimes they didn't. After the game last night, she'd already been sleeping when he came home from dropping Leah off at the resort.

Maybe Leah would want to stop by, watch the girls. No. She didn't want to spend all her time at the arena. He was lucky he talked her into the hockey game. Plus, he'd be working and wouldn't be able to sit and talk.

But it wouldn't hurt to ask. He could spend his lunch break with her, at least, tease her into trying a hotdog. The thought made him smile. He spun on the snowy ice to shout for her to wait up, but she'd vanished. He scanned the ice, but he didn't see her.

He blew out a breath. She must have caught a ride after all. An ATV, a snowmobile, they zigzagged the ice all day. Anyone going in the direction of the resort could have given her a lift.

He should take that as an omen. He didn't need to spend any more time with her than necessary.

Disappointed, and a little worried, he searched the ice one more time. Something fluttered near the frozen surface. He squinted. A hand shot up out of the water.

"Shit."

He dropped his coffee.

It splattered, black against white.

He started running. "Help! I need some help over here!"

Several people looked his way. When someone called for help on a frozen lake, that usually meant only one thing.

Someone had broken through the ice.

CHAPTER THREE

The ice wasn't thin enough he needed to snake toward her, though once he rescued a dog chasing a ball that forced him to belly his way toward the break.

Thankfully, he was able to run straight to where Leah broke through, and grabbing her jacket, he pulled her out of the jagged hole. The water was so cold that just in that brief amount of time, he lost feeling in his hands.

She huddled over, gagging, shivering so hard he hoped she didn't bite her tongue off.

Missy rushed to them carrying a blanket that would do little good, but he wrapped it around Leah's trembling shoulders anyway.

"Leah, are you okay? Are you okay?" he kept asking over and over, as if he could warm her with his words alone.

"N-n-n-n . . ." was all that came out of her mouth.

James stopped Jared's truck next to them, and he sent up a prayer in relief.

"Thanks, man," he said, picking Leah up off the ice, her jacket and snow pants stiffening in the frozen temperatures. "Can you drive us?"

James gestured like a madman. "Yeah, yeah, get in, get in."

Someone helped him climb into his truck. Leah wasn't heavy, but her sopping wet coat and boots weighed her down.

She shook in his arms, and he held her to him, pressing his lips to her forehead and whispering words he didn't understand.

James careened into the resort parking lot spitting snow and slammed on the brakes in front of the main entrance. "Get her dry, and get her warm," he said, scrambling out of the truck. He ran around the hood and opened the passenger door. Carefully, he helped Jared step out of the truck without losing his balance, or his grip on Leah.

"We're gonna get you warm, baby, we're gonna get you warm," he murmured against her cheek. Blue tinged her lips, and she trembled violently in his arms.

"I'll park your truck. Let us know how she is."

Jared didn't acknowledge him, only carried Leah across the lobby, and he had to waste precious seconds at the reservation desk to ask what room belonged to her.

With two quick taps, Sophia said, "204."

"Thanks. Leah fell through the ice. Can you send up some coffee? Decaf? And lots of it."

"Sure thing, Mr. Hollister. I hope she's okay."

Going as fast as he could, he went up the steps to the second floor, and following the gold signs on the wall, he found her room without any trouble. He guessed maybe fifteen minutes had passed since he pulled her out of the icy water, and desperately he patted her down, looking for her key.

"Key, Leah, I need your key."

"In-in-inside," she said, gesturing at her jacket in jerking motions.

He unzipped her coat and searched the pockets, finally finding the old-fashioned metal key attached to a plastic keyring.

He tried to jam the key into the lock, his hand shaking from fear and cold, though if he could think past her wide, vacant eyes, he knew she would be okay. She hadn't been in the water long. Thank God.

What spooked him was if he hadn't turned around, if he hadn't thought to invite her to watch Briar skate, how long would she have fought in the water before someone spotted her. She'd been far enough away from everyone . . .

His stomach clenched.

He pushed her into her room, ripping off her jacket, nudging her into a chair to pull off her boots.

The faster he tried to move, the slower time crept by.

"J-J-Jared—"

"I'm going to start the shower. You need to warm up." He trotted into the bathroom and ran the water. Not too hot, lukewarm. He couldn't warm her up too fast or she'd go into shock.

He rushed out of the bathroom, and she sat stunned, too cold to move.

"Come on, baby, let's get you warm." He grabbed her frigid hand and led her into the bathroom. He didn't like the way she walked, like in a dream, a blank look in her eyes. He'd need to call the nurse line or bring her to the ER if he couldn't pull her out of it.

Someone knocked on her door and he blessed the quick service, but he didn't want to waste the few seconds it would cost him to let them in. "Just leave it in the hall, thanks," he called.

Leah wore a grey sweater, and he pulled off the soaked material revealing a grey and black lace bra. At any other time he would have lingered appreciatively over lingerie that couldn't be found in their tiny department store, but not now. He peeled the thick leggings from her legs and found she wore matching panties.

"You've got some good taste there, Miss Bristow," he murmured, impatiently shoving aside the shower curtain. He lifted her into the bathtub and guided her under the spray. She swayed woozily under the shower head.

"Dammit," he growled.

He tore off his coat and left his clothes in a pile in the hallway. If this made her mad, it made her mad. There wasn't anything he could do about it because he wouldn't leave her in there alone.

Wearing a pair of black boxer briefs, he joined her in the shower and cuddled her to him. Her cold skin touched his and he shuddered, but he wrapped his arms around her and she rested her chilly cheek on his shoulder.

As they stood under the spray, he slowly increased the water's temperature until steam filled the bathroom and her shaking subsided.

He leaned his back against the tile, letting it bear the brunt of their weight. He closed his eyes and enjoyed the feel of her body, her soft skin. She was too skinny, but her breasts were high and perky against his chest. She molded to him, like she'd been made for him.

He didn't know how much time had gone by when she lifted her head. Her lips were back to their delicious pink, her cheeks rosy. Her hair stuck to the sides of her face, the ends dripping water down her cleavage.

"How are you feeling?" He pushed away the desire pooling in his belly, and lower.

"Warmer."

"Good."

She laid her head on his shoulder and wrapped her arms around his waist.

Knowing she was going to be okay, he relaxed, his hand rubbing soothing circles between her shoulder blades. "Can you tell me what happened?"

"I was walking," she murmured, her lips fluttering against his skin. He could barely hear her. "I didn't feel like I was on a lake, you know? It felt like walking across a parking lot covered in snow, but all of a sudden I couldn't breathe. I thought I was going to die. I watched a horror movie about that once. A woman fell through the ice, but the current swept her under. She couldn't get her head above water and she drowned."

He'd heard stories of that happening as well, real stories, and his arms tightened around her. "I'm so sorry, sweetheart."

"How did you know I fell through?"

"I turned around to invite you to the arena tonight. I didn't see you, and I thought maybe you caught a ride. I stared long enough I saw your hand poke out of the water."

"Thank you."

"You don't have to thank me. I'm sorry Rocky Point isn't giving you a very nice welcome."

"It's been okay," she said, nudging his shoulder with her cheek.

"That's kind of you to say, but we know it's not true. Mostly that's been my fault. Come on, I think we can get out now. You're looking better."

He turned the water off, and gripping her arm, helped her step onto the bathmat. He handed her a towel off the rack above the toilet. "Can you dry off by yourself or do you need help?"

"I'll be okay."

"Okay." He was reluctant to leave her alone, but he'd be on the other side of the door.

He grabbed a towel then stepped out of the bathroom and shut the door, trapping her in the warmth. After drying off in the hallway outside the bathroom, he tied the towel around his waist and rolled the coffee tray inside the room.

In a billow of steam, she came out, one towel wrapped around her body, another in a turban-style twisted around her head, exposing her slender, elegant neck.

"Do you want some coffee?" he asked.

She stared at him, her eyes wide.

"What? Are you going into shock again? What's wrong?"

"Nothing. Just—nothing. I didn't expect . . . You look . . ." She cleared her throat. "I don't feel like coffee. I'm tired, and I think I just need some sleep."

His wet briefs would feel terrible under his jeans, but he nodded and scooped up his clothes. The drive to his house took ten minutes—five if he hit all green lights—and he could be uncomfortable that long. Leah needed the rest, and he needed to get to work.

"Okay. Call me or Marnie if you need *anything*. Especially if you don't feel good. We have a twenty-four hour ER, and it wouldn't take long if you needed to be seen, okay?" He started to tug his t-shirt over his head.

"Wait. I mean, you don't have to go. Or do you? You have to go to work. I'm sorry." She sank onto the edge of the bed, the towel clutched in her hands.

He paused. Maybe he should keep an eye on her, just to

be on the safe side. If she needed to go to the ER, his truck was right outside.

"I can stay. Are you sure?"

"If it's no trouble. I'm kind of nervous to be alone right now."

Throwing his t-shirt back onto the floor, he said, "Okay. I'll tell Marnie I'm staying with you. James drove us here, and she's probably going crazy."

He texted Marnie and told her Leah warmed up and planned to take a nap but he'd stay with her for a little while longer. Then he texted his second in command at the arena and said he wouldn't be in until later. He still hadn't resolved the popcorn machine problem, and the quick fix to get them through the Bears versus Jets game wouldn't last. Otherwise, things were under control.

With the towel wrapped around his waist, he sat on the bed. She laid with her eyes closed, and when he propped himself against the headboard, a pillow behind his back, she rolled over and cuddled into his side.

He wiggled down into a more comfortable position. That's all it was. It wasn't so he could snuggle her to him or unwrap the towel from her hair so he could press a kiss to the top of her head. It wasn't anything like that at all.

As he drifted off, he tried to keep the sense of foreboding from settling in the pit of his stomach. This had bad news written all over it.

Then why did the feel of her curled into his side, her breath feathering his chest, feel so damned good?

The churning in her stomach woke Leah from a sound sleep and her eyes popped open. Nuzzled into Jared's side while she napped let her sleep more deeply than she had in a long time, but the stress from breaking through the ice must have made her ulcer flare up. In too big of a hurry to reach the bathroom in time, she didn't care that she lost her towel, and she heaved into the toilet shivering in her bra and panties.

Jared thumped out of bed and pushed the bathroom door open, and she squeezed her eyes shut in humiliation.

"We need to get you to the doctor." He wet a washcloth and kneeled next to her.

She forced herself to speak through her embarrassment. "There's no need. I've seen plenty." They all said the same thing. Eat better and avoid stress. Sleep for God's sake. Try yoga. Get a massage. Relax.

They dispensed those wonderful pearls of wisdom like dentists handed out lollipops, not caring if she could follow their advice or not.

"But not after falling into a frozen lake. What if it hurt the baby?"

"Baby?" she rasped. Her throat burned. If her dip made her get sick, she'd be mad. Ulcer aside, she was healthy. Well, as healthy as a woman who could barely eat and hardly slept could be. She wanted to enjoy her vacation, not recuperate from catching pneumonia.

"Aren't you pregnant?" he asked, offering her the washcloth to wipe her mouth.

She reared away from him, pressing her back against the bathtub. "No! Why would you think that? Oh, God. I've been wanting you to kiss me, and you think I'm pregnant? No wonder why you won't touch me." She took the washcloth and pressed it to her lips.

"That's not why I won't—wait. You're *not* pregnant?

What's with the throwing up then? And you're always rubbing your stomach. Pregnant women do that."

She closed the toilet lid and flushed. They were arguing over a bowl full of her puke.

And sitting on her bathroom floor wearing nothing but their underwear.

"So do women who have bleeding stress ulcers," she said, standing too quickly. The room tilted. She grabbed at the sink before she fell, but he reached for her instead, steadying her against his body. His rock hard body. His rock hard body she hadn't noticed in the shower because she'd been too busy thawing out.

His rock hard body she was certainly appreciating now.

"Come on, you need to get back in bed. Are you sure you don't want me to take you to the ER?"

She let him tuck her in. "I'm on medication, but it doesn't help. The only thing that will is changing my lifestyle, and I can't do that."

"Seems to me if you don't, it's going to kill you."

Not like she hadn't had the same thought, but it wasn't a matter so easily fixed.

"Thanks again for helping me," she said, tugging the bedspread up to her chin.

"You're welcome. Stay warm, Leah." He smoothed his fingertips across her forehead, stumbling over the worry lines.

Leah closed her eyes and listened to him dress. He let himself out, and through her exhausted haze, she barely heard the click when he shut the door.

The next morning, she woke to the sun glinting off the slopes and feeling a little more human than she had the day before. At least, it didn't feel like battery acid filled her stomach. She pushed the cart of cold coffee into the hallway and ordered pancakes hoping to ease her discomfort the rest of the way.

She couldn't believe Jared thought she was pregnant, and she doubly couldn't believe she confessed she wanted him to kiss her. Something he ignored, and she didn't know if that was good or bad. Good because he didn't want to embarrass her more than she already was, or bad because he wanted to forget she even said it.

It wasn't her fault that looking into his eyes made her all melty inside.

God, she needed to leave him alone.

He was as small town as she was big city, and there wasn't any changing that.

She showered, ate, and decided how she would spend her day. Helen's plight bothered her. When she mentioned it, it'd made Jared angry, and that baffled her. Why would he care if she wanted to help a woman set her business to rights? She had more than enough time to help.

Her wet clothes laying in a heap stopped her. Crap. Her winter jacket, snow pants, and boots were gone. Jared must have taken them when he left yesterday. Well, she'd be at the Supply Company, she could always buy another jacket and pair of boots. The purchase seemed like a waste, but maybe she could donate what she didn't need before she went home.

She didn't know when she'd be back to her room and she called her grandmother, wanting to tell her good morning, but the nurse said her grandma was having a bad day and didn't want to talk.

Disappointed, she said, "Okay, thanks, anyway. You'll tell her I called?"

"I always do, Miss Bristow. Are you having a good vacation?"

"It's been an adventure, I can tell you that."

"Sounds promising. Call again tonight. She takes her meds at five."

"Thanks, I will."

She sat in the resort's shuttle wearing the coat Jared made fun of when he picked her up in Marengo, and her thin, useless flats. She never would've been able to ice fish in these clothes. She could have skipped it and avoided falling through the ice, but then she wouldn't have had the opportunity to take a half-naked shower with Jared.

Hmmm.

The driver let her out onto the sidewalk in front of the Supply Company and told her to call the resort when she needed a ride back.

"Thanks, I will, but I don't know what time."

The young driver saluted her, and he drove away, music blasting in the empty van.

Standing on the sidewalk, this time she studied the storefront with a more judgmental eye. A small FOR SALE sign leaned against the window inside, hidden by a thick coat of grime. Faded posters taped to the windows blocked out light that could be making the store look more cheerful.

She opened the door, and silence greeted her when cheerful Christmas music should have been playing to encourage people to buy.

"Leah, doll, it's nice of you to come back! How are you feeling after your swim yesterday?" Helen asked, standing near a register.

"Hi. You know about that?"

Papers cluttered the two cash register counters, plastic bags everywhere.

Helen had given up.

If she wanted to sell this place, she was going to have to put in a little effort.

"Jared called the DNR last night and bitched them out for a good twenty minutes, little Sabrina, she works concessions at the arena, said. Wanted the hole you fell into marked so no one else did the same thing. From what Sabrina heard, they're going to flag it to help people avoid it." Helen smoothed her Rocky Point Supply Company t-shirt over her hips. "It's all over town. Sabrina said she never heard him so angry."

She turned a creaking display of Welcome to Minnesota postcards. "He pulled me out and warmed me up. He was really nice about the whole thing."

"That's Jared. I bet you're in here for another jacket and some boots? What does Marnie have planned now?"

"Oh, nothing for a couple of days, which is why I'm here. I saw your sale sign in the window."

"You gonna buy me out?" Helen laughed. It was full of tension but maybe a little hope too.

"No, but I thought you might want some help fixing this place up. It's not going to sell like this."

Helen sniffed. "What's wrong with my store?"

She gestured to the fading posters. "May I?"

"What are you going to do?"

She climbed onto the lip of the windowsill and pulled the posters down, letting in the buttery light. "We need to perk this place up a little. Let the sun in. Change the bulbs in your lights. Put on some music. A lot of your racks are empty. Don't you have any stock?"

"I have stock, I can show you. I haven't been doing my best, and I know it. It's hard when you're by yourself."

Smiling sympathetically, she said, "I know it is."

Boxes and roll-racks of clothes filled the stockroom, and she sighed in dismay. It would take forever to put all this out, but it needed to be done. Someone could pop in, hoping to get some shopping out of the way, and they'd walk right out thinking they wouldn't find what they needed, like she had. "We need to put all this out, Helen. It can't sell back here."

"We?"

"I'll help you. I've got all day, and some time this week, too. We can get through most of it."

Helen wiped tears off her cheeks. "Now I know why Jared took a fancy to you."

She slid off her coat and hung it on a hook with her purse. "We're not a couple. Just friends."

"Friends is a good start."

But a start to what?

She helped Helen put stock out first. They folded jeans and filled the display squares that were built into the wall in the back of the store. Levi's, Lees, Carhartts. Mens and womens. The Supply Company even stocked Youth sizes, which would help parents a great deal if their kids suddenly needed new school pants due to ripping or other accidents.

It took some energy as Helen kept more denim in the stockroom than she did on her selling floor.

They moved on to boots and tennis shoes, jackets, mittens—sorry, choppers—scarves, and souvenir t-shirts and sweatshirts. She dressed mannequins and set up displays in the windows she wiped down with Windex and a rag.

Lunch hour was a quick fifteen minutes to gulp down a sandwich she ordered from the diner next door. Word spread she was helping Helen, and some stopped in to say hi, gossip, and shop. It broke up the monotony of the day, and despite the repetition of putting out stock, she enjoyed chatting about this and that with Helen and the people who lived in town.

She groaned in relief when she lowered to the floor to sort through boxes of hand lotion, lip balm, body wash, and handmade candles Helen sold for a woman who lived two towns over. She found an old display case in the stockroom and scrubbed it until the metal and glass sparkled. It would be perfect near the registers to use for stocking stuffers.

"How do you know all this?" Helen asked, marking prices onto bottles of hand lotion with a sticker gun.

"I work for Outdoor Wonders. It's how I know Marnie."

Helen laughed. "You work for an outdoor adventure chain like that, and you didn't know how to dress to visit a town so far north we're practically in Canada?"

"There may have been a slight . . . miscalculation on my part," she said, trying not to be defensive. "I didn't know Marnie would schedule things like a snowman-making contest. Come on. Besides, New York's close to Canada, too, and we have normal temperatures."

"Oh, you're from New York?" Helen asked, her face smoothing into mask she didn't like. "How do you know Marnie then? You said through work?"

"I hired her, and we talk on . . ." Would Helen know what Zoom was? "The computer, and through email. Phone conversations. We get along really well. It surprised me when she asked me to be a bridesmaid, but that's not something you turn down, is it?"

"Not usually," Helen agreed. "It's an honor."

"I had the vacation time, so I thought, why not?"

They arranged the priced products in the display, and after adding a holiday bow, Leah stepped back to admire her handiwork. "That looks great!"

"It does look nice, and now I can tell SarahBeth her products are finally for sale. Let me take a picture, and I'll text it to her. She's been after me something awful. "

She didn't blame the woman, especially if she depended on sales to pay bills.

"There're a couple of things left. Music and the lights."

"I have a ladder," Helen said, snapping the picture with her phone, "but we should wait and I'll hire someone to do it."

"That's okay. I can do the lights if you figure out the music. Or at least put the local radio station on. You have one here, right?"

"Sure do. That's a great idea."

On her way to grab the ladder out of the back, she spotted a black sweatshirt that a cat's ears, eyes, nose, whiskers, and mouth embroidered on the front. The hot pink curly-Q font said, "Welcome to Meownesota." Cheesy, but too adorable to pass up, she put it on over her t-shirt. She'd pay for it before she left. Maybe Helen would give her an employee discount.

Wobbling on the ladder as "Silver Bells" played over the speaker system, she was replacing the long-tubed fluorescent bulbs when Jared came in.

He stood at the foot of the ladder and glared, hands jammed on his hips. "What are you doing up there?"

"What does it look like I'm doing up here?"

"Get down."

"I'm almost done. Doesn't the store look great? We have more to do, but we got a good start."

She secured the last bulb in the fixture and fastened the plastic cover back in place. "You can turn the lights on now," she called. In the back, Helen flipped the switch, and bright light filled the store. "That looks so much better."

Carefully, she climbed down and hopped off the bottom step of the ladder. "What's up?"

"Besides watching you try to kill yourself twice in two days?"

She bit back a bitter retort. He made her sound like a puppy finding trouble every second. "No one's asking you to."

He scoffed. "I dried your jacket and snow pants, and I left them in a bag by the door. I couldn't do anything about your boots except put them next to the heating vents at the house. It'll take a few days for them to dry out. Sorry."

"That's okay," Helen said, walking down the aisle carrying a large shipping box. "I owe her a pair for the work she put in today."

"Great, that's just great." He turned and stomped to the door, pushing it open with a vicious shove.

"What in the heck was that about?" she asked, bewildered. Jared slammed into his truck and sped away.

"If you find out, let me know. But I can tell you one thing," Helen said, a twinkle in her eye, "despite the freezing temperatures, Jared Hollister might finally be thawing out."

"Calm down, Dad." Briar pushed a bowl of mashed potatoes closer to his plate. "Have some more potatoes."

"Don't tell me to calm down," he said, but obediently spooned up another helping of potatoes he didn't want. When he'd come storming home after seeing Leah at the Supply Company, Briar handed him a beer and steered him toward the table to eat dinner.

"You're worked up over nothing. So what if she climbed a ladder? I think it's sweet she's helping Helen. A couple of my friends texted me about it. They said the store looks a lot better, and poor Helen. She's been so lonely since Glen died. I bet having someone new to talk to has perked up her spirits."

The store *did* look better. The racks were full for the first time in a long time, and the radio gave customers something to listen to while they browsed. He couldn't remember when Helen stopped playing music over the sound system, but the Christmas carols had been a pleasant surprise when he dropped off Leah's jacket and snow pants.

"She looked happier," he agreed. "And the store hasn't been that organized in years. Leah knows what she's doing."

"I'll have to go in there. And I'd love to meet Leah. See what kind of woman has my dad so twisted up. You're usually so easy going."

"I'm easy going," he said. "Just not when someone's thirty feet in the air on a ladder that's as old as I am."

"You're always telling me I can do whatever I want."

"You have more sense, I hope."

"Why can't you admit you were worried she was going to hurt herself? It's okay to care." Briar sipped her soda.

He rested his elbows on the table and clasped his hands. "And what would you do if I fell in love with her? She's from New York."

She set her can down with a tinny thunk. "I . . . I don't know. I'm not ready to leave my friends yet. It's important to me that I graduate from Rocky Point High."

"I know it is, but I can't ask her to relocate here if I can't leave for her. Do you understand? I have no idea what kind of life she has in the city. Stop pushing me to get close to her. Be careful what you wish for and all that."

"I don't want you to miss out on a relationship because of me. It's obvious you like her."

He stood and picked up his plate and fork. "You're my daughter first, most, and always. Any choice I make, I will make with you in mind. Besides, *I* don't want to move to New York. I like Rocky Point, or we would've moved with your mother. She didn't want to choose between her career and me. I forced her to, and I lost. I won't put myself in that position again."

"You can be friends," she insisted, helping clear the table.

"Yes, we can be friends, with no benefits involved."

She laughed. "That's not up to me, though maybe a little 'benefit' would put you in a better mood."

It probably would, he thought, but he said, "I'm not talking about my sex life, or lack thereof, with you. If I need my bed warm at night, I'll turn on my heating blanket."

"That's romantic."

He turned the water off and dried his hands. "Look, I agree it's time I start dating. If I join an online site, maybe I can meet someone who lives in Marengo and we can take turns making the drive. Okay?"

Briar tucked her blonde hair behind her ears. God, she looked like her mother. Rocky Point wouldn't keep her here much longer. She'd graduate high school and go to college. Rita already started sending her university brochures, hoping Briar would choose to go to school in New York.

The city lights would lure everyone he loved away.

"Are you okay?"

Her voice brought him back to the kitchen. For now, she was here. He liked his job and he loved everything about Rocky Point.

Things were good.

"Yeah. I am. What are you going to do for the rest of the night? Do you have homework?"

She rinsed out her soda can and tossed it into the recycling bin. "I was hoping you'd take me to Marengo tomorrow. I want to find a dress before all the pretty ones are gone."

"Don't you have school?"

"If you paid attention, you'd know I have tomorrow off. It's a teacher development day."

He leaned against the sink and gripped the edge of the counter. He wouldn't miss anything at the arena if he took half the day off. "I suppose we can. I have a few packages to deliver, too."

"Awesome! I'll be ready by nine. Goodnight."

"Goodnight."

He wiped down an already spotless counter and turned off the light. He flopped into his favorite recliner and turned on the TV. Listlessly, he flipped through the channels, turning it off after a few minutes.

Usually, he loved evenings like this. Briar was happy, gossiping with her friends. Nothing at the rink that couldn't wait until the next day. He'd make a cup of coffee, bring it up to his room, and settle in bed with a book. But that didn't sound appealing, and he tapped the remote against his palm as he weighed his options.

He could text James, see if he had anything going on tonight. He could go to bed and try to sleep because God knew the next two weeks would be busy.

But nothing he thought of sounded particularly appealing, and they didn't because none of them included Leah.

Seeing her on that ladder freaked him out, but Briar was right. Leah was more than capable of changing out lightbulbs, and she'd jumped onto solid ground as gracefully as the cat on her sweatshirt.

It hadn't tamped down his anger, and he'd left before he tried to kiss the stupidity out of her.

Friends.

They couldn't be friends. Not when thinking about standing in the shower with her made him harder than ice in forty below temperatures.

Though, he should learn to spend time with her. For the sake of the wedding party. James and Marnie wanted their friends to get along. Leah was doing a fine job. He was the problem, and he needed to fix it.

He picked his phone up off the end table. Fifteen degrees, no wind. Clear sky.

He hadn't been snowshoeing for a couple of years, and the weather was perfect.

"Briar, I'm going out for a while," he called up the stairs.

She peeked around the doorframe of her room, earbuds in her ears. Smiling a knowing smile, she said, "Tell Leah I said hi."

"Know-it-all," he mumbled under his breath as her giggle followed him out the door.

He loaded his and Briar's snowshoes into the back of his truck. Rocky Point hadn't had fresh snow in a while, but the trails in the park would be quiet.

He brought his own snow pants and winter gear. He

hoped they could spend a decent amount of time on the trail—he needed the fresh air and the exercise would do him good—and a few hours alone with Leah without their friends poking their noses into their business wouldn't hurt.

Annoyed his heart was pounding, he parked his truck in the resort's lot. This wasn't a big deal, but he should have given her a heads-up. Or maybe . . . asked. His mouth quirked. Leah tied him up in knots, but that wasn't any excuse. Besides, she might not be here. James and Marnie were in the mood to party, and she could be downtown with them or in the lounge grabbing drinks with other members of the wedding party.

He made himself admit the truth. The real reason he hadn't asked? After the way he snapped at her at the Supply Company, he was afraid she'd say no.

Maybe he should have texted James after all.

He knocked on her door, but she didn't answer.

He waited for a few moments, but her room was quiet. Disappointed, he turned away. He could always go alone. Use the time to clear his head. He hadn't felt this mixed up since Rita told him she didn't want to live in Rocky Point anymore.

He was halfway down the hallway when Leah flung her door open. "Sorry, I was on the phone. Something came up at w— Jared. What are you doing here?"

The saliva dried in his mouth. She looked pretty dressed in black leggings and a blue and black sweater, her hair swirling around her shoulders. Pink stained her cheeks and suspicion colored her eyes, but she didn't look like a kicked puppy, the sad expression on her face a constant accessory. Relaxed, and almost . . . smiling . . . she leaned against the wall outside her door, her arms crossed over her chest.

"I, ah, wanted to ask if you had some free time this evening? You might have plans with Marnie, or Autumn, or you said you were on the phone. I should let you—"

"It was just a thing. It's fine. What's up?"

"Would you like to go snowshoeing? I brought Briar's with me if you want to give it a try. There's not much to it, not like downhill skiing, if you're afraid you're going to . . . hurt . . . yourself." She pressed her lips together to keep from laughing, and he glowered. "Fine. Be that way. A little concern, and you have to blow it all out of proportion."

"I appreciate it, I really do," she said, padding down the hallway, her feet bare. "I would love to. Can I go dressed like this? If you guessed I've never done it before, you're right. I'm sorry." She touched his arm.

Through his thick jacket, he didn't feel anything at all, but electricity still zipped through his body. "You'll need socks, and everything you wore ice fishing."

"Okay."

"I'll pick you up in the front."

He turned and started down the hallway before he could make an even bigger fool of himself.

There was something about her that drove him crazy, and he needed to find some control before he lost his mind completely. He didn't want to fall in love. He didn't.

The faster he fell, the harder he'd land.

The more he'd hurt.

He knew it for a fact, too. One winter he was pushing snow off his roof and slipped. Tumbled right off the top of the house. He'd landed on a huge snow hill, but he'd still gotten the wind knocked out of him and his back hurt for weeks afterward.

Same difference.

Leah's hands shook as she applied extra face cream and lip balm to her cracked lips. The colder temperatures hadn't been kind to her skin, and she learned to pay better attention. She chugged a capful of antacid, grabbed her gear, room key, and phone, and met Jared outside.

His truck idled under the canopy, and she hoisted herself into the cab, dragging her snow pants with her.

"You didn't have to work tonight?" she asked as he drove down the driveway.

"There's always work, and I could easily spend all my time at the arena if I let myself, but I was there for most of the day."

"I know how that is." She fell silent as the town slid by. Charmed by how the lights framed him through his window, she twisted, sitting sideways in the seat. He was handsome, though he clenched his jaw so tightly she wondered if he suffered from lockjaw.

The small-town Christmas sparkles disappeared behind them, and she asked, "Where are we going?"

"Out to Flat Stone State Park. It'll be quiet except for maybe a random snowmobile. We'll get there in about twenty minutes."

"Okay."

A comfortable quiet filled the cab.

The highway was clear of snow and ice, and he confidently handled the truck on the winding road.

At one point he slowed, and she asked, "What's that?" Eight pairs of glowy spots lit up the woods alongside them.

"Deer. I don't want to hit one."

"Oh," she breathed, her face pressed to the window. "I want to see."

"If we're quiet, we might see some on the trail."

"Really?"

"Yeah, sure. You never know." He turned off the highway onto a narrow road, and everywhere she looked was dark, dark, dark.

He parked in the empty lot, and they climbed out of the truck and wiggled into their snow pants. She took off her jacket and snapped the enclosures over her shoulders.

If he'd asked her to do anything else, she probably would have turned him down. His hot and cold attitude wore on her spirits. It wasn't like she didn't have enough on her mind without clashing with one of James's groomsmen.

"Marnie didn't put you up this, did she?" she asked.

He slid snowshoes out of the bed of his truck. They looked different from what she'd pictured. These were sleek and modern-looking, made of metal, not rope and wood. Thank God she hadn't told him. It would add to the things he already made fun of her for, and that list was long enough.

"Give me a foot," he said, and she complied, letting him buckle her boot into the snowshoe. "No. Why would you ask that?"

"Because you don't like me, and every time I turn around, you're in my face, criticizing something I'm doing. If you're keeping me company as a favor to Marnie, you don't have to. I can find things to do on my own. I'm used to being by myself."

"It's not that."

She waited for him to say what it was then, but he didn't offer an explanation, only attached snowshoes to his own boots. She took a tentative step. They were light, and she easily lifted her feet. He handed her two walking poles as well, and they set out.

Following him, she inhaled a deep breath of cold and earth. No, not the earth, but what grew from it. Foreign, gritty, but simple. Basic. He started them on a trail she never would have noticed if he hadn't pointed it out. The trees swallowed them, his truck disappearing in the dark.

The crunch of their snowshoes was the only sound in the entire world.

Evergreens, poplars, birches. Out of curiosity, she'd scanned the brochure tucked inside the desk in her room describing the land in northern Minnesota that made the resort such a beautiful and exciting getaway. Those trees loomed above her, and she craned her neck to find a glimpse of the stars sprinkled like glitter in the sky.

The path widened, and she caught up with him. They walked side by side, their shoulders brushing.

She bit the inside of her cheek to keep from asking what it was about her that bothered him so much. If he didn't want to spend time with her, why did he keep seeking her out? In the end, it didn't matter why he had such a conflicting attitude toward her, and she didn't ask. She'd be leaving in less than two weeks, and she wouldn't see him again.

Her stomach churned despite the hit of antacid she took earlier.

She gripped the poles and prayed her nausea would go away. He already saw her throw up once, he didn't need to see it again.

"What else do you do?" he asked, turning toward her.

"What?" He looked cute in his fur-lined hat and parka. He moved like he drove, with such self-assurance. Like he'd been born knowing everything.

"What else do you do? I know you work, and you used to be married. I'm sorry about that, by the way."

"You're sorry I used to be married?" *So am I.*

"No. When I asked you about it at the meet and greet, I made you cry. I'm sorry."

"Oh. It's okay. I'm still a little raw. It got nasty and drawn-out toward the end." Nasty didn't begin to explain what Max had done to her, but it wouldn't be right to describe such ugliness when they were walking in the midst of something so beautiful. "I guess when you get to be our age, there aren't many people who won't have baggage."

He blew out a breath. "Yeah."

"James and Marnie, though. They seem like they're a strong, happy couple."

"Yeah, they are. Dated off and on, saw other people. Did the career thing, got that sorted out. Met up again when the time was right. I envy them. They were patient and waited."

"You didn't?"

"Nope. I married Rita right out of high school. She got pregnant not long after that. We lived in a cheap little apartment above the drugstore downtown. Small-town life, at its finest. Scares me sometimes, that Briar's only three years younger than I was when I married her mom."

"Kids don't do that anymore, do they?" Not the kids she knew. They worked internships, used family connections to skip ahead. She'd worked with an intern or two at Outdoor Wonders, and they didn't talk about starting families. They talked about school, earning their graduate degrees. Making money. Ruling the world.

"You'd be surprised what kids from small towns still do. History repeats itself. What goes around comes around, you know."

"Yeah."

She did know. It's why she didn't think about kids much. It's why when she turned thirty her biological clock remained quiet.

What goes around comes around.

They reached a clearing, and he said, "Do you want to take a break?"

"Sure."

He unclasped the straps of her snowshoes, and she dropped into a tall drift. He unhooked his boots and did the same.

"Lean back and look up," he whispered.

Leah fell backward, letting the snow catch her.

"Look," Jared said again, pointing his mittened hand toward the sky.

Green fog drifted over the black, swirling, dancing, moving in and out of itself, and the sight brought tears to her eyes. "What is that?"

"The northern lights," he said, rolling onto his side in the snow. "Leah."

"It's gorgeous. Like fairy dust, real fairy dust, sparkling in the sky."

"Leah."

"Yeah?" She sniffled.

"I want to kiss you."

"You do?"

"Yeah. I've wanted to for a long time."

"Really?" She was talking too much. If she didn't shut up, he wouldn't want to anymore.

"Yeah. Since you told me you didn't want wild mountain lions eating your remains."

"I still don't."

"I won't let them if you let me kiss you."

"Okay."

He covered her mouth with his, gently at first, more of a nuzzle than a kiss, and she leaned in, asking him to give her more. The tip of his tongue nudged the seam of her lips, and she opened her mouth, letting him in.

When she thought she wouldn't be able to catch her breath, he leaned away and settled into the snow next to her.

"Thanks," he murmured.

"You're welcome."

As the light floated over the dark, she smiled into the sky, and something smoothed over her soul. When they stood up to snowshoe back to the truck, her stomach didn't hurt at all.

CHAPTER FOUR

It wouldn't mean anything. The kiss. He couldn't let it. But all he could think about was doing it again.

He gave in when they reached the truck, crowding her against the tailgate, and pressed his lips to hers, her scent clean, like the frozen outdoor air.

It would be his luck to fall in love with a woman who lived half a country away.

Who lived in a city that, to him, represented torn up families, career aspirations that meant more than love, greed, and selfishness.

He leaned back. "Did you like that?"

"Yeah, I did. Can we do it again?" she asked, gripping the front of his jacket and pulling him closer.

He kissed the tip of her nose. Any more kisses and he'd ask to go inside her room when he brought her back to the resort. Kissing was one thing, making love was another. Harmless kissing, flirting. Having a good time.

It's all his heart could afford.

"I meant the snowshoeing, little girl," he said, laughing.

"Oh," she said, then started laughing too. "It was fun. No deer though."

"No. Maybe some other time."

He stored the snowshoes in the bed of his truck and they sat, letting it warm up. He turned on the radio, setting a twenty-four hour Christmas carol station on low. "What will you do for Christmas?" he asked.

"Work. I don't have much family. After this vacation, I'll have plenty to do. How about you?"

"I'll take a couple days off and we'll drive down to southern Minnesota. My parents live there, where it's a bit warmer. They didn't want to leave the state, but they were tired of the temperatures. Last year Briar visited her mom."

"Marnie said Rocky Point goes all out for Christmas."

"Yeah. Sleigh rides, there're groups that go caroling. The city and the fire department put on a huge bonfire, but I forget the date. You might be gone by then."

He cleared his throat and shifted into Drive.

Silence hung heavy in the cab.

She looked out the window, and he couldn't see her face.

"I'm taking Briar to Marengo tomorrow, if you want to come along." He drove down Main Street, and he glanced at the Viking's parking lot. Maybe he'd stop in for a few minutes after he brought Leah back to the resort. He could ask her if she wanted to go, but he needed room to breathe.

"What for?" she asked, finally meeting his gaze.

"There's a holiday dance at school and she wants to buy a new dress, and I have a couple of packages to drop off."

"Are you driving?"

"No."

She bit her lip. "Are you okay with me meeting your daughter?"

Jerking a shoulder, he said, "If I wasn't, I wouldn't have invited you. I, ah, told her I got upset when I saw you on that ladder at the Supply Company. She might tease us a little about it, but she knows the score."

"And what's that?" she asked.

"That after the wedding you're going back to New York."

She leaned back and closed her eyes, and he stared straight ahead at the car in front of them stopped at a red light.

At the resort, he idled under the canopy, and she pulled her door key out of her pocket.

"Hey."

She twisted in her seat. "Yeah?"

He pulled off a mitten and brushed the hair away from her face. "Are you okay? Did I say something wrong?"

A smile trembled on her lips. "Nothing that isn't true."

"Yeah."

Bing Crosby started crooning "I'll Be Home for Christmas," and the mood in the cab dropped another notch.

"I'd like to go, if the offer's still open."

"Yeah, it is. I'll pick you up about nine-fifteen. We'll have lunch there, too. Maybe the food court at the mall, something simple like that."

"Okay. I'll see you in the morning. Have a good night, and thank you. I had a good time."

She jumped out of the truck and hurried into the resort, not pausing to wave or look behind her.

He sighed and slid his phone out of his pocket. He texted James, asking where he was.

Immediately, an answer appeared. *Viking.*

That was James's only reply, but it got the job done.

Ten minutes later he sat in a rickety chair in a corner of

the bar with Marnie, James, and a few other high school classmates who hadn't been in their group. Funny, after all this time, he still thought of them that way.

James slapped him on the back and pushed a beer across the sticky table. "What are you doing out past your bedtime, old man?"

"I just dropped Leah off at the resort. We went snow-shoeing, and I didn't feel like heading home yet. How's wedding stuff?"

James slid his finger across his throat. "Gail's having a hissy fit about the playlist for the reception, and my aunt isn't happy having to stay at the no-tell motel because she changed her mind at the last minute."

"Mom will have to get over it," Marnie said, leaning into James. "She hates that I love the soundtracks to the *Fifty Shades of Grey* movies. She thinks they're crass, but I'm not listening to Frank Sinatra all night."

"Seems harmless enough." He sipped his beer. He married Rita at the courthouse, and afterward, their parents took them out to dinner at the Rocky Point Bar and Grill, a seafood place located along the lake. His dad snuck him a beer, and the bartender looked the other way while Rita sipped champagne.

"Seems that way, until you have to hear over breakfast my aunt thinks her bed has bedbugs."

"She's staying at Kelly's?" he asked. At Kelly's Inn, bedbugs were a sure possibility.

"It's the only place we could get her into. You have a spare bedroom. You wanna take Leah and Aunt Ruth can have Leah's room at the resort?"

"Don't ask him to do that," Marnie said, frowning. "It's your aunt's fault. You asked her months ago if she was sure she didn't want to come. She did it to spite me, but she only hurt herself. Did Leah like snowshoeing? Helen can't shut up about how wonderful she is. Autumn said she interviewed her for the blog to help spread the word about the store, and Helen kept her for over an hour singing Leah's praises."

He leaned back in his seat. They did make a nice couple. Marnie and James, that was. They looked at each other with love, but underneath the starry eyes there was respect—something he didn't know a relationship needed until he didn't have it.

"We saw the northern lights. They're bright tonight. Marnie, you didn't need her to do anything tomorrow, did you? I asked her to go to Marengo with me. Briar needs a dress, and she's off school."

"No, we're not doing anything, but we lost our cake server somewhere. You're going to the mall, right? Can you go into the engraving place and buy a new one? Put our names and the date on it? Pretty please?"

"Sure, no problem."

Marnie leaned across her fiancé and gave him a smacking kiss on the cheek. "Thanks. We could drive up between now and then, but James's parents want to do some more ice fishing and we have marriage counseling scheduled with the pastor a few times at the church."

"You don't need that. You guys are great."

"We get a discount on our marriage license, so why not? James and I can bicker about how many kids and cats we're going to have after we buy our house."

"You guys looking? You're probably the only couple I know who didn't live together first."

"I have to sell mine before we apply for a loan. I'll miss Callie. She's a fun neighbor, and she's saved my ass a time or two. I suppose I should have done it sooner than this, but once James and I decided the time was right, everything moved so fast."

James wrapped an arm around her. "I was tired of hearing about you dating other men."

"Aww," she sighed and launched herself into his lap.

He lost their attention, and he divided his time between watching a couple of community college kids play pool and the TV above the bar showing sports highlights.

He bullshitted with a few friends who lived in town, and caught up with a few others who were there for the wedding.

When the time closed in on midnight, he pushed his chair back. "Text Leah about the cake server. I don't want to forget," he said to Marnie.

"I will. Hey, we're taking over the pool and hot tub tomorrow night. Desiree said she'd close it off for us this one time." Marnie wrinkled her nose. "She's charging me extra, too, the stuck-up little thing. Come over and hang out. We're going to order a ton of pizza, and earlier this afternoon James bought out the liquor store."

"If nothing comes up at the arena, I'll be there." Maybe he'd see Leah in a swimsuit.

After listening to the music blaring in the bar, his truck turned into a quiet haven. He blew out a sigh, his breath white in the cold air as the engine purred while it warmed up.

Marnie and James were a good match. He wanted to find a love like that again. What were the chances that the one woman to catch his eye since Rita left him came from the very city he lost his wife to in the first place?

His life had been just fine before Leah came to town.

Fuck.

Leah fretted over what to wear, but in the end decided on black knee-high boots, jeggings, a black V-neck sweater, and her dried-out white parka. Having flown over Marengo, she knew it wasn't a metropolis, and even if they decided to eat lunch somewhere other than the mall, she'd look fine almost anywhere. To glam up her plain clothes, she pinned her hair into a French twist and added little dangly earrings to her ears. She fiddled with her makeup for a few minutes, but she was ready by nine.

Meeting Briar made her nervous. Jared hadn't seemed to think anything of introducing her to his daughter, and that meant he either introduced Briar to all the women he kissed or he didn't think their relationship was anything to make a big deal about.

She liked neither of those choices.

Handsome and kind, with a good job, well, as good of a job one could have in a small town like Rocky Point, Jared shouldn't be single. The most likely explanation was the one Autumn and Marnie implied on the lake while they were ice fishing and the one he didn't deny. He wasn't over Briar's mother.

He shouldn't be kissing her then, putting ideas into her head.

Oh, and what ideas would those be, Leah? she asked herself, locking the door to her room.

He wouldn't pursue her because he knew she was leaving. Couldn't resist bringing that up last night, either.

Probably more for his benefit than for hers, but like falling into the lake, it had cooled her off.

She couldn't get invested. Couldn't think this was anything more than a fling. She wasn't one to indulge in things like that and she should keep him at arms' length until after the wedding, but when she was with him, all thought flew right out of her head and his kiss . . . hmmm . . .

She did a clumsy pirouette in the hallway, the rubber soles of her boots catching on the carpet. One of the maids stepped out of the room she was cleaning and laughed. "Good morning."

"Good morning," she said, blushing. "I'm in room 204. I'll be gone for most of the day, if you could clean in there?"

"Yes, ma'am."

"Thank you. Have a nice day."

She waited anxiously in the lobby for Jared to pick her up. She checked her messages to be sure he hadn't needed to cancel and read one from Marnie, asking them to buy a cake cutter and server. *Jared knows what I want.*

They'd be shopping for more than Briar's dress, then. Maybe she'd browse for a few things, too. Another dress, maybe. They still had over a week of activities, and tonight was a pool party. Oh! She needed a new swimsuit. If the stores carried anything like that this time of year.

Jared stopped his truck under the canopy, and noticing the passenger seat was empty, she frowned.

She opened the door. "Hey, where's—"

"Leah, this is my daughter, Briar. Briar, Leah. She's a bridesmaid in Marnie's wedding."

"You didn't have to sit back there," she said to the blonde teenaged girl sitting in the truck's extended cab. She climbed into the seat and shut the door.

"No worries. It's nice to meet you," Briar said. "Thanks for coming. I could use a woman's opinion on my dress."

"Hey, I have taste," Jared said, mock offended as he

drove out of the parking lot.

"If you had it your way, I'd go to the dance wearing a bedspread that covered me from head to foot."

"As your father, I see nothing wrong with that."

She relaxed as they joked, Briar speaking to her as if they'd known each other for years. Jared included her in all topics of conversation, explaining anything she needed to know to keep her from falling behind.

Briar teased her for being afraid to fly in the little plane, bragging her dad was the best pilot in Minnesota. She admitted that the takeoff and landing were smooth, and the stories Briar shared all the way to Marengo shortened the flight.

Jared borrowed a vehicle from the airport, a pretty little blonde thing handing over the keys with a smile and wink for him and a frown her way. Maybe the airport girl and Jared had a thing going.

None of her business, but her jealous bone twinged.

"I need to make a stop at one of the assisted living facilities," he said, pushing two boxes into the bed of the borrowed truck. "I have a couple of care packages to drop off."

She perked up, but she sagged just as quickly. Half the battle would be finding her grandmother a safe place to live, but she'd still have other things to worry about and they loomed large in a murky horizon.

She sat squished between Briar and Jared, closer to him than she would have liked—no, that wasn't true at all—Briar wedged next to the door. This truck didn't have an extended cab like Jared's huge truck did, and to make things more comfortable, he wrapped his arm around her shoulders.

Briar smirked.

Leah swatted her knee and she laughed.

He pretended he didn't see it, but she caught him smiling toward the window.

She snuggled into his side. Today would be fun, and God, did she need some of that.

"I really like her, don't you, Dad?" Briar asked, shuffling down the corridor under the weight of the box she carried.

They'd lost Leah at the nurses' station, a distinguished woman wearing a beige skirt suit hustling her into an office.

"Hmmm?" he asked, toting his own box and trying to look over his shoulder at the same time.

"I said, I really like her."

"That's good."

"Dad. Pay attention. She said she'd be ready to go when we are. You can let her be for half an hour."

He scowled. "I'm just wondering why she'd need information about this place."

"Maybe she doesn't. Maybe she wants to give a donation or something. I could see her doing that. She's really nice, like helping Helen. She's here on vacation, but she spent all day at the Supply Company, and she said she's going back tomorrow to help more. If I didn't have school, I'd help, too."

"When did she tell you that?"

"When we went to the bathroom at the airport."

"Oh."

He didn't have anything to say, but they reached Mrs. Yates's room, saving him from needing to come up with something. Briar could be like a puppy gnawing on a bone, and showing her he'd taken a liking to Leah had been a mistake.

The elderly woman sat in a rocking chair, reading a thick paperback novel.

"Oh, Jared, thank goodness! Owen said you'd be bringing me more books, and this is my last one. You have good timing, young man. And Briar, so good to see you again! Running errands with your father today?"

That's why the boxes were so heavy. Carrying a box that weighed fifty pounds while wearing his parka made sweat roll down his back. Mrs. Yates needed to switch to an e-reader. But Jared suspected she looked forward to the visit just as much as receiving the books.

"I'm going to the mall to find a dress for the school dance, Mrs. Yates," Briar said.

"That's fine, then. It sounds like a nice day. Oh, who's this? Oh, oh," Mrs. Yates said, tears welling in her eyes. "Look at you. You remind me of my daughter." She tugged a tissue out of the square box sitting on a small table beside her. "She passed away ten years ago. Breast cancer."

Leah walked past him, her boots squeaking on the waxed floor, and knelt at Mrs. Yates's feet, holding one of her gnarled hands.

Mrs. Yates smiled through her tears and patted Leah's arm as she began telling Leah a story, forgetting all about him and Briar.

Feeling out of place, he set the box on the bed and rubbed the sweat off his forehead. Without a word, he backed out of the room, letting Mrs. Yates spend time alone with a woman who reminded her of a daughter passed away.

A lump formed in his throat, and he tried to swallow around it.

The picture Leah made, on her knees like she was meeting the Queen of England, listening to an old woman she'd never met before.

"See, I told you."

"I know what you told me, Briar, and remember what I told you. After Marnie's wedding, Leah's going home."

"I wish there was a way."

"You and me both, kiddo. You and me both. Come on, I'll buy you a cup of coffee."

The engraving store had an entire corner devoted to wedding items, and he asked Leah to choose the cake server. He didn't care what Marnie wanted.

"Do you think you'll ever get married again?" he asked. The store offered several types of frames, stock photos of happily married couples beaming at him through dusty glass, and he considered buying a frame and having it engraved with Marnie's and James's names and their ceremony date, as a wedding gift.

Briar looked at jewelry across the store, but he kept his voice low.

"Maybe. I don't know. You've been divorced longer than I have. Do you think about it?" She picked up a wedding album that had space for names and dates to be engraved on the cover.

"I know Briar wants me to. I don't want her to stay in Rocky Point because she thinks I'll be lonely if she's gone. She could do a couple of years at our community college, but even though I love the town, I have to admit there's not a lot of career opportunity there."

"What does she want to do?"

"Her mother talks about fashion all the time, and Briar does love clothes, but I'm not sure."

"Why did your wife leave?" she asked, brushing her fingers over a wedding cake set decorated with sparkling crystals. "I like this one."

"She wanted to work at a fashion magazine and moved to New York. She writes articles for *Vogue* now, and she's, I don't know, their jewelry editor or something. I'm not exactly sure what she does, though it sounds like she parties more than she works. Maybe that's part of the job."

"Schmoozing is definitely part of the job," she agreed. "I bet she goes to all the fashion shows. It would have been impossible for her to have a job like that in Rocky Point. I'm sorry."

He chose a frame. "I'm going to buy this too, as a gift. Do you want to go in on it with me?"

"Sure. That's a great idea."

"I blamed her for a long time, for breaking up our family, but the fact is, we could have gone with her."

She traced her fingers over his cheek, and he caught her hand.

"That wouldn't have been a life for you," she said, gripping his fingers. "I've had a glimpse of how you live, how liked and respected you are. You have a place in the community, and you would have lost that moving to someplace as big as New York. There's a saying that New York will chew you up and spit you out. It's true. I have bite marks all over my body."

"Then why don't you leave, Leah?"

"I have responsibilities I can't turn my back on. You know how it is."

"I do, yeah."

"Dad, can I get this keychain and put my name on it? It's really cute, and I don't have anything personalized."

"Sure, bring it up to the counter. We're done, too."

Well, that's that, he thought as the cashier wrote down what needed to be engraved on which item and rang up their purchases.

His mind may have understood what she said, but his heart didn't have to like it.

"Text me when it's time to pay," Jared said, kissing Briar on the cheek.

Barely looking at Leah, he left them at the mall's entrance of a large department store.

"He's not in a very good mood all of a sudden. Did something happen?" she asked, walking with Briar toward the dress section. He hadn't received any phone calls or texts that she was aware of, but maybe their conversation about marriage crawled under his skin.

"Dad gets sad this time of year. He doesn't want me to know, but he feels guilty Mom isn't around for Christmas."

"I'm sorry."

"I'm not as unhappy as he thinks I am. Mom wanted to do something different. Can you resent someone for that?"

If her whole life revolved around that person, she bet she could resent, even hate, someone, for turning their back on her. "Depends on the circumstances, I guess."

"She's been gone for years, and I don't think about it much, not like it's always in the back of my mind, you know? We talk a lot, and everyone's happy. She's doing what she wants and I didn't have to leave school and my friends. Dad's the only one who can't let it go."

She knew why, and as intuitive as Briar seemed, she was surprised Briar didn't understand her father was still in love with her mother.

Holiday dresses filled the racks, but after looking through all of them and trying on several that would either need altering, were the wrong color, or were, quite simply, just plain ugly, Briar sighed. "I'm not going to find anything here."

"Nope. Come on, there're other stores."

"Dad was hoping I'd find something here."

"Well, you have to look at it this way, buying a dress that doesn't fit and bringing it to a seamstress could easily add a couple hundred depending on what you need done. It doesn't come cheap."

"Yeah. I know."

She bought them smoothies, and in a different store, they laughed and browsed while walking down the wide aisle to the formal wear department. Briar needed more than a few minutes of searching, but finally, on a sale rack hanging on a hanger that an incorrect size clipped to it, she found a navy blue cocktail dress that made her eyes pop. Silver stars sewn into the tulle made it a keeper.

"Oh, Briar, that looks gorgeous on you. You have a lovely figure."

Briar tugged at the price tag hanging under her arm. "It's too much money. Dad gave me a limit, and it's a hundred dollars over, even on sale. I shouldn't have tried it on."

"Never say never. I'm sure we can work something out. Let's look at shoes, and maybe some earrings."

She found silver heels on clearance, and silver star

earrings, also in the clearance bin.

"Here try these on," she told Briar, shoving them at the girl, ecstatic she made the find. "They match your dress."

Briar put them in her ears and admired the stars in the oval mirror sitting on the jewelry counter.

"Did you grow up in New York?" Briar took the earrings out of her earlobes and fastened them to the plastic.

"Yeah. After my grandfather passed away, we moved around a lot because my grandmother had a hard time paying rent."

"What happened to your mom?"

"You know. Sometimes people . . . can't."

"My mom said she couldn't do a good job raising me because she didn't want to live in Rocky Point and her unhappiness would have turned her into a bad mom. Kind of like that?"

"Kind of." Her own mother had too many problems to explain, especially to a sixteen-year old girl whose only worry should be finding a dress to wear to a school dance.

"Let's pay. I found a store coupon on my phone, and I have points to redeem on my credit card. If your dad gets mad, he can get mad at me. He'll forget about it when he sees how pretty you look."

Briar bit her lip. "Are you sure?"

"I'm sure. With the coupon and my points, the dress is practically free."

"I don't know. He told me . . ."

"I know, but he never said I couldn't buy you a Christmas gift, right? There're ways around what your dad said."

She didn't feel right asking Briar to go against Jared's wishes, and it was clear Briar was torn between listening to her and buying the perfect dress or doing what her father asked. He was her father after all and she didn't know anything about raising kids, but the dress looked perfect and she had more than enough points on her credit card to use for the purchase.

"Okay, but let me help at Helen's store tomorrow when I get done with school. Will you still be there?"

"I'll make sure I am."

Briar hugged her as they waited in line for the cashier. "Thank you. I don't . . . hang out with other women very often. I mean, besides my friends." She blushed, clutching the dress to her.

"To tell you the truth, neither do I. I'm having a good time, thanks for asking me to go."

"I think Dad likes it, too."

"Maybe."

They found him outside a small bookstore, reading the new Stephen King.

Briar plopped onto the loveseat next to him, her eyes sparkling.

"You're done? You were supposed to tell me so I could pay."

"I paid. I hope you don't mind," she said, but the scowl on his face told her that he did. "I had points on my card, and I wasn't going to use them for anything else."

"Did you say thank you?" he asked, glaring at Briar.

She flinched. "Of course I did."

"Okay. Good. Is anyone hungry? Because I'm thinking we should head home. Marnie said there's a pool party at the resort tonight and she wants me to go, but I need to put in some hours at work if I want to have time for that."

"Yeah, I guess so," Briar said, gripping the handles of the shopping bag. "Leah bought us smoothies after we tried looking in the first store."

"Leah?"

"I'm fine."

"Good."

The atmosphere in the truck was chillier than the temperature outside, and Jared didn't speak to either Briar or her on the way to the airport.

He asked her to sit in the back of the plane, keeping Briar next to him, and she stared out the window as they flew over the snow-covered earth. Without any conversation, the flight seemed longer, though the distance remained the same.

On the drive to the resort, he held on to his cool demeanor. She was once again ordered to the back of his extended cab, and she sat in silence. A greasy ball of unease rolled around in her stomach.

When he parked under the canopy, she couldn't scoot out of the truck fast enough, and she flung the door open. Briar turned around, catching her gaze before her boots hit the ground. "I'm sorry," she mouthed.

She shook her head. It wasn't Briar's fault. It was completely hers. If she hadn't insisted, none of this would have happened.

"Can I talk to you for a minute?" he asked, leaving his door hanging open and following her into the lobby.

The kid who brought luggage to the guests' rooms stared at them with curiosity, and she fidgeted under the unwanted attention.

"I'm sorry—" she started.

He grabbed her arm and pulled her away from the doors.

"You had no right to do that," he snarled, his face an inch away from hers. "I gave her a limit, and I expected her to listen to me."

"I'm sorry. It's just a dress." She tried to yank her arm out of his grasp, his grip hurting her. "You're making a scene."

"It's just a dress? I'm her father. You're not her mother, and don't you *ever* act like you are again. Do you understand me?"

She stepped back, blood draining from her face.

"I'll pay you back for the dress, I'm assuming she has the receipt. We're on a budget, Leah. I have to watch where my paychecks go. Fancy city women don't get that, do you?" He stomped out of the lobby, his hands clenched into fists at his sides.

The young woman working the front desk gaped at her, and a couple waiting to check in whispered to each other behind their hands, amusement lighting their eyes. A maintenance man carrying a huge red toolbox hurried by, his head lowered, ignoring everyone.

"I'm sorry," she croaked to everyone in the lobby.

She turned and ran to her room.

If she hadn't been here for a wedding, if being Marnie's bridesmaid hadn't meant so much to her, she'd go, leave now. Back to New York.

She was done being Jared's punching bag. He couldn't decide if he liked her or hated her, but he wouldn't have to make the choice.

She'd choose for him and stay as far away from him as she possibly could.

"You didn't have to be like that," Briar said, tears brimming in her eyes.

"Yes, I did. I told you how much you could spend, and you deliberately disobeyed me."

She opened her mouth to protest.

"It doesn't matter if she paid."

"I knew I should have told Mom I needed a dress. She's always offering to send me something."

"I can take care of you myself." He gripped the steering wheel, ashamed he'd lost control. It wasn't the dress or the money that sparked his temper. It'd been the happiness in Briar's eyes. Being a man didn't mean he was stupid. Briar enjoyed shopping with Leah, and that hurt him most of all.

"She said she had points on her credit card, that the dress would be free."

"That's not the point and you know it. We're a family. I'm your father and I expect you to listen to my rules. I've raised you alone for the past five years, and I'll continue to do it forever. I'll always be your dad. When you go to college, when you get married. When you have your own kids."

"It's not you and me against the world, you know."

He clenched his jaw. "Sometimes it feels like it. When you're a single parent, and God, I hope you never have to be, but when you're a single parent, things weigh a lot more heavily on your mind, and your heart." He turned into the driveway, clicked the garage door opener, and guided the truck into the dark garage attached to their small house.

He turned the key in the ignition, and the engine clicking as it began cooling down sounded louder than normal in the cold, lonely dark.

"I struggle with it a lot, Briar. Your mother left us because she was unhappy. She said it wasn't me, that she wanted a career. Would our marriage have worked if we would've moved with her? Or would things have stayed the same, leaving you and me stranded in a city we didn't want to live in? I would have given up my job, our house, on a gamble the city would have made your mother happy with me again."

Briar slouched in her seat and stared straight ahead. "You've never told me any of this."

"You were eleven when she left, and I never would have put my feelings on you. She wanted to work, and all you knew was that she couldn't do what she wanted to do here. That was enough. You didn't want to leave your friends or your school, but I didn't want to move, either. During our marriage, I was asking her to make all the sacrifices, when maybe I should have made some, too."

"I was the one who didn't want to leave, Dad. I remember when you and I sat down and talked it out. You would have given New York a chance if I had wanted to go with Mom, but I didn't. And I still don't." She leaned over and rested her head on his shoulder.

"You've grown up without a mother when girls need their mothers most. I've stayed up at night thinking about that."

"You've done a good job, and it's not like I never talk to her, you know. We FaceTime, write emails. Just because she moved doesn't mean she stopped being my mom."

"You're too forgiving."

"You're too hard on yourself. Staying here was the right choice."

"I hope so."

She pushed the door open. "I'm going inside. If you don't want me to wear the dress, I won't. I'll keep the tags on it and the next time we go to Marengo, I'll return it. The credit will be put back on Leah's card."

He rested his hand on the door handle. After their talk,

Briar would do what he asked, but the memory of the joy on her face as she and Leah walked toward him laughing, victorious they'd found the perfect dress, would taunt him.

"She said I could think of it as a Christmas present," she wheedled, the teenage girl coming out in her.

He could ask her to be grown up for only so long before she turned back into a sixteen-year-old girl. Huffing out a sigh, he pushed his door open. "No. Keep it. I'd like to see it."

"Okay." She paused. "I hope you weren't too hard on her. You dragged her away from the door and I couldn't see."

"I *was* hard on her. She's not your mom, and I know you told her what I said. She didn't listen. She's not a part of our family."

"But you want her to be." She slammed out of the truck and raced into the house before he could respond.

It didn't matter what he wanted.

If it did, Rita never would have left them.

The last thing he wanted to do was go to a pool party, but as a groomsman, he had wedding duties, and after James and Marnie went back to Decatur, it could be months, even years, before he saw them again. Time slipped by faster than he ever thought possible.

It'd been five years since Rita left. Five years and it seemed to have passed in the blink of an eye.

Briar had her driver's license, dated, and looked at colleges, and he remembered like it was yesterday going to her elementary school graduation alone.

He checked in at work and helped set up the new popcorn machine the school's superintendent ordered without letting him know—thank God, but what a hassle—and after sorting through a short stack of paperwork, he went home and looked in on Briar. "I'm going to the resort. Did you want to go swimming? I'm sure James and Marnie wouldn't mind."

"Are you going to see Leah?"

"She'll probably be there."

"I hope you apologize."

"I don't have anything to apologize for."

She looked up from the magazine she was reading. *Vogue.* Of course.

"Keep telling yourself that."

On the way to the resort, Marnie texted him, saying he could change in their room. They'd blocked it open for him and a few others who weren't staying there.

At a red light, he texted, *Thanks,* and after using their room to change out of his jeans and sweatshirt, he walked into the pool area wearing plain black trunks and a t-shirt.

Music blared, people playing in the pool shrieked, and the drinks flowed freely. The scent of pepperoni pizza fought with the pungent odor of chlorine.

Hoping he didn't look like he was searching for someone, he scanned the pool area for Leah, but he didn't see her.

Marnie sat in the hot tub with Autumn and some people he vaguely recognized, and James, Logan and a few others played water volleyball in the large, heated pool.

After the day he had, he didn't have the energy to swim. He poured a couple fingers of whiskey into a red Solo cup and walked over to the hot tub. Marnie wiggled over to make room, and gratefully, he tossed his t-shirt onto a table and sank into the hot water.

He sipped his whiskey, closed his eyes, and let the booze warm his insides while the hot water bubbled around him and eased his muscles.

"You look like you've had a rough day," Marnie said, holding a clear plastic wineglass filled to the brim.

"I had to talk to Briar about her mother. That's never pleasant."

"I'm sorry. James and I are going to start trying right away. My biological clock feels like a ticking time bomb."

"You and James will be good parents."

"You don't think you're a good dad?"

He cracked his eyes open, annoyed Marnie jumped to such a negative conclusion. He didn't usually feel like a bad dad. Most days he was proud of the woman Briar was growing into. But . . . "I think there are things I could have done differently."

"Anyone can say that," Autumn said.

He tamped down a scowl. Autumn didn't have children. She didn't know anything about raising kids. It's what he got for sitting with the women instead of playing ball with James and Logan. Men didn't talk about shit like this.

"If you asked, I bet your parents could give you a long list of the things they wish they would've done differently. But some things are out of your control and it's not your fault," Marnie said.

"That's what I was talking to Briar about. Rita leaving. That maybe we should have gone with her. Was I too inflexible?"

"She talked to me a little before she moved. She *really* wanted to go." Marnie pursed her lips.

He tensed. "What?"

"She really wanted to go . . . alone. She said she was

counting on your roots here to keep you from going with her. If it's any consolation, you gave her what she wanted."

He'd known that, deep down, but it didn't stop him from wondering how things would've turned out had he fought a little harder.

"How's your blog coming, Autumn?" he asked, guilt rubbing at him because of the cruel things he'd thought about her. She pulled the short straw when it came to love, and it wasn't her fault she'd never married or had children.

"Good! This wedding series is getting a lot of hits, and the editor's pleased with the content. So, thanks for getting married, Marnie," Autumn said. Marnie flicked water at her and she laughed. "I interviewed Callie and Mitch. I heard about the way they were treated at the hockey game, but I was on the other side of the arena with Leah and didn't see anything. Did Ed really ask them to leave? Do you know anything about that, Jared?"

He downed the last of his whiskey. "Yeah, and I have to do something about it. I tried to head him off, but he blatantly ignored me. I'm the manager of that arena, and he should have listened to me when I told him to leave Mitch alone."

"What are you going to do?" Autumn asked, but she set her pen down.

He scoffed in disgust. "I need to talk to the superintendent, make sure cutting Ed loose is the way to go. He'll probably need to check with the school district's HR to make sure that's on the up and up." Talking about human resources made him look for Leah again, but she hadn't come into the pool area.

"It's too bad. Callie wants things to change for Mitch, but she doesn't understand what's been happening. Maybe his interview will help a little. I have to interview Leah about falling through the ice, too, and we're going to lunch tomorrow. For someone with nothing but free time, she's hard to pin down. You talked to the DNR, right? What did they say about the hole Leah fell into?" Autumn dried her hands on a towel and picked up her pen again.

Grateful for the change of subject, he said, "Nothing much. Some jerks messing around. The guy I spoke to said there are probably more holes like that around the lake. The one Leah fell into had frozen over and snow was crusted on top, but nothing that would support a human, or even a dog. Someone who lives here might've been able to see it, recognize it as a danger, but Leah wouldn't have known that the area looked different. Wet. You know? Kind of slushy."

She jotted down a few lines in her notebook. "I'm not on the lake that much, I don't know if I would have been able to spot something like that, either. Is she okay? You brought her back to her room, right?"

He was going to need more to drink if Autumn kept asking him questions like this.

"Yeah. I shoved her into a warm shower. Luckily, she hadn't been in the water that long."

"Well, maybe she's feeling the side effects now," Marnie said.

He snapped his head up. "What do you mean?"

"She's not coming to the pool. She said she's not feeling well."

"Did she say why?"

Marnie sipped her wine. "Stomach thing, I think. She probably needs some sleep. She works hard, twelve-, fourteen-hour days most days, and that asshole she was married to put her through hell and back. Don't tell her, but it's one of the reasons I asked her to be a bridesmaid. She was so kind when she hired me, talked me through every little thing, and I wanted to pay her back somehow. I love her to death, and I knew she needed a vacation. A few months ago she told me her doctor wanted to prescribe high blood pressure meds. I'm not sure if she went through with it."

His heart slammed with remorse. Remembering the way she'd thrown up after he pulled her out of the lake made goosebumps prickle his skin, despite the hot water swirling around him. She hadn't said anything while they were shopping about not feeling well. She seemed have to enjoyed the flight. To Marengo, at least. He hadn't looked at her on the way back. He'd been too angry.

"Maybe I should check on her."

"She'll be okay. She's probably sleeping. Snowshoeing with you until late last night and then shopping today wore her out."

"What's that?" Autumn asked, raising her eyebrows.

"He took Leah snowshoeing last night and flew her to Marengo this morning," Marnie said, nudging Autumn's shoulder with hers.

Water volleyball was looking better all the time.

"Did you remember my cake server?"

"Yeah, we did. Leah picked it out, but I didn't think to bring it here."

They'd almost left the mall without stopping at the engraving store to pick up their purchases. Briar reminded him at the last minute, and thank God too, because he didn't plan on flying to Marengo again until after the wedding.

"That's okay, as long as you have it. Thanks again. Another thing I can mark off my list. I'm going to go sit in the sauna. Does anyone want to come?"

He declined.

Marnie and Autumn got out of the hot tub and walked toward the steam room, and he dried off. He put his t-shirt on and with a towel wrapped around his waist, went to Leah's room.

He knocked on her door, but there was only silence.

Leah laid in bed, the bedspread wrapped around her. She couldn't face Jared. The more she thought about what he said to her, the more humiliated she felt. She'd had no intention of trying to be Briar's mother, though Briar missed her mom more than the poor girl wanted to admit, and more than Jared could see, or wanted to see.

"Leah, are you in there?"

His voice floated to her through the door and she stiffened. No way in hell would she answer him.

"I'm sorry about what I said earlier. I should have thanked you, not yelled at you."

That's for damned sure.

"Are you okay? How's your stomach? Do you need to go to the doctor? I can take you. All you have to do is ask."

Surprisingly, her stomach handled him yelling at her, and she might even order dinner from room service after Jared gave up and left her alone. Marnie said there would be pizza at the pool party, but she didn't want to tempt fate. The grease might cause her stomach to act up again, and she should be trying to eat healthier. There weren't a lot of things she couldn't control in her life, but her diet was one of them.

"I know I deserve the silent treatment, but I'm worried about you. You don't have to talk to me. If you could text me that you're okay, I would appreciate it."

Like she owed him any favors. Let him worry. He'd

made a fool out of her in front of strangers and his daughter, when all she'd done was try to be kind.

Fancy city woman.

Where she came from had nothing to do with it.

"Please, Leah?"

Please, what? Give him another chance to yell at her? Give him another chance to humiliate her? There was plenty to do in Rocky Point that didn't include spending time with Jared Hollister. She could avoid him right up until the rehearsal.

"I'm sorry, Leah. I'll leave you alone. Thank you for going with us. Briar loved shopping with you. She couldn't stop talking about what a fun time she had."

She sat up. That's what bothered him. It wasn't the money. It was her. Briar liked shopping with her, and he hated her for that. Resented it.

Okay, then. At least she knew the real reason. She wasn't Briar's mother and she wasn't part of their family. He wouldn't let her be. There wasn't a place for her.

The empty space Rita left took up too much space to let her in.

The next morning, she took a hot shower to wash away her tears and called her grandmother, hoping to catch her after a good night's sleep . . . and her first dose of meds. Luck was with her, and maybe if it stayed with her all day, she'd be able to avoid Jared, too.

"Miss Bristow, the aide just finished giving her a bath, and she's feeling good. She said she'd like to talk . . . but she thinks you're her daughter."

Sometimes that happened, but she would rather talk to her grandma and pretend to be her mother than not talk to her at all. "Thanks for the warning."

"I'll transfer you to her room. The aide is still there and she'll give Della the phone."

"Thank you." She sniffed back tears. "You don't know how much I appreciate all of you."

"It's no trouble, Miss Bristow. We all love Della. One moment, please."

She waited on hold, classical music playing, and a moment later the aide answered and handed the phone to her grandmother.

"Hi, Gra—Mom." Quickly, she corrected herself. The nurse had a reason for warning her. If she didn't play along, it could cause her grandma to break down, and she'd be inconsolable.

"Emmy, how lovely to talk to you! You don't call nearly enough," Della said, her voice strong, though whisper thin.

"I know. I'm sorry. I work a lot, you know."

"How's Richard? You're cooking him dinner every evening, aren't you? Good wives do that."

She sighed. Her father. She'd never met him. When her mother found out she was pregnant, he took off. It had broken her mother. Her spirit. Her mind. Her heart.

"Yes, Mom, I do." Agreeing with the old-fashioned ideas made her pace the floor. She loved these conversations, but they made her remember what she put up with being raised by a woman who thought men deserved to be treated like kings while women were their grateful servants.

"Good. He works hard to take care of you, you know. He loves you. In return, you do what he says, do you understand?"

"Yes."

"You'll come to Sunday dinner. I'm cooking pot roast, and you know Richard loves my pot roast. You can't make it nearly as well."

"We'll be there, Mom. Thank you for the invitation."

"Wear a dress, but nothing too revealing."

"I will."

"You're giving him sex, aren't you?" her grandma demanded. "Husbands deserve sex whenever they want it. Men want babies, Emmy. Sons. You were such a disappointment when you were born."

The refrain familiar, she still flinched at the barb. She being a useless girl and not a boy was another burden her grandmother lived with when she'd taken her in, and she never let Leah forget it.

"Whenever he wants it," she repeated, her voice soothing.

"Good. Sunday, then."

"Yes. Goodbye, Mom," she said, finishing the charade.

"I'm done talking," her grandmother snapped to the aide, and Leah disconnected the call. Her grandmother would take a nap now, even though it wasn't yet ten in the morning there.

She sank onto the bed. Drained after pretending, she could use a nap, too, but today she was helping Helen at the store and she promised to meet Autumn for lunch. She needed to find Marnie, too, and apologize for missing the party last night.

Later she'd look at the schedule and guess what activities Jared would be more likely to attend and figure out a way to skip those.

She'd never learned to play chess, but during her marriage, she'd taught herself how to think two steps ahead.

CHAPTER FIVE

Leah pushed through the Supply Company's glass door and stopped, stunned.

Shoppers filled the store, and Helen stood at one of the registers, her fingers flying over the keys. Fifteen people waited to pay, the line snaking around clothing racks. The store had been open for twenty minutes.

"Thank goodness you're here!" Helen yelled over "Jingle Bell Rock." "One of my girls called in sick and I'm alone until noon. Can you help customers?"

"Sure. I better get moving." Being she'd put out stock the other day, she knew where everything was, and she helped three people before she could take her jacket off.

A lull came around eleven, and Helen sagged against the register. "I'm going to run out for a quick bite. Let me show you how to ring someone up."

"You want to teach me how to use the cash register?" she asked, humbled. Helen must trust her to leave her alone in the store.

"Do you mind? I haven't eaten anything yet today. I skipped breakfast because I thought Susan would be in. I guess the flu's going around and her temperature's up to a hundred and three."

"Umm, sure. I worked a bit of retail in college. As long as they don't need anything strange, I should be okay."

The cash registers Helen used at the Supply Company were old and needed updating, but she learned to punch in the prices of the items and total everything together plus the tax, if any, for the balance due. The register display spit back how much she needed to give in change, but most people paid with a credit or debit card card. Asking customers to swipe their cards seemed simple enough.

Before Helen left, she practiced ringing up a pair of choppers and a scarf for a woman purchasing them as a Christmas gift.

"I told Autumn I'd meet her for lunch at one, is that okay?"

Helen blinked, then burst out laughing. "For a second there, darlin' I thought you were my employee and I was wondering how I'd spare you. You're not on the payroll, but you should be. You can do whatever you please."

She laughed, too. She'd felt like Helen's employee all morning. Like she belonged at the store. "Don't worry, I'll come back to help for the rest of the day."

"Sounds good, and I appreciate it very much."

She introduced herself to Helen's noon employee, an older woman who worked part-time to have extra spending money. Thankfully, she'd come in a little early, and they both ran the cash registers when too many people were forced to wait.

When Helen relieved her at the register, she put out more product, customers flocking to the new items before she could cut the tape on the boxes.

At five to one, she gratefully grabbed her jacket out of the stockroom, helped a customer find a sweater in the size she needed, and hurried down the sidewalk to the diner. She hadn't done so much physical activity in a long time, and every muscle in her body ached. Autumn was slipping out of her jacket and unwinding a thick scarf from around her neck at a table near the window, and she dropped into a chair, needing the break. "Hi."

"Hey. You look sparkly."

"I feel good. Exhausted, but good."

"No, I mean, you're really sparkling." Autumn laughed. "You have glitter everywhere."

She brushed at her shirt. "Sorry. I was helping at Helen's again. Now that she has stock out, people are shopping like crazy. I don't know if she loves it or hates it."

"Oh, she loves it. She'll cry when that store sells," Autumn said, hanging her coat on the back of her chair.

"She seems happy today."

"You did a nice thing. I stopped in to buy a new pair of sunglasses and I haven't seen that many people in the store at one time in years."

"All I did was help put out stock."

"That's not all you did."

"Maybe."

She looked out the window at Rocky Point's main street. Most people were working and school still had two more hours before it let out for the day, but there were a few people on the sidewalk, some going into the drugstore across the street.

She couldn't get used to the . . . space. The crampedness of city living pressed in on her like claustrophobia, all the people, all the buildings, all the noise, but here, in Rocky Point, she could breathe.

"Anyway, how are you? We haven't spoken since ice

fishing," Autumn said, passing her a laminated menu tucked behind the salt and pepper shakers.

She waited for the waitress to write down their coffee orders and walk away, then answered, "Okay, I guess."

Autumn held her hand. "That was a complete one-eighty. I'm sorry if I made you sad."

"You didn't. I went shopping with Jared and Briar yesterday, and I bought Briar a dress. It was more than he said she could spend, but I didn't see the harm. He was furious, and I . . ." She tried to laugh. "I shouldn't let it bother me. I'm not going to be here forever so what do I care if I made him angry?"

"That's why you skipped the pool party last night."

"Yeah. He said some pretty nasty things."

"He never mentioned it, but he was upset when Marnie said you weren't coming."

The waitress served their coffees and pulled a pad and pen out of her apron's pocket. Autumn ordered a BLT and French fries and because she hadn't looked at the menu, she ordered the same.

"He came to my room and apologized through the door. I didn't want to talk to him after what he said. By then it was too late, he'd told me his true feelings. You and Marnie were right. He's not over his ex-wife. He told me to stop acting like Briar's mom."

Autumn paused, her coffee cup halfway to her mouth. "Oh, honey."

She unrolled her silverware and used the napkin to wipe her eyes. "And the funny part is, I had no thought in my head I was acting like her mom. I was trying to be her friend."

The waitress poured them more coffee and set another

dish of cream on the table. "Your order will be up in a minute."

"Thank you," Autumn murmured, and then to Leah, "How are you feeling after your polar plunge? I'd like to include it in my newest blog post, if you don't mind."

"It's fine. I'm okay. Jared . . ."

"Took care of you."

"Yeah."

"Do you have feelings for him?" Autumn asked.

She smiled wryly. "Is that going in the blog?"

Autumn put her pen down. "No. I'm asking as a friend."

She wrapped her hands around her mug and stared out the window. "If my ex-husband . . . some couples, they divorce without fighting. Without getting nasty. Not many, but some. If my ex-husband had been . . . kind . . . maybe this would feel . . . I don't know."

"Marnie said your ex was an asshole."

"Yeah. He was. Is. It's been hard to let that go. And Jared . . . he's hot and cold all the time. Kissing me one minute—"

Autumn's eyes widened.

"Yelling at me the next. I'm confused about my feelings, but it's nothing compared his mood swings."

"He hasn't dated anyone since Rita left. He probably doesn't know what to do."

"Why didn't Rita want to be a bridesmaid?"

Autumn pursed her lips.

"You can tell me. I know I'm the odd one out here."

"No, you're not. Marnie considers you one of her best friends. She said so last night. Rita . . . hasn't come back to town. Not once. When she sees Briar, Briar flies to New York. When she was little, that was hard on Jared, putting her on a plane and hoping she arrived safely. Even with the flight chaperones, he hated it."

"I see." She didn't blame him for worrying about his daughter flying alone. She hated to travel, and she was a grown woman.

The waitress set their plates in front of them, asked if she could get them anything else, and moved on in disinterest before they could say no.

She met Autumn's eyes and laughed.

"Tell me about your icy dip and what you're doing at the store," Autumn said. She popped a French fry into her mouth and picked up her pen.

The rest of the meal passed by in a pleasant haze of coffee and gossip.

A little boy walking with Cole stopped in front of the window, and he pounded on the glass with his mittened hands, joy lighting his face.

Cole grinned at them, and Autumn blushed. Amused, and maybe a little concerned, she tilted her head in speculation. She'd thought something was going on between them, but whenever they were together, they weren't happy.

They walked into the diner and made a beeline for their table. Cole helped the boy settle into a chair, his short legs jutting out from the seat, feet heavy in blue and green snow boots.

"Hello, ladies," Cole said, flopping into a chair close to Autumn. She leaned away.

"Who's this handsome man?" she asked, earning a grin full of baby teeth.

"This is Tyler, Ty for short," Autumn said, introducing them. "He's my nephew."

She looked at the two of them. Something Autumn said during the hockey game snagged her memory. Cole had been, or still was, married to Autumn's sister. And she thought her love life was in shambles. Being in love with someone you couldn't have would definitely hurt.

She was lucky she wasn't in love with Jared—

Crap.

That couldn't be why he had the power to hurt her so badly, was it?

Did she light up around Jared the way Autumn shined for Cole?

No, she didn't think so. Her stomach had done a little thing when he kissed her while they laid in the snowbank, but it hadn't been because of him. She liked being outside watching the lights, feeling free of the city. And kissing him in the parking lot, leaning into his chest under the stars, she'd been swept up in the romance of it. That's all. She'd had very little romance in her life, and after Max, she didn't want to say she was susceptible to such a small crumb of affection, but the fact was, it'd been a hard year. Jared looking at her like she was as beautiful as the northern lights would make any woman's heart beat a little faster.

It didn't mean she was falling in love.

Ty chatted excitedly about playing outside, words and babbles blending together in pure happiness. Like everything else about Rocky Point, Ty charmed her, and when she stood up to go back to the Supply Company to put stock out for the rest of the day, she couldn't resist leaning in for a hug and damp kiss.

"It was nice to see you again," she said to Cole, pushing in her chair.

"Marnie has a fancy dinner at the resort planned for Wednesday night. I'll see you there?" he asked.

"I haven't looked at the activities sheet, but I'll be there. It sounds fun. I need to get back to help Helen. She's expecting a truck, thank God, because clothes are flying off the racks. Nice to meet you, Ty," she said, running her fingers through his hair. "Have a good afternoon, you two. Thanks for lunch, Autumn."

"I'll see you later," Autumn said.

Cole lifted a hand and Ty waved.

Leah stepped outside, her heart light. A feeling she hadn't had in a long time.

Passing her on the sidewalk, a woman said hello to her by name, and surprised, she returned the cheerful greeting.

She walked by the diner's window and peeked inside. Cole spoke to Autumn, a hand on her shoulder, but she turned away, tears dripping down her face. Ty, thankfully oblivious, scarfed French fries, a small glass of chocolate milk in front of him.

She hurried away before Autumn caught her spying.

Poor Autumn. Cole seemed like a nice guy, but if being around him made her cry, then he should stay away from her.

That was none of her business, though it hurt to see one of her friends hurting. And Autumn was her friend.

Autumn considered her a friend, too. It'd been a long time, since Marnie, really, someone called her a friend. Her life hadn't had the room, neither had her emotional or mental health. Max had taken and destroyed everything she could offer anyone.

She held the door open for a gentleman who was just about to push through the Supply Company's glass door, his arms laden with bags.

"Thank you, young lady," the man said, nodding at her.

"You're welcome."

The For Sale sign still leaned against the glass, sparkling now, because she'd hired a cleaning company to wash the windows. Helen had approved, of course, but there would be a lot more she'd want to do with the store, if it was hers.

What if she . . .

No. That was stupid.

She couldn't move here.

What would she think of next? Having babies?

Ty's smile dazzled everyone in the diner, as brilliantly as Autumn's tears sparkled in the sun.

People had problems in small towns, too.

Moving to Rocky Point wouldn't solve hers.

Sighing, she went inside.

She worked the cash register for the rest of the afternoon, Helen saying she'd rather hide in the back and unpack stock. She didn't mind. She loved talking to the customers as she rang up their items, listening to stories about life in Rocky Point or how grateful they were that Helen was once again showing interest in the store.

She heard more than once if the store closed, it would create a huge retail hole in Rocky Point.

A lull in customers allowed her a much-needed break, and she was sipping a bottle of water when Briar walked in.

"Hi!" she chirped, tugging off camel-colored choppers. "I'm here to help you and Helen."

She paused.

Helen waddled up the aisle holding a large box. "Leah, could you tag these when you get a chance . . . hi, Briar. What brings you in? Does your dad need you to pick up something?"

"No. I've come to help. Leah bought me a dress yesterday and I want to pay her back."

Helen set the box on the counter near her register and backed away. "That's sweet of you, and I'll leave that up to her, if she's got something you can do. I'll be in the stockroom if you need anything." She retreated, the racks hiding her figure.

"Briar—" she started.

"I know my dad was mad," Briar said.

She stepped from behind the register and adjusted the hem of her blouse to give herself a moment to think. "Come here," she said, leading Briar to a bench cranky husbands used as a resting and gossip stop while they waited for their wives.

"What your dad said . . ." She trailed off. She hated to hurt Briar's feelings, but she had to respect Jared's wishes. She already made a mess of things.

"What?" Briar licked her lips.

"He doesn't want you spending time with me." It was too much to say, yet not enough. She didn't want to put the girl in the middle. Briar had done nothing wrong.

This was between her and Jared.

"But why? That doesn't sound like my dad."

She smoothed a hand over Briar's blonde bob, but she let it drop.

The gesture belonged to a mother.

"He doesn't want you to get hurt when I go home, sweetie," she said. "I didn't listen, before, but I should listen to him now. Okay?"

Briar looked down at the choppers laying in her lap. "I don't know why he would say that."

"You should talk to him about it." She would never repeat the hurtful things he yelled at her.

"I'm sorry if—"

"You didn't do anything wrong. Please believe that. Your dad's a good man, and he's trying his best. But he's been hurt . . ." Too much, her brain screamed. Too much.

"By my mom," Briar whispered.

Regretting this conversation, she tucked her hands between her knees. Maybe she should have just let Briar help. She and Helen could have worked in the back, and everyone would have been happy.

"Yes. But that doesn't . . . I mean . . . that's none of my business. All I can do is what he asked. I didn't listen before."

Briar slid off the wooden bench and jammed her hands into her choppers. "I get it."

Her heart thumped painfully as Briar walked out of the store, her shoulders slumped in dejection.

"That was tough," Helen said, coming up behind the bench.

"On who? Briar or me?"

"On Jared. I can't imagine him hurting that much he'd tell you to stay away from Briar."

She stiffened. "Well, he did. I told Briar the truth. He can't stand the thought of me leaving."

Helen's faded brown eyes gleamed. "Really?"

"It's not like that."

"Then what's it like?"

"He doesn't want me to hurt Briar like her mom did. He's being a good dad, that's all."

"And that's it?"

"That's it."

Helen opened her mouth to say more, but a large group of people bustled their way into the store. A Canadian tour bus parked outside, letting out shoppers who wanted a good deal before Christmas.

"We better get to work," she said. "I can give you a few more hours. Especially with this crowd."

"Thanks, darlin'. You're a good girl."

She and Helen swapped places—Helen was better at figuring out the exchange if they paid with Canadian currency—and she put out stock and tried to push Briar out of her mind.

Jared was afraid Briar would get hurt when she went home after Marnie's wedding, but she, he hadn't bothered to think about, was in the same situation.

Build up the wall, like she had when Max left her. Don't let people in. She was becoming attached to Rocky Point, and Briar wouldn't be the only one hurting when she left.

She'd start with the Supply Company. Stop working here. After her shift, she'd tell Helen she needed to do more for Marnie and the wedding. Helen would understand.

The thought made her sad.

Her stomach churned.

Jared opened the door to his house, desperately wanting a beer. He couldn't get Leah's face out of his mind. The pain in her eyes, the way her cheeks paled leaving her pasty, clammy.

He hadn't heard a word from anyone all day. Didn't know how she was doing. He told himself every five minutes it wasn't his business. He'd done what he needed to do to protect Briar. Since Rita left, that'd been his only priority.

Before he met Leah, he'd been doing fine. His and Briar's relationship was strong. He'd gotten her through her period—though her mother told him what type of pads to buy—and he'd taken her bra shopping in Marengo because she'd been terrified to bump into someone she knew in town.

Boys.

Sleepovers.

Mean girls.

He helped her through it all.

He'd had no choice. And while things hadn't always been smooth sailing, they'd made it through with respect for each other and their senses of humor intact.

Now ripples of tension invaded their home.

Wearily, he trodded up the stairs. Too tired to cook, he decided to order out and needed to ask Briar what she wanted for dinner. He could relax in the living room, drink a beer, and flip through the channels like he had before Leah disrupted his way of doing things.

Damn her.

He knocked on Briar's door.

He didn't get a response, and it was like déjà vu standing outside Leah's door at the resort. He pushed it open. "Do you want—"

She laid on her bed staring into space, tears soaking her pillow.

He sat on the edge of the mattress, but she didn't look at him. "What's wrong? Something with Skyler?"

She shook her head.

That's good, at least. All that fuss about her dress would

have been for nothing if her boyfriend had broken up with her.

"Something happen at school?"

Again, she shook her head.

He wished Rita was here. These were the moments he hated most, when she didn't feel like she could talk to him because he was a man.

He'd learned a long time ago not to push. "Okay, if you feel like talking, I'll be downstairs. I'm going to order out. It's been a long day."

When he reached the door, she whispered, "She sent me away."

"What?"

She focused her blue eyes on him. "She sent me away."

"Who did?"

"Leah. After school, I went to the Supply Company to help. To thank her for the dress. She worked there all day, and Helen didn't pay her. I wanted to volunteer, too. She sent me away."

He sat on her bed again. "Why would she do that?"

"You told her to. You told her you didn't want her spending time with me."

A chill spread over his skin. "It's not exactly like that."

"It *is* like that. Is it the dress? She said because she didn't listen."

"It's not the dress, Briar. She's leaving after Marnie's wedding."

"So what, Dad? I have friends who live far away. I still talk to Hannah, and her family moved to Iowa two years ago. I still talk to Ryan, even though his parents had to move to take care of his grandparents. With social media, distance doesn't matter anymore."

It did to him. Distance mattered. When he would lie in bed so lonely he felt hollowed out. When he woke to an empty bedroom. When he made coffee for one in a cold kitchen.

Emails, phone calls, texts. FaceTime. Zoom. Those things couldn't take the place of a hug or a kiss.

Couldn't take the place of his heart tangling with hers as they made love.

One of his favorite things he'd had with Rita was walking up behind her and wrapping his arms around her, pressing his lips to her neck, feeling her heartbeat pulse beneath her skin.

She'd tip her head and purr, and they'd stand that way, silent, as he poured love from his soul into hers.

He couldn't explain that to his daughter. He couldn't explain that he needed more than an email.

"I don't want you to get hurt," he finally said.

"Having her in my life a little is better than none at all."

"Are you sure, Briar?"

She lifted her chin in a gesture he knew so well. She wouldn't budge.

"Yes."

"Okay. I'll go talk to her and apologize." *Again.*

He heaved himself off the bed, her bedroom decorated all pink, flowers and hearts. Her pompoms sat in a corner, crinkly and sparkly.

"Dad."

"Yeah?" He looked at his little girl, cheated out of a mother because he hadn't been man enough to keep his wife by his side.

"Remember when you're talking to her, you weren't looking out for me. You were looking out for yourself."

Leah's arms ached, and as she walked down the hallway toward her room, she looked forward to changing out of her clothes and either taking a bath or Marnie texted her earlier and said she and a few others were meeting at the pool if she wanted to grab her swimsuit and join them. Being alone sounded better after chatting with customers all day, but since she wouldn't be here if it weren't for Marnie, she should spend some time with the woman who would be getting married in less than two weeks.

Pulling her phone out of her pocket to check the time Marnie said they would be meeting, she didn't watch where she was going and stumbled into someone loitering by her door.

She staggered backward, an apology on her lips, but she looked away and dug her room key out of her purse. "What are you doing here?"

There wasn't any point in being polite. After the things he said, when she'd only been trying to be nice, he didn't deserve any more of her patience.

"I want to talk to you about what happened between you and Briar today."

She jabbed her key into the deadbolt. "I did what you asked. Or did I misunderstand what you yelled at me yesterday? You made it very clear you didn't want me around her, and that's fine. You're her father, and you have the right to make those kinds of decisions. I'm meeting Marnie. If there's nothing else, I need to go."

She cracked the door open, intending to slip inside and shut the door in his face.

"When I got home from work, she was in her room, crying."

She wilted, and sighing, she held the door open. "Come in."

Dumping her purse on the desk, she tried to think of what she could say without sounding like she was blaming him. All this was his fault, but it would make things worse if she defended herself by pointing it out.

"I didn't mean to make her cry, but I thought after what you said to me in the lobby, it was the best thing to do. It hurt, you know, accusing me of trying to be her mother. I would never assume I could do that. Even from New York, Briar's mother can do a better job than I would ever be able to do."

"Why would you say that? Can I take my coat off? Do you mind?"

She minded. She wanted him to go, but she shrugged and took off her jacket too.

He sat on the bed. "It didn't occur to me to ask if you had kids. I assumed since you were divorced you didn't have any."

"I don't. Max and I talked about it. He seemed to like the idea, having a boy to take after him, but he was as demanding as an infant. We didn't have room in our lives for a baby. I had the smarts to know early on I couldn't take care of him in the way he expected, care for a child, work full time, and everything else on top of it. I had an IUD inserted behind his back, and it probably saved my life. It certainly saved me a custody battle. A battle he would have won because he has more money than God and doesn't let me forget it."

"I'm sorry." Strain lined his face and worry wrinkled his forehead.

She spoke to her hands, unable to meet his eyes. "No, I am. I didn't mean to get into that tonight. This is about Briar. I still think I did the right thing, and I think you should go, because the fact is, you're right. I told Helen I can't work at the Supply Company anymore, and I'm going to stop having lunch with Autumn. I'm not a part of Rocky Point. I'm not a part of anything here except a wedding party that won't have any reason to see each other after the reception. We can be civil, can't we? Civil until the wedding's over."

"No."

"No, we can't be civil? Then what are you doing here? What do you want?"

"I meant, no, I'm not right, Leah. This is all wrong." He stood from the bed and cradled her face in his hands. Echoing his daughter, he said, "I'm not afraid for Briar. I'm afraid for myself."

Leaning into her, he breathed in the scent of cold air, cardboard boxes, dust, and something that would always belong to Leah. That it was probably a perfume that cost hundreds of dollars a bottle didn't make him hate it, but it should have.

On her, the scent smelled right, and it didn't make him hate it, it made him sad.

"I don't understand," she whispered.

He rubbed the pad of his thumb over her lips, nudging her against the wall, trapping her. "I get tired, being alone, and I tried hard to keep you at arms' length, but you're so fragile, so delicate, all I want is to keep you safe. I can't because you're not mine, and how can you be when your home, your career, are thousands of miles away?"

He thought thinking those things hurt, saying them aloud shoved a knife into his heart.

"What do you want to do?" she asked, gripping his wrist.

"Can we . . . have tonight? And the rest of your vacation? Can we have those minutes, those hours, before you go?"

"Will you be able to do that? Because I don't think you can. You're friendly, then you're not. Then you're kissing me. Then you're yelling at me. You're spinning me around in circles."

And you're making me sick. She didn't have to say it, not with the way she clutched the material of her blouse over her stomach.

"I'm sorry." He echoed Briar's words, admitting the truth in them. "Having you a little is better than none at all."

"I won't put up with you snarling and growling and snapping at me. Not anymore. If you can't do this without treating me with respect and kindness, then I don't want to be a part of it. I've done nothing wrong, and I don't deserve it." Tears filled her eyes.

"You're right, and I don't want to keep hurting you. I want to be with you, for as long as I can." He hoped she wouldn't make him beg because he would. From the minute she sat in his plane when he picked her up at the Marengo airport, he knew this would end up happening. He'd tried to hide from it, tried to push her away, but those things did the opposite of what he wanted them to do. Protect his heart. Because when she hurt, he hurt.

"Okay." She blew out a breath, and a smile trembled on

her lips. "Will you kiss me, then? Will you make love to me tonight?"

"Are you sure?" he asked, kicking himself for giving her an out. He'd be a very broken man if she took it.

"If I wasn't sure, I wouldn't ask. I want to be with you, too. You can hurt me because I—"

He placed a finger over her lips. "Let's not say things we can't take back."

She held his hand and kissed his palm. "But you feel it."

"Yeah." God help him, he did.

He leaned his arm against the wall above her head, and he kissed her, his hand caressing her damp cheek.

She opened her mouth, and he accepted the invitation, delving into her sweetness. She wrapped her arms around his neck and raked her fingers through his hair. He tried to stay in the present, tried not to calculate how long it'd been since a woman held him this way.

"You feel good," he murmured when he came up for air.

"It's been a while, since a man has . . . touched me like he cared."

"Come to bed, sweetheart, and I'll keep showing you."

He began to unbutton her blouse, sure she would stop him, but she didn't. He parted the silky material, revealing a cream-colored bra. Tenderly, he traced the lace, his fingertip barely grazing her skin, and he smiled when she shivered. "You're so beautiful."

"You're not so bad yourself," she said and unbuttoned his plaid flannel shirt. "When we were in the shower, I didn't realize . . . I was in too much of a shock to appreciate what you had going on under your clothes."

"Here I was concerned you almost died, and you were gawking at me."

"The gawking started after I warmed up."

Chuckling, he slipped off her shirt and undid her slim belt. Her belly quivered under his touch as he unzipped her slacks. "You can say no anytime, sweetheart. I promise I won't get angry."

"Thanks, but I'm good."

"Good." He kissed down her stomach, over the waistband of her panties, to the apex of her thighs. Her musk filled his nose, and he pressed his lips to the damp satin.

"Jared," she moaned.

"Take your shoes off and crawl into bed." He kissed the inside of her thigh and stood.

His erection strained against his jeans, and he prayed he could make this good for her. He hadn't slept with another woman since Rita. No one had opened his heart the way Leah did. Maybe it was her vulnerability, maybe it was the way she cared about everything and everyone around her, maybe it was the way she wanted to befriend his daughter and do something sweet, or maybe it was all those things wrapped into one, but she had something he hadn't found in another woman. Something he wanted to keep.

He kicked off his boots and shoved his jeans down his legs.

Debating if he should take off his briefs, he stood at the edge of the bed, but then she unhooked her bra and threw her panties on the floor near the rest of her clothes, and it would have been stupid to get into bed in his underwear.

He pulled off his briefs, and her eyes widened.

"It's been a really long time for me, too," he said honestly, "but I won't hurt you, I promise."

"I know you won't."

She turned down the bedspread and he followed her between the sheets. Immediately, she wiggled under him and spread her legs. This was going a little quicker than he would have liked, but he couldn't complain as she held his cock in her warm hand, and tilting her hips, urged him inside her.

"You're still protected?" he asked, gritting his teeth.

"Yes. Fill me up, Jared. It's been too long."

He did as she asked, sliding inside her silky heat and settling his weight on top of her. She wrapped her legs around his waist, bringing him closer, until he couldn't go any farther.

"This what you want, baby?" he asked, his breath warming her ear.

"Yes, please, Jared, please."

He withdrew, then pushed into her, then withdrew, unhurried, steady glides, his hand under her head, covering her lips with his. This was the way he made love. Quietly, slowly. Oh, he had his fun, and if he and Leah ever made it back into bed, he would show her that too, but for now, he'd let her know how deep his feelings went.

Her muscles quivered around him. She was almost there but needed one last thing. He reached between their bodies and a simple touch sent her over.

She cried out into his neck, hugging him to her, and he let himself go, giving her a part of himself that he hadn't to another person since his wedding day.

Leah whimpered, hot tears wetting his skin, and he tumbled.

She rolled over and rested her head on Jared's chest. She wanted this, and she didn't have any regrets, but come morning, things might be different. It was always much easier to hide in the dark, and in Minnesota, when the darkness closed in at five in the afternoon, there was that much more of it.

"How long were you married?" he asked.

She should have expected the pillow talk but she didn't want to talk about Max. Though if forced to choose between talking about things she wanted to avoid and Jared dressing and leaving, the choice was easy.

"About three years. I didn't work for Outdoor Wonders then. Max started his own financial consultation firm, and he needed a partner. I worked for a headhunting company, and I helped him find someone that met his specifications. After Max lured him away, he kept in touch with me. Coffee led to lunch, lunch led to dinners, dinners into late-night drinks, drinks turned into breakfast in bed. He had a ring on my finger before I knew what was happening. He's ten years older than I am, and I got carried away." She sighed and pressed a kiss to his skin. "I sound like I wasn't thinking for myself. I was. Or I thought I was. I was dazzled by the glamour of it. I didn't grow up with money, and he has gobs of it."

"Three years isn't very long," he said, hugging her to him.

"I suppose it's not, but it feels like it when every day is hell." She propped herself up and looked into his kind hazel eyes. She kissed him, soft lips, a little tongue, and he rubbed his knuckles up and down her back. She shivered.

"Did you leave him?"

"No. I don't think he would've let me if I tried. He left me for a junior consultant—someone I headhunted for him, if that matters. We lived in a huge apartment, and when I came home from work one day, there was nothing left. Only my clothes. He said my replacement had bigger boobs than

I did and nothing I owned would fit her. He wasn't so crass, Max is all class, but I knew what he meant."

He swore. "He left you with nothing?"

"He gave me my freedom. But . . . I had financial responsibilities. I had to take out a loan to make ends meet, and I was lucky I found a bank that approved one. Outdoor Wonders offered me a job, and it paid well, with better benefits than what I had headhunting, so I took it. I've tried to be happy there, they're a good company, but times were hard for a while."

"You said it wasn't that long ago."

"No. About a year. The divorce went through quickly. He got what he wanted because I couldn't afford to fight, but that doesn't mean he leaves me alone. He picks at me whenever he can."

"Bastard."

She laughed. "Yeah. But I'm happier in my little walk-up struggling to make ends meet than in our fancy apartment where Max would go ballistic if there was even a speck of dust in the living room. Which was always my fault, never the cleaning service, because he liked to blame me for whatever he could."

"Did he hit you?" he asked, gripping her hair, forcing her to meet his gaze.

She bit her lip.

"Leah."

"No. He didn't. He didn't," she insisted when he raised an unbelieving eyebrow, "but the way he looked at me, the way he acted, every minute we were together, sometimes I wished he would have just gotten it over with. His new wife got pregnant the first month they were married. I feel sorry for her."

"I'm glad you're out of there."

"Me too."

She brushed a hand over his hard cock, and he surged beneath her fingers. She wiggled until she was poised above him, his tip nudging her.

He filled his palms with her breasts, and she steadied herself, gripping the headboard.

"You said that Outdoor Wonders pays well. Why do you struggle?"

"Oh, you know . . . bills . . ." She slowly sank onto him. "Did you want to keep talking?"

"There's time enough for that."

"That's what I thought."

They sat on her bed and ate hamburgers room service delivered and sipped beer.

He'd never seen another woman look so beautiful, her hair mussed from his hands being tangled in it, her lips swollen from his passionate kisses. His whiskers had chafed her cheeks, but she didn't complain.

The time neared ten o'clock when he put on his jeans. He'd like to stay later, but didn't want Briar alone in the house overnight. "What are you doing tomorrow?"

Wearing her robe, she slid off the bed. "Is there anything on the activities sheet?"

"I don't think so. Fancy dinner thing coming up, but tomorrow's free. James and Marnie are going snowmobiling. Do you want to go?" he asked, shrugging into his jacket.

"Don't you have to work?"

"I blocked out days a long time ago. That's probably the

only nice thing about weddings . . . things are planned out far in advance. I can take half the day if I stay later."

"If it's no trouble, I'd love to go."

He cuddled her to him and kissed her. She tasted of beer and salt, and a flavor he'd never tire of. "It's no trouble. I want to see you as much as I can."

"Even if it hurts?" she asked, smoothing her fingers over his jaw.

"Even if it hurts." He paused. "If you don't—"

"I do."

"Good. Meet Marnie and James in the lobby at ten. We'll stop for lunch at a resort a few miles from here." Halfway out the door, he stopped. "And Leah—"

"Dress warm. I got it."

He kissed the tip of her nose. "Goodnight."

"Night."

This was right. How it should be, he thought, sitting in his truck while he let it warm up before the ride home. Take what he could get, make each hour count.

Better than nothing.

At least, he tried to tell himself that.

CHAPTER SIX

The day dawned sunny and bright, and Leah squinted as she stepped outside the resort with Marnie and James.

James's had father dropped off a snowmobile a few minutes earlier and they were waiting for Jared, who'd texted her he was on the way.

"I didn't hear from you last night," Marnie said, looking at her out of the corners of her eyes.

"I was going to text you but Jared stopped by my room."

Marnie frowned. "You two aren't fighting again, are you? I've never known him to be a jerk, at least, he wasn't in high school. I guess people change."

"We weren't fighting. We . . . patched things up."

That was the closest she was going to get to admitting she and Jared slept together last night.

James, sitting on the snowmobile and sipping coffee out of a disposable cup, smirked, amusement sparkling in his eyes. "You can take that to the bank."

"What do you mean?" She didn't know James very well, and her cheeks flamed.

"My cousin's on the other side of you, and at breakfast this morning she was telling me all about how her neighbor has been so quiet, until last night."

"That's not true! We were quiet!" She slapped her mittened hand over her mouth. Dammit.

Marnie laughed but gave her a tight hug. "I'm glad you two are getting along. Jared's a really nice guy, and as much as I love Rita as a friend, I think what she did wasn't right," she whispered in Leah's ear.

She was saved from responding as Jared drove into the parking lot, a huge, vicious-looking snowmobile strapped in the bed, its rear jutting out of the open tailgate. "Good God. Am I going to be riding on that thing?"

"It's the same size as this one," James said, swinging his leg over the snowmobile and throwing his cup into the outdoor trash bin. "His is a couple of years newer." He clapped his hands, and his choppers snapping as the leather connected. "Let's get going," he called to Jared.

"I'm on it," he said, waving.

"He's such a cutie," Marnie murmured, nudging her shoulder.

"Yeah, he is."

No use denying it.

Jared used a ramp to push the snowmobile off the truck. James helped him slide it back into the box and Jared locked his truck. He started it, the engine growling, and rode the giant machine toward them, kneeling with on one knee on the seat instead of sitting. He stopped, lifted his sunglasses, and met her eyes, his guarded. "Good morning."

"Good morning," she said, shuffling to the snowmobile, her thick layers making it difficult to walk. Her hearting fluttering, she reached onto her toes and kissed him, taking the chance he hadn't changed his mind.

Instead, he took his mitten off and brushed her hair out of her eyes. "You sure?"

She looked over her shoulder at Marnie and James, a know-it-all glint in their eyes. "They already know. Apparently, we were noisy last night."

"Well, then." He lifted her into his arms and covered her mouth with his.

She melted, parting her lips, wanting more.

Only Marnie's and James's hoots and howls made him release her, and he grumbled his displeasure under his breath.

"I'd say get a room, but you already did," James said, laughing.

"Shush," Marnie admonished, but she laughed too, and settled onto the back of James's snowmobile. "We'll break for lunch in a couple of hours. Try not to have to pee before then. There's not a lot of places to go."

"I'll try not to," she said, meeting Jared's eyes and grinning.

"Ever been on one of these before?"

"Nope."

"You're having lots of first times."

She straddled the seat and wrapped her arms around his waist. Squeezing the gas, he lurched them forward, and in anticipation, she tightened her grip.

Yeah, she was having a lot of first times, and so far, they were all wonderful.

The roar of the machine buzzed in her ears and thrummed under her butt.

The men tore across the lake, and as the miles flew by them, she relaxed into Jared's back.

Marnie pointed to a bird flying in the sky, but in this cold, she didn't know what would still be this far north. A hawk. Maybe a falcon. She'd try to remember to ask Jared at lunch. Asking him now over the rumble of the snowmobiles would be impossible.

The white expanse of the snow-covered lake met the bright blue sky, and Leah had never seen anything so stunning.

Freezing air burned her lungs, but she drew in deep, greedy breaths, the crisp coolness of it revitalizing her.

She didn't grow bored like she thought she would. Two hours of nothing but white and blue, green sometimes, evergreen trees that dotted the shore or grew on small rocky islands the men drove around in large, looping turns.

She was almost sorry when they reached the other resort, James and Jared parking the snowmobiles in a line that reminded her of the Wild West when cowboys tied their horses to a post before going into a saloon.

"How'd you like that?" Jared asked, standing and stretching.

She did the same. "It was fun. How fast were we going?"

"About eighty," James said, helping Marnie off the snowmobile.

It hadn't felt like they were going that fast at all. "Are we in Canada?"

Jared patted her butt to get her moving toward the resort. "Almost, but not quite."

The resort's bar was packed with others doing the same thing—taking advantage of the clear winter day to ride, meet up with friends, and relax.

They managed to snag a corner table a waitress cleaned off just as they stepped inside, and everyone needed a good five minutes to pull off hats, choppers, scarves, and jackets. Snow pants stayed on, but she unclipped hers and let the top bunch around her waist.

She leaned into Jared, and he draped his arm over the back of her chair. He played with the ends of her hair, then rested his hand on the nape of her neck.

It surprised her how natural it felt. Out with friends, chatting, laughing. Drinking coffee and eating chicken strips off the limited menu the resort provided. The weight of Jared's arm around her shoulders, the shared smiles.

But something writhed in the depths of his eyes when he looked at her, and she turned away. Their time was limited. No one knew that better than her.

After they ate, Marnie asked her to go to the ladies' room while the men paid the bill. She almost offered to pay for her meal, but she didn't want to make Jared angry. She'd been doing a good job of that, and he asked her to go.

"You and Jared are getting along better now," Marnie said, washing her hands.

"We've come to a truce, I guess."

"Doesn't that make you happy?"

"Yeah, it does, but it'll make it harder to go back to New York after your wedding."

Marnie threw her paper towel away. "Who says you have to? You're not married anymore. Max can't tell you what to do."

She hadn't been thinking about Max at all, but now that Marnie brought him up, her lunch rolled in her stomach. "No, he can't but that doesn't mean he'll leave me alone, either."

"Fuck him. You don't owe him anything. He left you and good riddance."

"I know, but where would I work? Where would I live?"

"You mean besides sleeping at Jared's?"

"Yeah, besides that."

"You're not considering the cost of living. Houses in Rocky Point are cheap. The rent for your walk-up costs more than what you'd pay for a mortgage payment every month. Ask Autumn."

That made sense. But . . .

"What about my job? There isn't anywhere to work in Rocky Point."

Marnie studied her face in the water-stained mirror and fluffed her platinum bangs. "It's a good thing I'm marrying James now. My looks are going."

"They are not." She tried to laugh, but Marnie mentioning moving to Rocky Point upset her. She didn't know if Jared would want her to, and she'd already wasted three years on a man. She wasn't going to quit a job that paid her bills and take her grandma away from the care-givers she knew for a whim. For a dream.

Max beat those dreams out of her. Maybe not literally, like Jared asked about last night, but figuratively. Mentally exhausted, she didn't need any more turmoil.

"Where *couldn't* you work?" Marnie asked, picking up the thread. "You headhunted remotely, right?"

"I went to an office when I did that."

Marnie scoffed. "All you did was find people online because the companies who hired you were too busy to do it for themselves or they didn't have the connections you had."

She coated her lips using a tube of vanilla Chapstick. "Point taken."

"You could do that again, or you could get an HR job in Marengo and work from home most days. The commute isn't so terrible you couldn't drive there once or twice a week. Plus, I'd get to see you more. Being we'd be in the same state and all."

"You mean you'd get to see me, period."

Marnie opened the bathroom door. "That too."

They stepped outside to the snowmobiles and Jared grinned at her.

Her heart hitched.

She could relocate. She could pack up her things in a shoebox, secure medical transportation for her grandmother, and move. Say goodbye to New York. The thought of never having to see Max again lightened her heart.

Jared kissed her forehead. "Are you okay?"

"Yeah. Marnie's giving me a hard time."

"I'm giving you simple solutions to the world's toughest problems. I'm like a rep at the Apple Genius Bar."

"And this is coming from the woman who can't turn her phone off and turn it back on to reset it." James yanked Marnie into a bear hug, lifting her off her feet. "Love you, babe."

"You better," she squealed.

Their happiness made her uncomfortable, and she shifted her gaze.

"Let's go feed the chipmunks." Jared shook a brown paper bag.

"What?" she asked, thinking she misheard.

"There's an area over there where you can feed the chipmunks. If you sit still, they'll eat off your hand. Come on. It's why we came here. I wanted to show you."

She sat in the snow with Jared and let the little creatures climb on her looking for snacks.

He kissed her, and she leaned into his embrace. Startled, the chipmunks scurried away.

Her heart dipped.

On the ride to the resort, she tucked herself against his strong back and realized why she felt so unsettled.

She was happy, and she hadn't experienced that light, carefree feeling in a long time.

Sadly, she quietly admitted to her broken heart that she never had.

"Did you apologize?"

"Did you do your homework?" Jared asked instead, hating to be grilled by anyone, but especially by his own daughter. Too smart for her own good, her interference grated on his nerves.

Briar had been sleeping when he came home last night, and this morning before he went snowmobiling, he'd gotten a couple hours of paperwork done at the arena. It wasn't to avoid Briar, at least, that's what he told himself. He liked sitting in his office with a cup of coffee, the arena quiet. A lone figure skater finding extra time to practice before school, the blades of her skates scraping against the ice.

He managed to avoid being questioned until dinner. He made it a priority to cook and sit down with her to talk about their days. The time was important to him, no matter how brief, otherwise, they could go days without speaking, passing each other in the hallway on their way to their bedrooms. He didn't want to parent Briar that way, and though sometimes dinner ruffled her feathers because she'd rather be doing something else, it felt right to sit and catch up. He wouldn't let her turn into a stranger, not like Rita, whom he one day looked at and didn't know anymore.

"I did my homework in homeroom. All we're doing is taking tests before winter break."

The question was automatic. He didn't need to police Briar's school work. She consistently pulled As with a B or two mixed in, but he wasn't as hard-assed about that as some parents. As long as she tried her best, that was all that mattered to him.

"Good." He slid a glass baking dish out of the oven. He tried to cook different meals every night, but he made the same things more often than not. Briar never complained, and tonight was no exception. Chicken bake, again, but it'd been too late to change his mind when he remembered he put the same meal together last week.

"I answered yours, now will you answer mine?" She asked, setting the table.

"Yes, I apologized. She'd like to say she's sorry, too, and you can see her tomorrow night if you go to Marnie and James's dinner with me at the resort. Marnie wanted an excuse to dress up. You can wear one of your old dance dresses, and we'll make a night of it."

"That sounds fun. You were out late," she said, looking at him out of the corners of her eyes.

"We were talking."

"Ah-huh."

He clamped his mouth shut and set the hotdish in the center of the table. The less he told her, the easier it would be. If she found out he slept with Leah, she'd get her hopes up, and he didn't want that. It would get his own hopes up, and that was the last thing he needed.

He tried to push away how good it felt to be in her bed,

to sink into her heat, to feel her arms wrapped around his neck.

He'd missed the connection. He'd craved the intimacy.

But it wasn't only sex. Watching her laugh in wonder at the little chipmunks who were brave enough to climb into her lap and shove peanuts into their cheeks made tiny cracks in his heart.

He hadn't thought there'd be room for any more after what Rita had done to him.

He was wrong.

Steering Briar away from the subject, which was easy to do as she loved to talk about her friends, school, and figure skating, he ate dinner in peace.

They hadn't made plans to see each other later, but when Briar said she was going to Skylar's to study for an algebra final, nudging his foot under the table, he took the hint and texted Leah. While he waited for her to answer, he did the dishes, letting Briar out of kitchen clean up and giving her extra time to stop by the Dairy Queen to pick up ice cream to bring to her boyfriend's for dessert.

Leah texted back saying she'd been invited to James's parents' house to play cards but she could get out of it if he wanted to do something.

He debated asking her to cancel her plans. She was in town for the wedding, but everyone was pushing them together and he doubted Marnie would give her a hard time about backing out if she knew Leah was doing it to spend time with him. In the end, he let her decide, and she said she didn't know how to play poker anyway and that he could stop by whenever.

That left him wondering what they could do. If he was going to keep her from participating in wedding activities, he didn't want to share her going to the Viking or the movies, even if the Rocky Point Multiplex wasn't as large as the name implied.

No, he liked Linda and Roy, and if he wanted to spend time with Leah around a bunch of people, he could go to poker night with her.

He mulled it over on the way to the resort, and he was still at a loss until she opened the door dressed in several layers. "You take what I say to heart," he said, tugging on her sweater.

"What do you mean?" she asked, letting him inside her room. "Oh."

"Dress warm," they said together, and she laughed.

"Yes, whenever we have plans, I always assume you're going to bring me outside."

"I wouldn't want to disappoint," he said, suddenly having a destination in mind, "but you won't need your snow pants."

She stepped into his arms. "It's nice to see you."

His chest tightened. "You saw me this morning," he said, trying to be nonchalant.

"Yeah." She smiled.

He huffed a laugh. "Come on."

They drove out of town, his headlights cutting through the darkness.

"Are we going to the park again?" she asked, holding his hand.

"Close." He squeezed her fingers.

His truck handled the road drifted over with snow without trouble, and he parked in front of the Rocky Point water tower.

"What are we doing here?" She leaned against the dash to look up at the tower through the windshield.

"I want to show you something." He met her eyes in the dark cab. "Do you trust me?" *Do you trust me to keep you safe? Do you trust me not to break your heart?* He wanted her to say no, to bring her back to the resort, because he was afraid he wouldn't be able to keep from doing either of those things. When all was said and done, they'd both end up bruised and bloody.

She brought his hand to her lips. "Yes."

"Okay."

The metal stairs were clear of snow, and he helped her step over the single chain intended to stop the curious from climbing the tower but did a poor job of it.

He asked her to go first in case she slipped and he needed to catch her, but she stepped confidently, her mittened hands gripping the rails.

Climbing silently, they reached the top of the spiraled stairs, and he said, "This way," his voice sounding too loud in the quiet.

Neon graffiti sparkled on the white paint, though the town's mayor tried his best to keep it clean. It was harder to do in the winter, and fresh designs and block letters he couldn't read covered various parts of the tower.

He led her around to the side that looked over the lake.

The frozen water spread out before them, dark and vacant, except for the lights blinking on the horizon, snowmobiles and ATVs, their drivers on an evening excursion.

"This is beautiful," she said. "So much space. I would never get used to it."

"It can make you crazy sometimes," he admitted, resting his forearms against the metal rail.

"How?"

"The isolation. The emptiness. The temperatures.

Leah, it can get cold enough that when you take your phone out of your pocket, it freezes and shuts down."

"I don't have my phone with me."

He bit back a retort. He wanted her to understand how lonely it could be living in Rocky Point. He wanted her to understand how lonely *he* had been since Rita left him. How devastated he'd be when she went back to New York after the wedding.

"Not everyone can live like this," he warned, but he didn't know why. She never said anything about staying here.

"Not everyone wants to," she whispered, staring across the ice.

"That's true. Come sit," he said, nudging her away from the rail.

He lowered onto the grated platform and leaned his back against the cold metal. His ass would be numb in a matter of minutes, but besides that, the evening temperature was tolerable and they'd be able to stay out here for a while yet.

She sat sideways between his legs and hooked her knees over his thigh, resting her cheek on his jacket.

He wrapped his arms around her.

"Autumn said Rita never visits. That Marnie asked her to be a bridesmaid, but she said no."

"Yeah. When she left, she said she wanted a clean break. A fresh start. She didn't want to look back."

"Don't her parents live here?"

"No, not anymore. They didn't want to live in the cold anymore and moved to Kentucky to be closer to her mother's family. They weren't close, Rita and her parents, I mean, and when we married, they said she was mine to take care of. I think that had a little to do with her being able to leave so easily. Rocky Point didn't feel like home."

"You and Briar weren't her home."

"No, we weren't. I tried my best, Leah."

She brushed her lips over his jaw, and he sighed. "That's all you can do, and then you make peace with it when it's not enough."

"Sometimes you can't," he said.

Leaning away, she met his eyes, and hers were so sad. "Sometimes you can't," she agreed softly. "And you live with it until you can't anymore."

Luckily, she'd never been scared of heights, otherwise looking over the lake would have made her queasy. But calm, she took a deep breath of the clean air, scanning the dark vastness of the frozen water. She would have described it as otherworldly, almost magical.

The stars were bright and she could've spent the rest of her life counting them and never come close to counting them all.

She understood what Jared said about the isolation. The silence could eventually crush someone if they let it. It wasn't so quiet that she felt suffocated, and if she listened closely, the hum of a motor carried across the ice and Jared's breathing was soft in her ears. The slight winter breeze shook the trees, and every once in awhile the ice shifted and cracked, the breathtaking snap breaking the stillness.

A woman could wish for more, living in a little town like this, if she'd never had it, but she knew the city, knew that what it offered she didn't want.

"Do your parents live in the city?" he asked. "Do you have any brothers or sisters?"

"No, I'm an only child. I never met my father. When my mother got pregnant with me, he took off. She didn't take it well."

"I'm sorry."

"We would've been okay, maybe, if my mother would have been stronger, but my grandmother, my mom's mom, she's very . . . old-fashioned, and she blamed my mother for not being able to keep her husband happy. My mother couldn't handle the shame, and after I was born, she disappeared. I haven't seen her since."

His arms tightened around her. "Who took care of you?"

"My grandma, but she wasn't happy about it and she made that loud and clear. She resented me and said my father wouldn't have left if I'd been a boy. Since I wasn't, a boy, that is, she raised me to be a good wife and taught me to cook, how to do laundry. How to sew. I can mend a hole in your sock, if you have one." She tried to sound light but failed. "She wanted the first man who was interested to get me out of her house. I was able to escape sooner than that, I earned a scholarship to go to college and I lived in the dorms, but . . . I guess that's why I let Max sweep me off my feet. I wanted the fairy tale. I didn't know how quickly it would turn into a nightmare. My grandma thinks I can't get pregnant and said it was my fault he left. Men should have sons."

"What about her husband? Your grandfather?"

"He was a womanizing alcoholic who had a gambling problem, but my grandma stood by him until the day he died, even though he drank and gambled all the money away. She said that's what wives did. Stuck by their men, no matter what. A heart attack killed him when I was fifteen, and I think more than a little piece of my grandma died with him that day."

"Is she still alive?"

"Yeah, but she doesn't like talking to me since Max left. She sees a woman's worth in a man's eyes. I'm nothing if a man doesn't want me."

"You've been alone for a long time."

"I've lived all my life in a city with millions of people." She twisted toward the lake. "This is being alone."

"Yes, it is, and I've felt it every day since Rita said she didn't want to be my wife anymore."

She knelt in front of him, even though the cold metal dug into her knees. "Kiss me," she said, cupping his face between her mittens.

He complied, gently covering her lips with his.

She shuddered and wrapped her arms around his neck. She'd try to help him feel not alone.

At least, for a little while.

They ended up in her bed, making love as their coffee grew cold on the nightstand. The evening had been worth freezing. Their talk brought Leah a little closer to him.

He breathed in her scent while she dozed in his arms, and hesitantly, cautiously, he started to think of ways they could still be together after the wedding. A dangerous preoccupation at best. And at worst? Well, he wouldn't think about that.

The more he learned about her life, the less impressed he became. Her dirtbag of an ex-husband and the grandmother who wrote her off for things that weren't her fault. He hadn't asked what tied her to the city, those elusive responsibilities she didn't explain, but, until he told her he loved her, it wasn't any of his business and telling her that was miles away, even if that's how he felt. Afraid she'd say, thanks, but no thanks, he'd keep his feelings to himself. At least, until the pressure pushed him to the breaking point.

"Thanks for shivering with me at the tower," he said, nuzzling her mouth with one last kiss. It was late, and though she hadn't texted asking when he'd be home, he didn't want Briar to worry.

"Thanks for bringing me there. You give good date, Jared."

He laughed and grabbed his jeans. "I'm glad you think so, but I'm running out of things to do."

"This is good, too," she said, hugging him from behind.

"Too good," he agreed, tilting his head and giving her room to nip at his neck. "What's up for tomorrow?"

"I'm helping Helen until Marnie's dinner. I know I said I wasn't going to anymore, but she called earlier and asked for help. She doesn't feel well, I guess she caught the flu that's going around, and she needs someone during the day until her evening person can come in and close."

He lifted her into his lap. "You're a nice person."

"I can appreciate the situation she's in. She doesn't want to hire more people because she doesn't know what will happen to the store. I think she's still hoping to sell it. She's got a better chance now, at least. The store looks profitable with people actually shopping there."

"Thanks to you."

"It was nothing."

"Probably not to Helen. You saw she needed help, offered it, and came through. Not many people do that."

"You didn't want me to."

He let her crawl off his lap. He needed to get dressed anyway, though going out in the cold to drive home didn't sound good at all. "No, I didn't. I didn't want you to become a part of this community. A part of my life. You did both anyway." He tried not to sound bitter, and he snuggled her against his chest to lessen the sting.

"I only wanted to help." Her breath feathered against his skin.

He kissed her cheek and stood, the mattress squeaking as it gave up his weight. "And you did. The Supply Company looks amazing. But you've become Helen's friend and she turns to you when she needs someone. What is she going to do when she can't do that anymore?"

She wrapped the sheet around her. "I didn't think of it that way."

"You don't need to think that way, but I'm trying to make you understand that you're becoming part of this town and I won't be the only one who will miss you when you're gone." He cleared this throat. "I'll see you tomorrow night, okay? Have fun at the store, and no more ladders."

"I promise. See you tomorrow."

He left her sitting on her bed in the dark room, coffee cold, his side of the bed empty.

He could try to show her the hole she'd be leaving in Rocky Point after she left, but he couldn't make her stay.

He'd already tried to force one woman to stay where she didn't want to be, and he'd be damned if he'd do that again.

All the lights in his house were ablaze when he turned onto his street, and his heart hammered. Briar should have been in bed.

His hand shook as he jabbed the garage door's clicker, and he bolted inside the minute he parked.

"Dad!" Briar yelled from the living room, and he rushed through the mudroom, clipping his hip on the dryer in his haste.

"Are you okay? What are you doing up?" he asked, his boots leaving clumps of snow on the floor.

"Hello, Jared."

"Mom came to visit! Can you believe it?"

"Yeah . . . I can see that."

Rita sat on the couch, the same one they'd owned when she lived there, sipping a glass of wine he'd been given as a gift. He didn't drink wine very often, and he pushed it to the back of the cabinet a few months ago.

Briar snuggled into her mother's side, and Rita wrapped an arm around her while staring at him in defiance.

"What are you doing here?" he asked, lowering into a chair to untie his wet boots.

"I decided to go to Marnie's wedding. And I wanted to see Briar, of course. She's been telling me about school, and Skylar."

"Why didn't you tell me you were coming?"

"I wanted it to be a surprise."

"Well, it is."

"Not a good one," Rita said, and Briar looked up.

He glared. They wouldn't do this in front of their daughter. "Briar, you need to go to bed. It's late, and you have school tomorrow."

"Give her a few more minutes. I haven't been here long."

"Please, Dad?"

"No," he said, frowning. "If your mom's going to Marnie's wedding, she'll be here for a while yet and you'll have plenty of time to catch up. School first. You have finals." He resented being put in this position, playing bad parent to Rita's good parent because she'd been away and Briar had missed her.

Briar kissed Rita's cheek and raced up the stairs, not sparing him a glance.

He sat on the edge of his chair, studying the woman he hadn't seen in five years. Her blonde hair looked lighter, her frame thinner. She'd lost the curves he'd enjoyed when they were in bed.

"How did you get here? You should have asked me to pick you up."

She smoothed her hair and licked her lips. "I was afraid if I told you I was coming, you'd say no."

The city hadn't beat out her mannerisms, and he was somewhat grateful his wife was still under all that gloss.

"I wouldn't tell you that you couldn't visit. I don't hate you. I've never hated you."

"I didn't want to take the chance. The resort's shuttle happened to be at the airport, and I hitched a ride."

"Do you have a reservation there?"

"No. I was hoping I could stay in the guest bedroom. I want to see Briar as much as I can."

She knew where to hit him, bringing Briar into it, but it made sense she used the spare room.

"You'll have to move some stuff around."

"Okay." She stood from the old couch and hesitated in front of him. Tentatively, she sank into his lap. "I missed you."

He gave in and hugged her, but she didn't feel right,

didn't fit in his arms like she used to. "I missed you, too. I've been lonely, Rita."

She shifted and pressed her face into his neck. "It's been hard."

"Yeah."

"Where were you? You never stay out this late."

"I was with—" *Leah*. He tried again. "I was showing one of Marnie's bridesmaids around. I brought her up to the water tower."

"The same place you asked me to marry you."

"Yeah." His heart slammed with guilt. He hadn't thought about Rita when he and Leah were there talking, not in terms of missing her or what he'd lost when she left. More in the sense of accepting he and Briar hadn't been enough to keep her in Rocky Point and moving on from that. With Leah. He wanted to get to know her, and he'd encouraged her to open up. Bit by bit she was starting to share her life with him.

"Kind of a romantic spot to bring one of Marnie's bridesmaids."

"Does Marnie know you're here?"

"No. I wanted it to be a surprise." She lifted her head and met his eyes. "You don't want to talk about her."

He smoothed his finger over her jaw. Skin so soft it glowed. Her blue eyes regarded him thoughtfully, her head tilted in contemplation. "No, I don't. You left a long time ago. Did you expect me to stay single forever?"

"Not forever," she said, leaning away. "It's been five years, but that's not long, not when we're talking about our whole lives. These past few years I've tried to build a foundation, a career I could be proud of." Tears filled her eyes.

"It seems you did that," he said. "So why are you crying?"

"Marnie's wedding isn't the only reason I came back. I want you and Briar to move to New York with me. I want us to try again."

Leah called her grandmother before she left to spend the day at the Supply Company. There was a lot of trial and error during the past few months, and she found Della seemed to be at her best after her breakfast and morning meds. The aide put her on the phone, but despite her timing, her grandmother seemed surly and out of sorts.

"Are you okay?" she asked Della, disappointed she didn't want to participate in the conversation.

"I'm tired. I didn't sleep well last night," her grandma said, her voice distracted and muffled, "and I miss Emmy. Do you know where she is?"

She wasn't sure whom her grandma thought she was speaking to, but she answered the question honestly, hoping the nurses didn't have an emotional mess to clean up after she said goodbye. "I don't know, Grandma. I haven't seen her in a long time."

"Try to find her for me," Della said, near tears. "I need to know where she is."

"Okay, I will. Rest now, okay? I'm sorry you had a rough night."

"Thank you, goodbye."

She expected the aide to offer reassurances they'd take care of her grandma and help her back to bed, but the call disconnected and her cell beeped.

She swallowed a lump in her throat. Her grandma

hadn't been in her right mind for years, but she was all the family Leah had, and she missed her.

Working at the Supply Company lifted her spirits and she rode the shuttle downtown to open the store, grabbing a spare set keys from the short order cook at the diner who had opened the restaurant for the breakfast crowd hours earlier. She bought a cup of coffee to go and spent the next eight hours filling racks, ringing up customers, and singing along to Christmas carols.

A fancy dinner with Marnie and her new friends would put a bright red ribbon on a perfect day.

She paid special attention to her hair and makeup as she dressed for dinner. She could understand why Marnie wanted to host an elegant evening. Little Rocky Point didn't have a dressy, trendy downtown, not like the larger cities, and a woman could easily spend all her time in jeans and sweatshirts, never having a reason to do more than put her hair up in a ponytail.

She smoothed the silver dress over her hips and added diamond earrings. Imitation, of course, as Max had taken all her real jewelry, but she didn't care. Fakes sparkled exactly the same. Whenever she looked at Max, no one knew that better than she did.

She fluffed her hair and gave her lipstick one more glance in the mirror. She grabbed a small clutch and locked her door.

She hadn't heard from Jared all day, and he didn't tell her what his plans were before dinner, though she assumed he went to work. After the lecture he gave her about the cost of Briar's dress, she thought maybe money was tight for him, too, and he needed the hours. She should be more careful about the time they spent together, but if he had the evening off, maybe they could slip away early and go back to her room. If he had time.

When she stepped into the small room Marnie rented, she waved at the bride-to-be, laughed when James winked at her, and searched the room for Autumn. She hadn't arrived yet, and she wondered if Cole would be with her. She never did ask what made Autumn cry at the diner. Autumn never mentioned Cole in a personal capacity, only professional, and she wouldn't pry.

Because Marnie's parents knew why Leah backed out of poker night, they teased her about skipping cards at James's parents' house, and while sipping a glass of champagne, she let Gail poke fun at her for choosing a man over Texas Hold 'Em. "Although, I don't blame you, dear," she said, holding her champagne flute near her mouth. "Jared's quite the catch . . . if you can reel him in."

She'd never felt more included or welcome.

"Hi, Leah," Autumn said, walking quickly through the dining room in a cloud of cold air and floral perfume.

"Hey. You're running a little late. Are you okay?"

Autumn slid her winter jacket off revealing a navy blue cocktail dress. Silver accents matched her silver heels. "I'm fine, but thanks for asking. I was at the office updating the blog. It's fabulous Marnie planned this dinner, it will give me more to write about. And you need to update me on the Supply Company. I heard you worked at the store again today."

They sat at a table away from the other guests and chatted about how the blog was going and her time at the store.

Feeling guilty she hadn't taken the time read Autumn's blog on the newspaper's website, she promised herself she would do that soon. Especially since she'd been featured a time or two and shoppers at the store were always giving her positive feedback. She didn't have any trouble believing Autumn did a good job. The woman was an excellent writer and was very easy to talk to. It helped her ask for a favor.

"How easy is it to find someone?" she asked, nodding at a server who started placing bread baskets on the tables.

Autumn lifted a shoulder. "Depends. Are we talking a kidnapped child? A runaway? Someone who faked their own death? There are varying degrees of 'missing.' If you're talking about high school classmate and you want to reconnect, probably all you need to do is search for her name on social media and she'll pop right up."

She hadn't considered looking for her mother simply by doing an internet search, but she should have. When she was headhunting, she searched for people all the time. This was just a different kind.

"What about someone you haven't seen in over thirty years?"

Again, Autumn shrugged. "It really depends on what they're doing now. If they don't want to be found, that's a bit different, but if they're living an everyday life, it might be easier than you think." She paused. "Do you mind telling me who?"

"My mother. She disappeared after I was born. My grandma asked me to look for her."

"Sweetie." Autumn placed a hand on her arm.

"No, it's fine. I don't know if she wants to stay hidden, or if she's even still alive. I thought as a reporter you might have some resources, but I never tried looking for her myself. Maybe I should try that first before wasting your time."

"No, don't. It's not a waste time. I'm happy to help you, however I can. I have access to a couple of different people searches and research sources, and someone in the police department owes me a favor. We'll see what we can find, okay? I don't want you to do that by yourself."

"Thanks. That would be great." She checked her phone. Maybe she missed a call or text from Jared saying he'd be late or couldn't make it after all, but there weren't any messages or missed calls and she slipped her cell into her clutch, disappointed.

"Oh, my God," Autumn murmured.

"What?" Leah asked, looking up from her purse.

Jared stepped into the room, Briar on one arm and a blonde woman who could have been Briar's twin on the other. "Who—" she started to ask, but Marnie's excited squeal cut her off.

"Rita!"

Jared met Leah's gaze across the room, his eyes tired and resigned, and she forced herself to smile.

His ex-wife had come back, and by the way she clutched at his hand, they'd reconciled. Or at least, they were talking about it.

Her stomach burned, and the sensation caught her off guard.

For the past few days she'd been feeling almost normal, as if maybe she didn't have to live with a searing pain in her gut. As if maybe she could be happy.

Everyone circled around Rita, welcoming home a woman who hadn't been back in five years. Even Autumn shifted, excited.

"Go see her," she said. "She's your friend, too."

Autumn bounced to her feet. "I'll be right back."

She should wait, sit through the meal before running back to her room like a broken-hearted coward. She owed it to Marnie and the rest of the wedding party to meet Rita, possibly give up her place as a bridesmaid. Then Marnie could have her high school friend by her side the way she wanted.

But there would be time for that, and she gulped the last of her wine and stood.

Keeping her head low and avoiding eye contact with everyone, she pushed through a side door the serving staff used to replenish their tables.

Bright fluorescent lights lit the white service hallway, and a waiter dressed in black pants, white shirt, and a dirty black apron rushed by, not giving her a glance.

She turned around and walked in the other direction, hoping to find an exit and the signs that would lead her to the lobby, but the hallways were like a maze and she found herself in a laundry room, huge industrial washers and driers lining the walls that hummed and shook as they spun. A woman folding towels lifted her eyebrows in puzzlement and directed her out another door. Gratefully, she retreated, and she stepped into a hallway near the ballroom where Marnie and James were going to have their reception.

A smattering of applause met her ears, the ballroom full for an event.

She leaned against the wall in relief.

If anyone questioned why she disappeared, all she would say is that she felt sick. It was the truth, anyway, even if it was a cop-out.

Knowing where she was now, she went to her room, but she paused outside the door.

All dressed up and nowhere to go.

The resort boasted an elegant lounge she hadn't seen yet, and she followed the arrows carved into gold plaques attached to the hallway walls.

A fire crackled in the fireplace, and a large picture window looked over the ski slopes. Well, what she imagined were the slopes. It was nighttime, the dark thick and inky black, and her figure reflected back at her, blocking her view of the outdoors.

A man dressed in a business suit sat a table near the fireplace and appraised her appreciatively but didn't rise to approach her.

She nodded at him, acknowledging his choice to leave her alone, and she slid onto a stool at the bar.

"What can I get you?" the bartender asked.

"Do you have any blackberry brandy?" She wanted something stronger than wine, but she hated the taste of whiskey and scotch.

"Yes. Do you want it over ice?"

She shook her head. "No, thank you."

The bartender served her a lowball glass of the purple brandy, and she sipped it, trying to relax. She felt like a fool running away, but she couldn't sit there and watch Jared and Rita.

Leaning against the bar, the bartender asked, "What brings you to Rocky Point?" Leah grimaced, and she flinched. "Sorry. You don't have to talk if you don't feel like it."

Her hair was fastened into a messy ponytail, and dark circles shadowed her eyes. Though she wore the standard black pants, white shirt, and black tie all the staff at the resort wore, the woman appeared unkept, her clothes wrinkled, her tie askew. She *didn't* feel like talking, but the poor woman looked more miserable than she felt.

"No, it's okay. Marnie Zimmerman's wedding. Do you know her?"

"We were in high school together, but we weren't friends. She was popular, you know? Still is. Has a nice family, a cushy job, now a good-looking, rich husband. I'm not saying James isn't a nice," she added, abashed, "but you know how it is."

"I do. Privileged from the start."

The bartender stared across the room to the fire. "Yeah."

"You never fit in no matter how hard you try," she said, glancing at the bartender's nametag.

Surprised, Ivy said, "You don't look like you know anything about that."

"Oh, trust me," she said, her throat burning. "There are other ways to feel left out. It's not only money or social class."

"Family."

She sipped her brandy. "Family. You got that right."

Her footsteps heavy, Ivy shuffled to a couple sitting near the windows who looked like they were on a date.

She would never fit in with Jared's family. Not that she expected to or wanted to try. But because of their talk at the water tower and the way he'd made love to her afterward, she'd thought that maybe they could have some kind of future. Which was stupid. Dating her would be like dating his ex-wife, and why would he want her when he could have the woman he still loved, the mother of his child. He hadn't made those sacrifices for Rita. Why in the hell would he make them for her?

Moving to New York.

No one in their right mind would move there when they had a perfect life here in Rocky Point.

Hadn't she been trying to think of a way to stay here?

She wouldn't take such a leap of faith for a man, ever again. She'd trusted Max and look what happened. If she made any kind of move, she'd do it for her grandma first, herself second, and a man third. In that order. Her grandma had loved her husband more than she'd loved her. In fact, she hadn't loved her at all, but her grandma hadn't thrown her onto the street, and she could have. She very well could have.

"You're the woman Jared pulled out of the water," Rita said, sitting on the stool next to hers and crossing her legs.

She stiffened. "How do you know?"

She doubted Jared would talk about her. The second he knew Rita was back in Rocky Point, he probably hadn't thought about her at all.

"I read Autumn's blog. You're lucky you're okay. I lived here most of my life and I've never fallen into the lake, frozen or otherwise."

"Jared's been very kind. At Marnie's request, of course," she added.

"Of course," Rita agreed, the corners of her mouth lifting into an insincere smile.

"Hi, Rita, what can I get you?" Ivy asked, placing a coaster on the bar in front of her.

"Whatever Leah's drinking," Rita answered, not bothering to look at Ivy, and Ivy turned away, the skin pinched around her eyes. She felt for the woman, and though she wouldn't ask, she wondered just how far down the high school hierarchy Ivy had been.

"Your dress is gorgeous. Donna Karan, the Fall collection, 2020, right?"

"Yeah." She bought it when she and Max were first married, when he told her he wanted her to dress "appropriately." She'd been expected to be by his side during all the social events he attended for his consulting firm.

"I heard the rumors." Rita picked up the brandy Ivy set in front of her, not bothering to say thank you.

"What rumors?" She should have gone back to her room, but in a small town like Rocky Point, there would be no escaping the woman and it was best they got this confrontation over with. She'd tell Marnie she'd bow out of the ceremony and let Rita have her place. Her dress wouldn't have to be altered that much. They were both slim, though Rita was a couple inches shorter. A seamstress could easily fix that.

The thought hurt her heart, but she didn't belong here, and she didn't have the energy to make it so.

"That you've been spending time with my husband."

"He's been doing his part as a groomsman, that's all," she said.

Cutting lemon slices, Ivy looked at them out of the corners of her eyes.

"I heard it's more than that, and I want to thank you."

"For what?"

Rita sighed. "I know I hurt Jared and Briar when I moved to New York, and if I could do it all over again, I'm not sure what I would do. I love my job and I love living in the city, but I divorced a man who loved me and I left my daughter when a girl needs her mother. I'm thanking you because you reminded Jared that it's nice to have someone, to be part of a couple. He hasn't dated since I left, and he hid that part of himself away. He's receptive to the idea of us getting back together because you reminded him he's lonely."

"You had what a lot of women want," she said bitterly.

"A caring husband, a lovely daughter. Friends in a tight-knit community."

"And you have what I wanted, what I have now. A glamorous job, the party scene. Designer dresses and Tiffany."

She drained her glass. She didn't have those things, not any of it.

She lived in a run-down walk-up without a way to do her laundry and rode the subway to work every day. She may have a closet full of old designer clothes, but she had nowhere to wear them, nor did she want to. And the closest she ever came to visiting Tiffany was watching the movie that starred Audrey Hepburn.

"Those are things, Rita. You gave up your family for things. I hope you and Jared work it out. He's a good guy and didn't deserve what you put him through." She dug into her purse and pulled out a twenty. Glaring at Rita, she slapped the bill onto the bar. "Thank you, Ivy. Have a good night."

She went back to her room, hope and dread tangling in her heart. She wanted Jared to look for her, yet, she didn't. She knew what he would say. He'd break things off. No more snowshoeing in the dark, no more snowmobile rides. No more making love because he'd be doing that with his wife. Ex-wife, but maybe they'll remarry.

She listened for a knock until midnight when she finally fell asleep, but no one looked for her at all.

Autumn didn't disappoint her, though, and the next morning over coffee and an English muffin she had delivered to her room, Leah received her text.

Come over any time. I don't have to go to the paper until this afternoon. An address followed, and though Autumn didn't say, she assumed it was for her house.

I'll be there in an hour, she replied, giving Autumn a heads up. She didn't want to waste any more of Autumn's time than she had to.

Pushing down disappointment Jared didn't look in on her last night, she showered and dried her hair. She called the front desk and asked when the next shuttle was going into town, and Sophia said she could leave whenever she wanted because the driver was free.

Autumn's house was little and painted white, located in an older part of town on a postage stamp yard where huge trees grew near the street. The floors were hardwood, the atmosphere cozy, and two cats slept next to each other on a worn couch.

She envied her immediately.

"Thank you for doing this," she said, taking off her jacket, wishing she'd brought pastries or something.

"It's no problem. Where'd you go last night? I looked for you. Then Rita disappeared, too."

"I wasn't feeling well," she said, her eyes downcast.

"Ah-huh. Seeing Jared and Rita together made you sick, huh?"

"Something like that," she muttered.

"If it makes you feel better, he didn't look happy. Briar's ecstatic her mom's back in town, but he's going to have a huge mess to clean up when Rita leaves after the wedding."

She followed Autumn into a bedroom she'd turned into an office, a sleek Mac monitor, mouse, and keyboard sitting on a white, uncluttered desk. "According to Rita, that's not going to happen. She hunted me down in the bar."

"That doesn't sound good," Autumn said. "You didn't get into a fight, did you?"

She scoffed. "Over what? She was clear she wants Jared to give her a second chance, implied it was a sure thing. Knowing him, though I can't claim to know him as well as you, or James, or Marnie do, I think he will, to give Briar her mother back."

Autumn sank into a mesh desk chair and wiggled her mouse to wake up her computer. "I don't know. Someone doesn't get over something like that very easily. It's tough to forgive."

"You sound like you know what you're talking about."

"Doesn't everyone know what betrayal feels like?" Autumn opened a search page. "Anyway, sit down and we'll start with what you know and go from there."

She sat on a kitchen chair next to Autumn. She must have moved it into the bedroom before Leah got there. "My mom's name, when she gave birth to me, was Emmaline Bristow. She took my dad's last name when they married."

Autumn's fingers flew over the keyboard. "Is this how you spell it?"

"Yeah."

Autumn pressed Enter.

"She was a character on *Murder She Wrote*," Autumn murmured as she skimmed the search results.

"You're kidding."

"Nope. But that doesn't help us. Let's keep looking."

"There's a social media account under that name, but it doesn't have any content."

She leaned closer.

"It looks like an Emmaline Bristow is a blogger. Could this be her?"

"Without a photo, I can't be sure," she said.

"Her avatar's empty. We'll keep going." Autumn returned to the search results. "There's an Emmie Bristow, but she's a young girl in college. That could be the blogger from the university, so we'll rule her out."

After a half an hour of searching without finding any results, Autumn said, "Do you know her maiden name? Let's try that."

"Her last name was Harris. My grandma's name is Della Harris, if that can help you at all."

"There are a lot of people named Emmaline Harris," she said, turning the monitor. "Scoot over and you'll be able to see better, unless you think I'll bite."

She huffed a laugh and nudged her arm.

It didn't take Autumn long to narrow down the search.

"There," she said, pointing at the screen. "That woman. We have the same hair and eye color. Our noses aren't similar, but I've never met my dad so I don't know for sure how much came from him."

Autumn clicked on a social media profile that happened to be public and scrolled through the woman's photo albums. Leah's heart sank. This Emmaline Benson, née Harris, was indeed her mother, as one of the children in a family photo looked exactly like she had when she was a toddler.

"She remarried." Under the About tab of the woman's profile, Autumn read, "She listed her birthplace as New York City, she has two daughters and a son, and six grandchildren. She's a receptionist in a dental office, and they live in Iowa. Do you know her birthdate? She made it available."

Through her tears, she studied the woman who beamed

into the camera, a baby sitting in her lap. "That's the birth-date I know. My grandma had to give it to me when I filled out my college application." She sniffled. "She looks happy."

"Yeah, she does. She never tried to find you?"

"No. I don't want to understand, but I do. My grandma's mental health has never been great. It makes her difficult to live with."

"That doesn't mean once she was in a better place she couldn't have come back for you."

She pulled a tissue out of a box on Autumn's desk and wiped her eyes. "I don't know how I would have taken that. Briar's happy her mom came back to town, but they stayed in contact and maybe their relationship didn't deteriorate. My mom never wrote me a letter, never called. Left me with her own mother who wasn't exactly abusive, but, well, if *she* didn't want to be around her anymore, why did she think she could raise me? I didn't grow up with any love. I would've rather been raised by a woman who loved me even if we struggled, than by my grandma who was only doing her duty and made sure I knew it."

Autumn rubbed her back. "Maybe when your mother was younger, she didn't know how to love anyone. Your grandma didn't love you. Maybe she didn't love your mom, either. You said her husband left her. That's a lot of pain, Leah, and most people have to dump it somewhere."

She stilled. Her mother hadn't loved her. Didn't know how because her own mother and husband hadn't. But Leah would have. She would have loved her mother with all her heart.

"But that doesn't mean she wouldn't welcome you into her life now."

"How long did it take us to find her?" she asked.

Autumn glanced at the time in the corner of the screen. "About forty-five minutes."

"And me, search my name. How long does it take to find me?"

Autumn returned to the search page and typed in her name. She pressed Enter and her social media profiles came up, along with Autumn's blog series about Marnie's wedding. Under Images, several photos of her popped up, including her staff photo for Outdoor Wonders.

"There are a few women named Leah Bristow, but it wouldn't take long to figure out who's who," Autumn said.

"See? If my mother wanted to find me, she could do what we did, but she's never been in touch. She started her new life and left the old behind. Not everyone is strong enough, or heartless enough, to do that, but she did."

Autumn slid an index card off a thick stack on her desk and clicked the back arrow for Emmaline's information. "Maybe not heartless. When we reach the point of desperation, sometimes all we can do is put one foot in front of the other and try to survive. Here's her mailing address, if you want to write her a letter. Maybe she'd be willing to explain."

She shook her head. She didn't want an explanation.

"You don't have to use it, but it's here, in case you want to get in touch." She paused. "What will you tell your grandma?"

"I don't know. Knowing my mom is out there but hasn't bothered to contact us . . . it might be easier to tell her I couldn't find her and leave it at that. My grandma's mental health is fragile and the truth might do more harm than good."

"I'm sorry."

"It's okay. I didn't know what we'd find. I mean, is it

better knowing she's safe, that she's happy, than not finding any trace of her at all? If she would have dropped off the face of the earth, would I have stayed up at night wondering what happened to her? Maybe she was homeless before she was able to get out of the city. Bad things can happen and I should be happy she's okay, but she doesn't care if I'm okay, does she?"

She started crying, and Autumn hugged her.

"But you *are* okay, and that's the most important part. You got out of a crappy marriage and didn't let him break you. You have a good job and have given many people good jobs, too. You have friends who love you. You could have let her abandonment hurt you, but you didn't. You should be proud of yourself."

It was nice to hear someone praise her when all her grandma ever did was belittle her. She *did* get through a crappy marriage and she *was* proud of the work she did when she was headhunting, in her position at Outdoor Wonders, and working at the Supply Company. She was valued, and sometimes it was difficult to remember that.

"You're right. I'm doing fine on my own."

"But you're not alone. Remember that."

She met Autumn's eyes, thoughtful, yet sad. Autumn couldn't hide the hurt, and she gripped her hand. "And you're not alone, either. You've turned into a good friend, and if you need anything, *anything,* tell me."

Autumn smiled. "Thanks. Are you hungry? I'll make lunch then drop you at the resort on my way to the office. No need to wait for the shuttle."

"That sounds good, thanks."

They spent a pleasant hour chatting over tomato soup and grilled cheese sandwiches, but in the back of her mind, she forced herself to admit that even without Rita coming back to Rocky Point, she and Jared didn't have a future.

Her mother was a stranger, but she was just like her. She didn't know how to love anyone. Both raised by the same unkind and unfeeling woman, both divorced because their husbands didn't want them.

She was better off alone, taking care of herself.

"You'll do no such thing!"

"But Marnie—"

"No. I asked her, and she said no."

"Did you ask her before you asked me?"

"I'm not going to answer that because there's no right answer. You didn't hire a dummy."

"No, I didn't," she murmured.

Marnie stood in front of the mirror attached to the wall above her room's desk, curling her hair, the curling iron plugged into the lamp's electrical socket. "Then you're going to be my bridesmaid whether you want to or not." She lowered the wand. "Unless you really don't want to anymore. You and Jared were getting close, and if it hurts you to be here . . ."

She stopped pacing. "I wouldn't have met him if it hadn't been for you, and I won't back out of your wedding because of him."

"Good. Then it's settled." Marnie turned the curling iron off and grabbed her makeup bag. "I need to try on my dress. I wasn't going to until later, but it can't hurt. Being on vacation and eating whatever I want, I feel like I've been gaining weight. Or . . ."

"Or what?"

Marnie looked up from a tube of foundation. "I went off the pill last month. My gynecologist said it might take my body a few cycles to get back into the swing of things. But . . . I'm late."

She opened her mouth, but Marnie cut in. "I know, I know. That could be part of my body going back to normal. But Leah," she said, her eyes shining with possibility, "I feel like I could be. I have this sense that I am." She dropped the tube onto the desk and pressed her hands to her belly.

"I'm so happy for you," she cried, giving Marnie a hug. "I know how much you want kids."

"I really do. I feel like we're starting so late. I mean, Briar's sixteen!" She eased away, laughing. "But don't tell anyone. Not yet. Not until I know for sure. I don't want to take a test until after the wedding. If I'm pregnant, I want to tell James on our honeymoon. Won't that be romantic?"

"It will be," she agreed. "You two will be great parents."

"Are you doing anything right now? Can you come with me? Autumn's at work and I haven't seen Callie around. So much has been happening with Mitch and his parents. James wouldn't want to go, and he's at his parents' place fixing their furnace anyway."

Before Rita came back to Rocky Point, she might have been meeting up with Jared or visiting him at the arena, but her day was free. "No. Jared hasn't talked to me since . . ." Since the night they'd made love in her room. "Since the other night. I mean—"

Marnie began rubbing foundation into her skin. "I know what you mean, and I'm sorry, Leah. I had no idea Rita was coming to the wedding, or I would have warned you. I hope you believe me."

"I do, and there's no hard feelings. Briar's sweet, and I wouldn't resent her having her mother back."

"But you were thinking about moving here and everything."

"That was Zamboni rides and snowshoeing under the stars. I wouldn't make a life change like that for a man. For three years I lived my life the way Max wanted me to, and it was hell. If I moved here, a relationship with Jared would be icing on top of a very important cake. I still want to be a bridesmaid, but it will be rough getting through to the ceremony. I was starting to . . ."

"Fall in love with him."

She sank onto the bed. "Yeah. I guess I'm lucky Rita had such good timing."

"He might not want her back." Marnie applied mascara to her eyelashes, thick and black.

"That's what Autumn said, but he didn't text or call after I snuck out of dinner last night—I'm sorry about that—and I haven't heard anything from him today. It's his way of letting me down gently, and I get it. We don't want to ruin your wedding, and I'll do my best to stay out of his way."

Sucking in her stomach and looking at her figure in the mirror, Marnie said, "The only thing that could ruin my wedding is if my dress doesn't fit. There's still over a week before the ceremony. I'm going to have to stop eating whatever I want, and drinking, too."

"You should stop drinking anyway," Leah said. "If you're pregnant."

"Yeah. Trying to explain that to James will be interesting. He knows how much I love Prosecco. It's a good thing I have the dress excuse, he'll believe that. Let's go. Your bridesmaid dress will be there, too, but you guys don't have a final fitting until next week."

Marnie drove them to the dress boutique, and she promised herself she'd put her heart into the wedding and nothing more. She wouldn't give Jared the privilege of ruining her vacation. The day her divorce was final was the day she said she wouldn't live her life for another man, ever again.

She'd do better at being there for Marnie, and she'd go home confident she'd been the best bridesmaid she could be and leave the hope of Rocky Point behind her.

CHAPTER SEVEN

"I did a bad thing."

James lifted an eyebrow. "I haven't heard you say that since the night you TP'd Mr. Erickson's yard because he gave Rita a D in Algebra."

"She worked her ass off. He could have fudged a bit and upped it to a C. Her parents made her take summer school for that D. I was pissed."

"I remember. What'd you do this time? What's it like having Rita back?"

He knelt on the floor, a wrench in his hand. The old furnace sitting in James's parents' basement wouldn't last the rest of the winter. It was too old to eke any more time out of it, and the temperatures were too cold to ask it to do anything less than what it needed to do: keep two humans in their late fifties from freezing to death.

"Briar loves it. Didn't want to go to school today. She can't miss school for the next week and a half so she's going to have to get over it. Rita's taking her to figure skating practice tonight, then they're going out to dinner. They invited me to go, but I was thinking since I had the evening free, I'd see Leah."

"Is that the bad thing you're talking about?" James asked, sinking to the floor. "Fuck this. I don't want to go back to Decatur after the wedding and worry for the rest of the winter if their furnace is going to break down. I'm buying them a new one. They won't like it, but they have no choice."

"What will Marnie say?"

"That I'm being a good son?" James asked, frowning. "What's that about?"

"Nothing. It's something Rita would've given me flack for."

"And Leah wouldn't?"

He shrugged, but he knew she wouldn't. Not when she worked at the Supply Company and didn't ask Helen to pay her a single penny.

"Comparing the two won't get you very far, very fast. Either you're in love with one of them or you're not."

"It's not that."

James threw a screwdriver into a beat-up black toolbox. "That's all there is."

Jared slanted him a glance.

"No, that's all there is. If you can't say you're still in love with Rita, tell her, and tell her fast. Briar too, because the last thing you need is her believing her parents are getting back together. And if you're not in love with Leah, at least do her the courtesy of telling her it's not because of Rita."

"You don't know what's going on between Leah and me. She hasn't been in town that long."

"I know you looked pretty damned cozy the day we went snowmobiling. I know you kept looking at her when you went to dinner last night, and you didn't stop until she snuck out with her tail tucked between her legs."

"She doesn't have any plans to stay here."

James scoffed. "She won't think she has a reason to if you don't talk to her." He paused. "Does she have a reason?"

"Yeah."

"She's not going to know if you don't say something."

"No. I'm not asking her to stay. She'd be bored to tears in under a year, then she'd move back to the city and I'd be right back to where I was five years ago. I told you, I need to find a woman who'll be happy with small-town life. This is *my* life. I went to school here, I have friends here. My job's here. Briar goes to school here." He lowered to the cold concrete floor. "Rita isn't staying. She wants us to move to New York with her. How do I tell her I don't want to go?"

"The same way she told you she didn't want to stay. Be honest. Relationships need compromise. There has to be some give and take or one person ends up doing all the giving and the other all the taking, and that's not fair."

"I know. That's why I can't ask."

James slapped him on the back. "Then maybe it wasn't meant to be. Sometimes that happens and it's no one's fault. Look at Cole and Autumn, and Logan and Ivy. Too much baggage, too much history. You aren't the only one still licking your wounds. Marnie's told me a little about Leah, and she's had it rough. If you love her, tell her, and figure the rest out later." He sighed. "Are we done here? We did what we could to fix this old dinosaur. Let's break it to my parents that Christmas is comin' early to the Fox house."

"Yeah, sure."

There would be some tough conversations ahead. Thoughts and feelings and emotions he'd been able to bury for the past five years had started to surface, and he didn't like it. In this situation, no one was going to win.

Least of all, him. He'd fallen in love with Leah, and he couldn't ask her to stay because he wasn't willing to go. James didn't have to tell him that.

He needed Leah to want to stay all on her own. Staying for him wasn't enough.

Rita leaving made that loud and clear.

"Thanks for telling me you were here," Autumn said, plopping onto a bench in Marnie's fitting room and pulling out her phone.

"No pictures. You'll leak them to the press."

Autumn laughed. "*The Rocky Point Daily Journal* is hardly Page Six."

"You know Page Six?" Leah asked.

"Sure. It's where I get all my Ben Affleck gossip. I won't leak your pictures, but can I report on the style? The color? It's not white. It's not cream, either. Eggshell? A delicate baby powder. For the blog, of course."

"Of course," Marnie said. "I don't care, but no pictures. I want James to be the first one to see it."

"You mean besides us, your mother, James's mother, and the woman coming to do our hair? Who was that again?" Autumn asked.

"Daisy. From the Curl-E-Q."

"God, could that name be any more horrible?" Autumn asked, moving her tongue around her mouth like she just tasted something bad.

Leah smothered a laugh.

"She graduated top in her class, and she's cheap. Our updos are only going to cost ten bucks apiece. I promised her I'd give her some leftover cake, and that's all she wanted."

"Where did she go to school?" Leah asked.

"Comet Cosmetology."

Autumn straightened. "Wait. Was that the school a woman taught out of her garage? Or am I thinking of something else?"

"That was a different one. Have some class. Comet used to be in Marengo, but it burned down. One of the students spilled fingernail polish remover all over the floor and then 'accidentally,'" Marnie said, using exaggerated air quotes around the word, "dropped a match when she was lighting up a joint."

"Good Lord," Leah gasped. "Was anyone hurt?"

"No, but a few hair mannequins melted to oblivion before the ceiling sprinklers went off. I remember it because Callie's dad volunteered her to fill in for someone, and she helped put the fire out. She said all that burning product stank to high heaven." Marnie gently slid the dress off the hanger. "This color is Winter White, and I thought the name was perfect."

"Daisy's doing your, I mean, our hair, the dress is Winter White. What style is that?"

"Princess, I think. I needed the skirt to hide these hips. Rita would know." Marnie winced. "Sorry."

Leah scowled. "You can talk about her all you want. I told you if you want me to step aside—"

"No!"

"Leah!"

"Okay, but you don't have to treat me with kid gloves

just because Jared and I slept together a couple of times. We're adults, and it was mutual. Things happen."

"Like falling in love," Marnie said dreamily, clutching her dress to her breasts.

"They weren't lying when they called it falling. It sure as hell hurts when you land. Anyway, enough of that or I could wallow in it for the rest of my time here and I don't want to do that. Marnie? Do you need help? It's why we're back here with you."

"Can you keep my boobs from spilling out of this dress? I told you, I need to lose weight or I'm preg—"

"Oh, Marnie!" Autumn said, jumping off the bench and dancing around the puddle of lace. "I can't even hug you or I'll step on your dress."

"Do *not* say anything. I don't even know for sure yet. I feel . . . puffy. I needed to know I can still fit into this thing."

"Besides the boob issue?" Leah asked, doing the buttons at the small of Marnie's back.

Marnie tried stuffing her breasts down into the bust. "God. Can I lose twenty pounds in a week?"

Shaking her head, Autumn said, "Not safely. Especially if you're pregnant."

"Take your bra off," Leah said. "You don't need the support and that will give you a bit of space."

"Good idea."

Her phone rang, and she stepped back. "Can you help her, Autumn, and undo the buttons I just did up?"

"Yep."

She hurried to find her phone in her purse hoping to catch the call before it went to voicemail. Maybe it was Jared wanting to see her.

The name of her grandma's assisted living facility

flashed on the black screen and her heart started to pound. "Hello?"

"Hello? Is this Miss Bristow?"

"Yes, speaking."

"This is Amy, one of Della's aides. She had a stroke, and an ambulance is taking her to the hospital."

She swallowed. "Which one, please?"

"Mercy Vale General. It's not far from us."

"Yes, I know it. I'm out of town at the moment, but I'll fly back as soon as I'm able to make the arrangements."

"Thank you, Miss Bristow. She'll be happy to see you."

"Please tell her, if she's lucid enough to understand."

"We'll pass the information to her doctors."

"Thank you."

She disconnected the call and sank onto the bench, her hands trembling.

Marnie knelt in front of her and touched her arm. "Are you okay? What happened?"

"My grandma had a stroke. I need to go see her."

"Shit. Okay. We'll help you. Autumn, can you get me out of this dress?"

Autumn helped Marnie step out of the voluminous skirt, and she quickly dressed, leaving the gown in the fitting room.

"Autumn, can you book her a flight out of Marengo?"

"Yeah, but—"

"I'll drive her to the airport. Unless, Leah, did you want to ask Jared to fly you there? It will be faster than driving."

"No. I can't bother him. He's with his family, and I can't —" She followed Marnie and Autumn out of the dress boutique, tears sliding down her cheeks.

"Okay, it's okay. It's a two-hour drive. Do you need to go to the resort first and grab anything?"

"I need to know which airport you want to fly into," Autumn said, tapping on her phone. "Do you use a middle initial?"

"JFK is fine, and no, I don't. I should check out. I don't know when I'll be back."

"But—" Marnie said, opening her truck's door.

"She can stay at my place," Autumn said, pushing her into the cab. She squished in next to her and pulled the door shut. "I'll help you pack."

"Thank you."

Her grandma was the only family she had left. Her mother didn't want to be her mother, and she didn't count the sisters and brother she'd never met that Autumn helped her find. Max had left her, and her grandpa was gone.

If her grandma died, she'd be alone.

Completely alone.

"Your ticket's ready. One way from Marengo to New York. You have a three-hour layover in Chicago, but that was the best I could do with such a short notice."

"I appreciate it," she said, squeezing Autumn's hand. "I'll pay you back."

"Don't worry about that now."

They quickly packed her suitcases, and they rushed through the lobby. Marnie stopped her in front of the reservation desk. "Can you not check out? Would you mind if we moved James's aunt into your room? I know it's a horrible thing to think about at a time like this, but—"

"That makes sense," she said, dismissing the thought. She didn't care what happened to her room. "Where should I put my luggage? I don't want to bring it with me."

"We have to drop Autumn off at her car. It's still at the dress shop. She can bring your suitcases to her house and they'll there when you come back, okay?"

"You guys have thought of everything."

"That's what friends are for. When we get on the road, I'll call James to let him know what's happening."

Marnie tried to distract her while they drove the empty highway between Rocky Point and Marengo. She appreciated her friend's attempt, but she worried about her grandma all the way to the airport.

Jared watched Briar and Rita drive away in Briar's little car, and he breathed a deep sigh of relief. They were going to the arena and then somewhere to have dinner, giving him the evening free to find Leah and explain what in the hell was going on.

Driving through the dark to the resort, he tried to think of what to say. Why he hadn't been in touch since Marnie's dinner. All he'd done since meeting Leah was hurt her, and once again, he found himself in front of her door, his hat in his hand, hoping she would accept his apology one more time.

He knocked, and he shifted on his feet, waiting for her to answer.

The door opened.

Too much of a coward to meet her eyes, he stared at his boots, the snow melting and dripping onto the carpet. "Leah, please give me a chance to explain."

"I don't know what you've done, but you have the wrong room."

A vaguely familiar woman peered at him through the crack in the door, a towel wrapped around her ample figure, her hair wet. She appraised him, her eyes widening in recognition. "You're Jared, James's friend. It's been a while since I've seen you, young man."

"You're not Leah," he said stupidly, his tongue thick in his mouth. Sweat covered his skin and he unzipped his jacket, desperately needing air. He struggled to breathe.

"No. I'm Ruth, James's aunt. You remember me, don't you? He found me a room and got me out of Killer Kelly's."

"Killer Kelly's? Where's Leah?"

"I don't know where Leah is, but the name fits because one more night in that dump would have killed me. Thank God I can spend the rest of my time here. I felt filthy staying and my shower lasted a whole hour."

"The rest of your time?" he asked, ignoring everything else the woman said. He didn't care about anything except finding Leah.

"I'm staying here for the next week and a half. Marnie said whoever was in this room didn't need it anymore."

Backing away, he said, "I'm sorry I disturbed you, Ruth."

"It's no problem, young man. Poker at Linda and Roy's later, if you want to stop by."

"I'll see what I can do. Thanks."

"Leah's one of Marnie's bridesmaids, isn't she?"

"Yeah."

"I hope nothing bad happened."

"Me too."

Jared trotted to James and Marnie's room, hoping someone was there. He could be at his mom and dad's if they were having people over again. Treating the two weeks leading up to the ceremony as a never-ending party turned the Fox house into wedding central, and the kitchen was never empty of family who hadn't seen each other in years catching up on gossip.

James opened the door, the TV playing a football game behind him. "Hey, what're you doing here? Where's Rita?"

"She and Briar are at the arena. Briar has skate practice tonight. Where's Leah? I stopped by her room but she wasn't there." He stepped inside and waved off the beer James tried to hand him. He didn't feel like drinking. Too scared, too worried about the reasons why Leah wouldn't need her room anymore, and in a downright panic because he didn't know where in the hell she was.

"She got a call this afternoon when she and Marnie were at the dress shop. Her grandma had a stroke and she went back to New York. She promised Marnie she'd come back as soon as she could."

He raked a hand through his hair, frustrated. "She's not coming back if she gave up her room."

"Calm down. If you don't want a beer, drink this," James said, pouring a couple inches of scotch into a plastic cup. "I take it you didn't talk to her?"

"No." He sipped the drink and let the warmth loosen his muscles. Breathe. Leah would be back for the ceremony. Breathe. She's coming back.

"The women already decided she's going to stay in Autumn's spare bedroom. Marnie's on the road. She drove Leah to Marengo."

He scowled. He didn't like the idea of Marnie driving back to Rocky Point on the snowy roads alone, and he was sure James didn't either. "I would've flown her there. It's faster."

"Marnie suggested it, but Leah didn't want to bother you."

"It wouldn't have been a bother."

"You know that, and I know that. Marnie knew that, or she wouldn't have offered, but Leah doesn't know that.

From what Marnie's told me, Leah doesn't have many close friends. Doesn't know what it's like to have someone's support, no questions asked."

"I haven't exactly been showing her that, either." He drained his drink and let James pour him another shot.

"Nothing you can do now except wait. Come over to the house, a couple hands of poker will keep your mind off things."

"Thanks, but I should get some chores done. Laundry basket's full, run the vacuum, you know."

"All right, but the offer's always open."

"Yeah. Thanks. I'll catch ya later."

He rested his forehead against his truck's cold steering wheel. Leah went back to New York and didn't say anything, to a grandparent he barely knew anything about. Torn between letting himself become attached and keeping her at arms' length, he hadn't tried to get to know her. Hadn't wanted to because he knew the more he knew about her, the more of her there was to love.

He'd wait for her to come back, and then he'd tell her. Even if they couldn't have a life together, she'd know how he felt. That someone in the world cared about her.

That *many* someones in the world cared about her. Briar, Marnie, James, Autumn. Helen. She had people behind her, good people.

Parked in his dark garage, he pulled out his phone and opened his contacts. He could text her and tell her he was thinking about her, but he put his phone to sleep without sending a message. She was busy, possibly flying, and she wouldn't see it anyway.

He walked into his empty house and right back out again.

Feeling alone, he too, needed a reminder someone cared

about him, and sitting in a kitchen full of people who'd known him since childhood would be a good place to start.

He spent the rest of the night with James, Marnie, and their parents playing Texas Hold 'Em and waiting for news about Leah that never came.

The traffic and noise crushed her, the claustrophobia and anxiety gripping her lungs in a vise until she couldn't breathe. How had Rita traded the wide open spaces for this constant, painful buzz of energy? Some people thrived on it —maybe she had in the best of times, too—but no more.

The dirty air churned her stomach and bile rose in her throat.

She rode a cab from the airport to the hospital, the ride taking longer than she would have liked, sitting in a vehicle that stank of stale food. Traffic jams plugged the streets even though rush hour passed many hours ago.

It couldn't compare to driving through Rocky Point in Jared's truck, Christmas lights and empty roads, the spicy scent of his cologne permeating through the cold.

The driver let her out and she darted across the street past a taxi full of boys partying, yelling at her through half-open windows to watch where she was going.

The hospital's quiet lobby enveloped her, and she sank into a padded chair near a tree to give herself a moment to stop shaking. She needed a meal and a cup of coffee. She needed to text Marnie and let her know she landed safely, but before she did any of that, she needed to find out how her grandma was doing.

On wobbly legs, she walked to the information desk

where even at this late hour a middle-aged gentleman sat watching something on a tablet.

He looked up when she approached and smiled. "Can I help you?"

"My grandma was brought in from her assisted living facility down the street. Della Harris."

He tapped on a keyboard and squinted at the large monitor. "I see her. She's on the ninth floor in ICU. I can't tell you anything about her condition, but the nurses' station will be able to give you more details."

"Thank you."

Her stomach did somersaults in the elevator, her trembling fingers clutching the straps of her purse.

Nurses spoke in hushed voices at the large desk, whiteboards behind them annotated in brightly colored markers. She crossed the floor, the soles of her boots squeaking, and two of the nurses looked up from a clipboard as she approached.

"I'm here to see Della Harris. I'm her granddaughter, Leah."

"We were told to expect you," one of the nurses wearing mint green scrubs said. "Your grandmother's doing well. The stroke was mild, and physically, she may not have any long-term effects, but it's difficult to say if the stroke will aggravate her dementia."

"When will you know?" she asked, following the nurse down the hallway.

"There's no definite answer," the nurse said, stopping at a small room, large windows flanking the sliding glass door.

Her grandma laid on a bed attached to several wires and an IV. She wasn't intubated, thank God. She would've hated to see that. She'd never seen someone intubated in real life, but on TV it always looked serious. Thin, her skin pale, her grandma's condition looked grim enough as it was.

"When will she be able to go back to her assisted living facility?"

"We'll keep her here for another day or two. The facility where she's been staying is equipped to handle what she'll need as far as various therapies. In fact, we send stroke patients there if they need long-term treatment. She'll be well taken care of."

"That's good to know. I'm not in a situation where I can be an adequate caregiver."

The nurse patted her back. "Don't feel guilty. Keeping your grandma safe is the main priority, and her stroke aside, her dementia means she needs more attention than a typical person. You're doing the right thing."

"I never feel like I am."

"We hear that from a lot of our patients' families. You have work and other obligations, and your grandma could wander off and get lost while you go to the grocery store. The facility she's been living in is one of the best. You're doing all you can."

She was, and her pocketbook took a hit for it every month. So much so, a year later she still struggled to get back on her feet. If Max had been kinder in the divorce . . . but he hadn't and she stopped crying over it a long time ago.

She wasn't eating Ramen noodles for dinner every night, but she'd have to move her grandma somewhere else if her medical insurance and Medicare stopped paying their share of the facility costs. She paid the remaining amount and had just enough left over to pay bills and stock her kitchen with decent wine.

To afford to go to the wedding, she started saving money

the very second she'd accepted Marnie's invitation. Luckily, Marnie asked her six months ago, and she was able to put aside just enough to pay for her room at the resort and her bridesmaid's dress.

"You should get some rest. There's nothing you can do right now, and it's late."

The weight of traveling and missing Jared suddenly landed on her shoulders. She missed him more than she thought she could miss a man she'd met only days before. She missed Marnie, and Autumn, even poor Ivy who looked like she carried more than her fair share of problems.

She missed Helen and the store.

She missed her life in Rocky Point.

Would she still miss that life if she took Jared out of the equation?

If she *had to* take Jared out of the equation? For all she knew, he and Rita were back together. She hadn't heard a word from him, and someone would have told him by now she'd come back to New York to take care of her grandma. No way Marnie would keep that to herself. She'd tell James, and James would pass the information along to Jared.

Leah took a cab to her building and used her last remaining strength to walk up the stairs to her fourth-floor unit. Exhausted, she trudged inside her apartment, tears filling her eyes.

She'd turned the heat down low, thinking she'd be away for two weeks. That resulted in sleeping in an apartment that was only fifty degrees. She changed into pajamas, layering a tank top under a sweatshirt and putting on the thickest pair of sweatpants she could find, managed a quick text to Marnie, and went to bed.

Wrapping herself in several blankets, she shivered as

she fell asleep, finally allowing the tears of fatigue to trickle down her cheeks.

The watery sunlight trying to seep past the blinds woke her from a restless sleep. Tentatively, she eased her hand into the air to test the bedroom's temperature. The room had warmed overnight and she pushed off the pile of blankets and grabbed her phone off the nightstand.

No message from Jared, but Marnie and Autumn wished her well and Helen had tried calling her.

She tucked the reminder to return the call into the back of her mind and crawled out of bed.

The kitchen warmed up during the night, too, and she made coffee without shivering. She had to drink it black because she used the last of the milk before she left for Rocky Point. Try as she might to fly back as soon as possible, if her grandma's doctors couldn't tell her positive news, she'd need to run to the corner store. She didn't like coffee without milk or creamer, and she couldn't live on, or afford, hospital food.

She showered and dried her hair. Dressed. She didn't care what she wore and tugged on leggings and a worn sweater, her boots and jacket. She walked into Mercy Vale just before nine o'clock.

The elevator doors opened to the ninth floor, and she stepped out of the lift. A man standing at the nurses' station turned as the elevator dinged. Her throat worked and her mouth opened and closed like a guppy, but no sound came out.

"Leah."

She stood frozen in place, her hands useless at her sides. Hate and fear twisted her stomach. "Max. What are you doing here?"

He smiled, but she didn't see compassion or sympathy. The curve of his lips contained malice and disgust.

"I'm still listed as an emergency contact and someone called me early this morning. I came to see how Della was doing. If you didn't want to see me, you should have updated your records. You never did have your shit together."

She kicked herself. It should have been the first thing she did after she signed her divorce papers. Max's number was listed on all her personal forms at work, too. God forbid someone call him in an emergency. He'd probably let her die.

"I'll take care of it," she said, her lips trembling.

"Well, it did give me the chance to see how you're doing, and not well by the look of things. Why are you dressed that way? You look stupid."

Her toes curled in the boots Helen gave her in exchange for helping at the store, the ones she wore when she fell through the ice were still at Jared's, and she grasped her jacket, the zipper's teeth digging into her skin. "I've been away. Not that it's any of your business."

She hadn't thought of changing her clothes yesterday, too worried about her grandma to care. It hadn't been ideal clomping around the airports in her heavy pacs and they were far from the sleek leather handmade Italian boots Max bought her when they were married, but her clothes reminded her of Rocky Point, of the friends she'd made there, of spending time with Jared outside, and of the wide open space of frozen lake that somehow filled the wide open space in her heart.

"Away where? You can't survive anywhere but here. You're just a pampered princess who needs to be waited on hand and foot. Why do you think I got rid of you? I was tired of taking care of a woman who couldn't do anything for herself. You're pathetic. I thought Della taught you how to be a good wife. A credit to me. But you're a barren, frigid, selfish shrew."

She straightened her spine. What in the hell was she doing? She was better than this.

She wouldn't let this man, this *asshole*, who'd emotionally abused her only to kick her to the curb, penniless, treat her like this anymore.

She wasn't stupid. She found a decent job that offered good benefits, was able to pay to keep her grandma in one of the best facilities in New York, and still make ends meet every month. Without anyone's help, she'd kept her head above water after he took everything, and without losing her mind, too. She had friends who cared about her. Maybe Jared did go back to his ex-wife, but that didn't have anything to do with her. She couldn't blame him if he was still in love with Rita and wanted to keep his family together, but what he'd taught her was that she was still lovable. Damaged, maybe, but still lovable.

More importantly, Max hadn't destroyed her ability to love in return. She loved Jared.

Wrong place, wrong time, wrong person, but Max hadn't destroyed her ability to love.

He hadn't destroyed *her*.

Maybe Max didn't want her, maybe her mother had given her up, maybe Jared chose the mother of his child over her, but she'd find someone who wanted her. She'd never let someone tell her she was worthless. Not ever again.

With the memory of the last time she and Jared made

love lingering in her heart, she stood in front of Max and looked him in the eye. He couldn't hurt her, not physically. Security guards and nurses were stationed on every floor. And not mentally, because she wasn't the same woman she was when he divorced her.

She was learning her worth. She had value, and that didn't depend on anyone but her.

"I was on birth control when we were married because I didn't want your children, you stupid son of a bitch, and I was frigid because you make my skin crawl. We're not married anymore, and you have no rights when it comes to my life. You should leave."

"I'm happy I got rid of you," he snapped, his face red.

He turned toward the elevator.

"So am I."

He stiffened, but he didn't turn around. He punched the elevator's Down button and stepped inside, the doors hiding him from view. She hoped she never had to see him again.

She sighed and turned toward the nurses' station.

Four nurses stood behind the desk, staring.

Her cheeks burned.

Until they started clapping.

"Nice job."

"Asshole."

"What a loser."

"Thanks." Her voice hitched and she laughed. "My heart feels like it's going to explode."

"We have more good news to tell you. Later today we're moving Della to a room on the seventh floor. She's stable, and we think she'll be able to go back to her assisted living facility tomorrow."

She leaned against the desk in relief. "She's going to be okay?"

"It appears the stroke was minor. That doesn't mean side effects may not develop at a later date, but for now, she seems to be fully-functioning. She's been awake since four this morning, giving all of us a hard time. In a good way," the nurse added quickly when her smile faded. "You can speak to her if you'd like. She's eaten breakfast and has taken her medication, but I think she'll need to rest before too long."

"Thank you. Thank you very much."

She went to her grandmother's room and pushed a chair closer to the bed. She held her grandma's hand.

Della laid at an incline, a puffy pillow under her head, and she opened her eyes. "Leah."

"Hi, Grandma. How are you feeling?"

"I'm tired, and I miss my other room. Why am I here? When can I go home?"

She smoothed her thumb over her grandma's knuckles that were swollen with time and age. She needed to tell her grandma all the news while she was having a lucid morning.

"Soon, Grandma. You had a stroke, and they want to keep an eye on you. Then you can go back to your room."

Della nodded. "Okay. That's okay. They have good coffee here."

"That's good." She paused. "Do you remember asking me to find my mom? To find Emmy?"

Della's eyes watered. "Yes. Did you? Did you find my little girl?"

During the flight to New York, she debated for a long time what would hurt her grandma the least. Knowing her daughter was out there, happy, surrounded by her second family, or believing Leah hadn't been able to find her and living with the mystery for the rest of her life.

Emmaline hadn't looked for them. She hadn't come back.

She'd left them behind, and Leah knew how her grandma would feel knowing her daughter was alive and healthy and hadn't bothered to reach out in over thirty years.

"No. I looked everywhere. I even asked a friend to help me search, but there's no trace of her. Autumn's a reporter and good at finding people. She would've found Emmy if she was out there. I don't know where she is."

Some of the light slipped out of her grandma's eyes. "She's gone."

"Yes. I'm sorry, Grandma. I tried my best."

Della's face hardened. "Your best was never good enough. You were never good enough. Emmy should have had a boy. Richard wouldn't have abandoned his family if my daughter would have given him a son. Go away. I'm tired." She turned her head and stared at the cream-colored wall.

She was used to this. It didn't have anything to do with her dementia or her stroke. She'd grown up being given the silent treatment. Sometimes Della would refuse to speak to her for days, and she wouldn't know what she'd done to cause it.

It made her feel lonely, isolated. As she grew older, she didn't blame her mother for leaving, but she'd wished with all her heart that her mother would have taken her, too.

"Okay, Grandma. They're going to move you later, and I'll come back to visit, okay?"

Della didn't acknowledge her.

She smothered a sigh and stood from her chair. "I love you."

Still nothing.

"I made her mad," she warned a nurse sitting behind the desk filling out paperwork.

"People who don't feel well are often in poor spirits. We're used to it and don't take it personally."

"Her heart's a bit bruised as well."

The nurse smiled in sympathy. "Life's hard, Miss Bristow. Get some rest."

"Thanks."

She'd done the right thing. At least, she tried to convince herself she had. Her grandma may have blamed her for not being able to find Emmy, but she didn't mind taking the blame for that.

If she would have told Della she'd found Emmy and Emmy hadn't contacted them in all these years, Della would have blamed her, and that was the kind of blame she wanted to avoid.

As she walked the crowded sidewalks back to her apartment, she talked herself through all that, and by the time she reached her building, she felt better.

It also made saving the boxes of keepsakes she cleaned out of Della's last apartment almost pointless.

Keepsakes celebrated life.

There was nothing to celebrate when it came to her mother.

With a cup of coffee and a pastry she picked up from a corner street vendor, she settled on the floor surrounded by beat-up cardboard boxes.

There wasn't much to go through.

It seemed surreal that these few scant boxes contained

her entire history. Her grandma hadn't kept school drawings or art projects, from her or Emmy. She hadn't kept report cards or student-of-the-month certificates. She'd wanted Little League trophies, football trophies. Little girl things hadn't mattered to Della.

She learned quickly they wouldn't be treasured and stopped keeping them, sometimes throwing them in the trash on the way home from school.

Her grandma gave her a roof over her head, food in her belly, and kept her dressed well enough she wasn't teased at school. She taught Leah how to sew, how to cook, things that gave a woman worth, but underneath the time had been the idea she was a chore, a duty, an obligation.

Then thinking she was escaping her grandmother's indifference, she married those same feelings.

She opened a box and took out her christening gown. A stained photo of her in her grandma's arms standing next to a priest laid under the yellowed lace. Her face pinched, Della stared into the camera, frowning, the priest's smile hesitant on his lips.

An empty baby book.

A rattle.

Pink baby booties.

A single picture of her and her mother.

Taken right after Emmy had given birth to her, Emmy rested in bed, exhausted, looking as if she still hurt. Leah laid swaddled in her arms, a newborn hat covering her head. Even through the picture, she could feel Emmy's disconnect.

All because her father abandoned them.

She was half of her father, and that made it impossible for her mother to love her.

It was more than that, and she understood.

She'd been raised by Della, too. Failure to keep her man had broken Emmy.

In Della's mind, keeping a man was a woman's priority, and Emmy failed.

So had Leah.

But the difference between her and her mother was that she didn't want a man who didn't want her. Who wouldn't treat her with the love and respect she deserved.

Emmy hadn't been strong enough to raise her alone, and she ran. Leaving her behind like Emmy's husband left her behind.

In a burst of misery, she threw the picture against the wall. The glass shattered and the frame broke.

A piece of pink paper fell out from between the picture and the back of the frame.

She picked through the glass and unfolded it.

Dear Leah, she read in a handwriting not familiar to her, *I named you after your father's mother. Did you know that?*

She didn't know. There would have been no way for her to know unless Della told her, but all the information Della ever offered her about her father was that he wouldn't have left Emmy if she'd been a better wife.

It was an attempt to get him to come back to us, but it didn't work.

I don't know if you'll ever find this letter, but I want you to know how sorry I am. I love you. You won't believe that, but I do. I'm sorry I couldn't do better by you. I hope, Leah, you grow into a strong woman. Fearless. Live life on your own terms. I buckled because I'm weak. I bent under my mother, and I let your father break me the rest of the way. I could ask you not to hold that against me, but you will. And you should. I'm leaving. Tonight. I can't take you with me. I hope one day you can understand. Oh, my sweet girl—

Tears smeared the ink, and the writing abruptly stopped. It looked as if her mother wanted to continue, the pen pressed to the paper, but there wasn't any more.

Her mother had been young, and selfish, and heartbroken.

Mix that with a mother who blamed her daughter for everything and, well, she could sympathize.

She still didn't forgive Emmy for leaving her behind, but her letter made it easier for her to move on.

On her terms.

She hated the city.

It was time she started living her life the way she wanted to live it.

She slid her phone out of her purse. Marnie had texted her, asking if she was okay and how her grandma was doing.

No word from Jared, but she hadn't expected there to be. She hoped he would've at least had the courtesy to tell her they were finished, but that was okay. She didn't need him to be happy.

She found the Supply Company's number in her contacts and pressed Connect.

When Helen answered, happy to be hearing from her, she knew she was doing the right thing.

"Helen. How much are you asking for your store? I want to negotiate."

CHAPTER EIGHT

Jared missed Leah so much. She'd been gone only two days, but those forty-eight hours felt like a lifetime.

He asked Marnie how she was doing, but all Marnie did was narrow her eyes and say, "Ask her yourself."

He couldn't.

Growling, he kicked a chair in his office. He couldn't call her when Rita slept down the hall hoping her visit would repair their relationship and their family. He didn't work that way.

Rita cooked dinner last night, and they sat at the table, chatted about their day the way they used to before she left.

Then, after they all went to bed, Rita had slipped into his. They kissed, but all he could think about was Leah and the way they'd made love at the resort. He told Rita he couldn't do it, and she ran out of his room in a puddle of embarrassed tears.

To say breakfast this morning had been uncomfortable would have been a gross understatement.

What he needed was some time in the air. He hadn't

flown since bringing Briar and Leah to Marengo to go shopping. He hadn't flown for the hell of it in months.

He'd go in the morning for a couple of hours. Then he'd tell Rita they weren't getting back together. His heart had moved on.

He prayed he hadn't blown whatever chance he and Leah had.

It was easy to forget she didn't live in town. She fit into his life, into the community, as easily as he feared she would.

On the flight, he'd need to decide how much of her he'd settle for to keep her in his life.

He missed her so much, he suspected he'd be happy with breadcrumbs. Anything to keep her from saying goodbye when she went back to the city after the wedding.

He met James that night at the Viking to watch the football game. Marnie was spending time with her parents, Linda and Roy were having a quiet evening at home, all the recent company wearing them out, and he didn't want to be at home, even though Rita and Briar made popcorn and asked if he wanted to watch a movie. It was too much of a family evening, one that didn't belong to him, not anymore.

"Rita tried sleeping with me last night," he blurted out, tired of keeping the secret and guilt to himself.

"Did you?" James asked, his hand paused over a bowl of pretzels, his eyes never leaving the giant flat-screen TV attached to the wall.

"No. I told her I couldn't. She started crying and ran out of the room."

James looked at him. "Marnie said Rita's different. She's not the same person she used to be."

"How can she be? Five years in New York City? We're probably lucky she hasn't changed more. I thought they kept in touch."

"They did, as much as two people can in circumstances like that, but people change. Even if Rita would've stayed here, it still could have happened."

"I'm not different," he said, leaning against his chair. "I'm the same man, working the same job, trying to take care of his daughter the best way he knows how."

James scoffed. "That's not true or you would have slept with Rita last night."

He sipped his beer. "I can't say what would have happened if Rita would've come back before I met Leah. Leah . . . I felt it when I picked her up at the airport. Five minutes in, and I knew my life would never be the same." He laughed. "That sounds stupid."

"No, it doesn't. The truth is, I never gave Marnie a thought. We were friends, you know, high school sweethearts, but we dated other people and I didn't care. Until one night we all met up at a party and this guy was hanging on her. She liked it, or didn't mind it, at least, but something clicked and I knew. Up until that point, I'd known her all my life, but like you said, in those five minutes I knew I didn't want her dating anybody else, ever again. I drove her home that night, laid it all out. I'm a lucky man she felt the same." James paused to glance at the TV screen. "You need to tell Leah how you feel."

Swallowing his pride, he forced himself to ask, "Will you tell me how she is? Marnie won't."

"She's doing okay. Her grandma's stroke wasn't as bad as it could have been." James sucked in a breath. "She told

Marnie she bumped into her ex-husband. Something about not updating emergency contacts. It didn't sound as buddy-buddy as you and Rita, but Leah's tough and she's okay."

Dammit. Guilt ate at him. If they would have been on speaking terms when she left, she would have felt she could talk to him about running into her ex-husband. He wanted to support her. He could have gone with her. But he'd been stupid, too stupid and stubborn to realize what avoiding her would do to them, and now she was dealing with an asshole of an ex by herself when he could have been there to defend her.

"Do you know when she's coming back?" He pushed the words out. "Or if she's coming back?"

"Nope. Sorry. She offered to let Rita take her place as a bridesmaid, but Marnie threw a fit. Leah's going to do her best to make it back before the wedding. That's all I know."

"Thanks."

"Yeah."

"How are things with you?"

Poking at his beer bottle, James said, "I think Marnie's pregnant."

He raised his eyebrows and lifted his beer in a toast. "Congratulations." He paused. "You don't know?"

"She stopped drinking. She said it's because she wants to lose a couple of pounds before the ceremony, but she loves wine too much to do that. She was all about treating these two weeks as a giant party."

"Are you ready for kids?"

James chuckled. "You know what? I am. I really am."

"I love Briar, but we were too young. I envy you, waiting and doing things right."

"Things turned out okay for you."

"If you can consider not going to college, or living in a

crappy apartment downtown, or not being able to afford a house until your daughter's five years old, or your wife leaving you to chase a more exciting life okay, then yeah."

"Things can go to shit no matter what you do. If you want to go to school, take night classes at the community college or enroll online. You and Rita were together for over ten years. Lots of couples don't make it past five. I love Marnie, and she makes me happy. I hope I make her happy, too. Rita wanted something that you couldn't give her. That Rocky Point couldn't give her. That's not your fault."

"Yeah, it is. You just said it. I didn't make her happy. That's on me. I should have tried harder. Anyway, I'm happy for you. Kids. If there's anything I *can* say, it's that Briar turned out to be a pretty wonderful person. Inside and out." Sighing, he threw a twenty on the sticky table. "I need to get home."

"You okay?" James asked, frowning.

He hadn't been okay since Rita left him. He'd been slowly getting back to feeling comfortable with life, being satisfied with the way things were.

Then he'd picked Leah up at the airport and his okay turned to anything but.

"I put in a long day at work. I'll talk to you later."

He left James at the corner table munching on pretzels, sipping beer, and watching the game highlights.

He envied James his place in life.

He needed to find his place, and the longer Leah stayed in New York, the more he suspected his place was with her, no matter where that turned out to be.

Rita didn't try to sleep with him that night, and she didn't meet his eyes over coffee the next morning. He told her he was taking a couple hours to himself up in the air, and she shrugged in indifference. Like a coward, he hurried out of the house while she showered, avoiding a fight that had begun a steady build-up since she'd run out of his room.

It made sense that Rita stayed with him and spent as much time with Briar as she could, but he wished she would've made other arrangements. Being under the same roof as his ex-wife was beginning to wear on his patience, and there were still several days until the wedding.

The open expanse of the airfield soothed his jangled nerves.

Grey colored the sky, but Minnesota in December, that was nothing new. The clouds would keep the sun out of his face. A light wind blew, but all in all, his time in the air would be smooth and give him time to think.

"It's a great morning to fly," the airport manager said, catching him outside the hangar that stored his plane. His Cessna shared space with a few others, and the hangar door was already open, another plane gone. "Did you want to file a flight plan? I'm heading inside if you looked for me."

Jared bit back a frustrated sigh. Normally he did file a flight plan when he was flying to Marengo on business or when he carried a passenger, but today he was flying for pleasure and he'd be alone. He wouldn't be gone long, he needed to get a few hours in at the arena this afternoon. The high school hockey team had another game coming up, and there were a quite few things he needed to get done before then.

Mainly, he wanted to try and forget about Leah for a bit, and it had been a long time since he flew over town and the lake.

He was making things worse between them, not texting or calling her, at least to say he was sorry about her grandma, but he couldn't bring himself to do it. He wanted to wait until he could see her in person and explain how wrong it felt to have Rita under his roof when they were no longer together.

When he was in love with Leah.

Dammit.

"No, not today. I'm flying alone and I won't be up there that long. Staying in touch with ATC will be enough."

"Alrighty. Weather says there'll be some wind, but we shouldn't see snow until tonight. Mike's in the tower," he said, pushing his wire-rimmed glasses up his nose, his dark blond hair blowing in the breeze that started to kick up. "He's in a good mood."

"Thanks."

He felt at home in his plane, and as he settled into his seat, the tension drained from his muscles. Flying reminded him of his grandma. They'd been close while he was growing up, and his happy childhood contrasted with Leah's unhappy one.

With his cheat sheet laying on his thigh, he went over his pre-flight checklist. Mike, the air traffic controller, left his radio open, and he was telling someone about a date he had last night.

Adjusting his headset, he laughed.

He taxied to the runway and paused to work out a route before taking off. He wanted to fly over the resort and take a look at how many people were ice fishing. Maybe fly over the resort where he and Leah fed the chipmunks. A leisurely flight would help him unwind, and when he landed, he'd call Leah and find out when she was planning to come back. He could make arrangements with her to pick her up in Marengo since Marnie had driven her there. They would have the flight to talk . . . alone.

He took off against a gust of wind, the propeller spinning so fast it turned invisible. The small plane easily handled Mother Nature's pushback, and a few moments later, Rocky Point was below him in a mix of green trees, brown rooftops, and white snow.

An hour into the flight, he decided to head back to the small airport. He could grab a late breakfast or early lunch. If he ate at the diner on Main, he could look in on Helen and ask if she knew when Leah was coming back.

Goddamn it. He was such a coward.

Turning sharply, he changed his mind. He wasn't ready to go back yet. He needed a few more minutes to hide.

Giant snowflakes started falling from the sky, and in typical Minnesota fashion, visibility went from miles to mere inches in seconds.

The abrupt change in weather didn't alarm him. He'd flow many times in inclement weather with and without his grandma. There weren't many situations he hadn't flown in, thanks to the wisdom of a woman who wanted to make sure he was prepared for anything, though he did stop thinking about Leah and concentrated on the flight.

Flying over a large expanse of farmland, he guessed he was about twenty minutes away from the airport.

The wind whipped snow against the windshield, and he steadied the plane as he navigated through a rough patch of turbulence, his hands sweaty.

Though his grandma made sure he could handle almost any situation, the one thing he never experienced was the engine suddenly sputtering to a stop and the eerie silence where the hum should have been.

"What the hell?" he muttered. "Hey, Mike?" he asked

the controller as he checked his fuel tanks. He flipped the switch, hoping to reengage the tanks. If the line was plugged, switching tanks would give him juice again, enough to turn around, but nothing happened, and slowly he lost altitude.

"What's up, Jared? You fly into some weather? We're seeing some snow."

"Yeah, but my engine stopped." He swallowed hard.

"Where are you? What's your read?"

He glanced at the GPS mounted to his instrument panel.

"I'm about twenty miles out, south, southwest."

"You have a place to land?" Mike paused. "You're flying over Anderson's farm. Should be open space. The old coot owns a few hundred acres."

"Okay."

The snow made it impossible to see, and he had to rely on his gauges to tell him where the ground laid beneath him. He concentrated on maintaining best-glide speed.

He tried to restart the engine, double-checking the throttle and the ignition. His hand shaking, he pulled the key out and pushed it back in, wiggling it, hoping for a spark.

Nothing.

He'd done emergency landings with his grandma before. Smooth, no-engine landings that were a piece of cake. Almost peaceful. She taught him to always have situational awareness, to know where in the hell he was in case he ever needed to land in an emergency.

Lakes in the summer were no good because his plane wasn't equipped for a water landing. A vacant highway, or a dirt road that connected farmland. Even a field.

His grandma's voice echoed in his head. "Watch out for

fences. See, different crops could be cordoned off with wire you can't see from up here. You don't need to be pulling out miles of fencing for some old farmer. They're busy enough, and it's costly too."

With the wind and snow whipping around him and his visibility zero, he didn't have a choice where he landed. Landing safely was his top priority, and Anderson's fences would be his last consideration.

"Mike, how am I looking? I can't see a damn thing," he said through gritted teeth. It would be his luck he'd have a wide-open space below him, completely fly past it, and crash into a grain elevator.

"Whatcha got?"

He read his GPS coordinates.

"You're okay if you're slowing down. Anderson's between two other farms. If you overshoot a little, you're covered, but if you go too far, Halverson has that dairy barn."

He remembered flying over that barn several times. The building was enormous, and not anything he wanted to clip flying over, or bash into while landing.

Switching off the fuel selector, he prepared for landing. He pulled the throttle back and unlatched his doors.

There was nothing but white and he could only hope he had a clear space. Sending up a prayer, he turned the battery and alternator off.

He braced a moment too late, and without warning, the plane slammed down.

"Shit."

He jerked in his seat, the plane plowing through the snowdrifts and crashing into . . . something. A fence, maybe. A hay bale.

The plane shuddered and settled, and he caught his

breath. His first thought was, thank God Leah wasn't with him because no way in hell would he ever want to hurt her. His second thought was, thank God Leah wasn't with him because she never would have flown with him again.

"Jared?"

Mike's voice buzzed in his ear followed by a loud burst of static.

"I'm okay. Landed as well as I could."

"Good deal," Mike said. "Blizzard conditions in Rocky Point. Travel not advised. Be a while before someone can get to ya."

"Copy that."

Mike left the line open, and he heard him shout to someone, maybe the airport manager, that he was all right.

He pulled his headset off and unbuckled his harness. Flexing his sore fingers, he thought about what he needed to do next. Always exit the plane. But until he calmed down, leaving the plane wasn't his first choice.

He wiggled his cell phone out of the holder mounted to his instrument panel and sent James a text. His phone said it was delivered, but until James texted back, he wouldn't know if the message had truly been sent or received.

The sudden snow could have caused issues for other planes as well, and he hoped the pilots who had flown out before him made it back to the airport.

He would have, if his engine hadn't failed. The FAA would investigate his emergency landing and find out what caused it, and he needed to know how much damage his plane sustained, if any. It'd be a while before he could afford to have it repaired.

The snow flew across the field and beat against the plane. Visibility was still at zero. It was safer to stay inside but sitting and doing nothing wasn't his way.

Luckily, the temperature hovered above zero, and though it would be uncomfortable, he wouldn't freeze to death if he was stranded overnight.

He checked his phone. James hadn't responded.

He texted Rita, but this time his phone didn't say it was delivered.

Well, he had to do something. His legs were starting to cramp and his back hurt. Either he needed to jump out and find his bearings in all the snow, if he could, or move to the backseats where he'd have a little more legroom. He might even find a snack, the late breakfast at the diner a dream now.

He moved to the back, unsure of what to do next. He sat in one of the seats and sipped from a bottle of water Briar left behind. No food, though.

He checked his phone hoping James or Rita had texted him back.

There was nothing. No bars, no signal.

Settling in to wait, he checked the time and groaned. Eleven o'clock. It'd be a long day if the snow didn't let up.

His stomach growled. Trying to ignore it, he reclined the chair as far as it would go, hugged his jacket around him, and closed his eyes. If he dozed, maybe the day would go by faster.

With the wind slapping against the plane, he daydreamed about making love to Leah, and he slipped into a light sleep, a smile on his lips.

Leah visited her grandma that afternoon. Della's doctor released her earlier that morning, and she'd been moved to her living facility. With new purpose, she'd thrown out everything she no longer wanted to keep. She saved the picture of her mother holding her in the hospital and the short letter. Her christening gown. Everything else were items from a past she didn't care to remember.

She'd make new memories, even if they didn't include Jared. Eight thousand people lived in Rocky Point, and as the new owner of the Supply Company, she'd meet new customers every day. She and Helen had come to a surprising and beneficial agreement for both of them, and any trepidation she might have felt choosing to move to a small Minnesota town dissipated. The deal Helen gave her made it more than possible to not only purchase the Supply Company, but it would enable her to set money aside for the repairs Helen hadn't bothered with after Glen died.

That didn't mean the move would be easy, and on the cab ride to her grandma's nursing home, she called the assisted living facility in Marengo. She asked if they still had an opening available, which, in retrospect, she should have done first, but luck was with her and the director said a lovely room off the garden opened up yesterday. If she put down a deposit, the room would be theirs. It didn't need to be said that the primary way a room turned available was when someone died, and she didn't want to think about that. It would be many years before her grandma passed away. Della was healthy, and if it weren't for the dementia, she'd still be living on her own in the small rundown apartment she moved out of to go to college.

Sitting in the lobby of her grandma's facility, she gave the director her credit card number and her grandma's Medicare ID. That would be enough to secure her room, for now. She couldn't depend on her medical insurance, as that would change. She'd be self-employed, and her medical coverage would be something she'd worry about later.

Medical transportation across half the country would be costly, but cheaper and safer than flying. Della had lived in New York all her life, and if she had good days while they were driving, perhaps her grandmother would enjoy sightseeing.

She'd need to move to Minnesota in stages. Perhaps putting in a four to six week notice at her job instead of two. She could hire and train her own replacement while she looked for a place to live in Rocky Point. Hopefully, if she saw her grandma settled in Marengo first, the rest would fall into place. It would be strange, living in New York while her grandma was in Minnesota, but she couldn't take a chance of the room becoming unavailable. Her grandma would be taken care of there, and that meant the most.

Maybe she'd need a little help, but there were people like Autumn she could ask. Out of anything, that might be the most difficult thing to get used to. Knowing she wouldn't be alone anymore.

"Grandma, how are you feeling?" she asked, walking into her grandma's room. Her hands hadn't quite stopped shaking yet.

"I'm fine, dear," Della said, a frowning. "Do I know you?"

"Yes, Grandma, I'm your granddaughter, Leah. I want to talk to you about something."

"Should we have coffee?" Della asked, her eyes lighting up. "We could have cookies."

"Of course," she said, hoping if her grandma was having a good day she would respond favorably to the news, even if she didn't understand what Leah was telling her.

She called the kitchen, and one of Della's aides brought in a coffee and cookie tray.

They took good care of her grandma here, and moving her was a risk. But moving to Rocky Point was a risk, and she was willing to take it. Willing to take it for a better life. Her grandma wouldn't be around forever, and she couldn't base her decisions solely on her grandma's welfare. She needed to do what made her happy too.

She sipped her coffee.

Della wouldn't make eye contact with her, treating her like the stranger she thought her to be. Before the silence became too uncomfortable, she said, "Grandma, you've lived in New York for a long time. Have you ever thought about moving?"

"Where would I go? Would you be with me?"

"I would be with you," she said, leaning forward and asking her grandma to meet her eyes. "I would take care of you, and I would make sure you were safe. Do you remember when I told you I was going to Minnesota to be in a wedding?"

"Y-yes," Della said, but a shadow moved across her face. She didn't remember.

"I was there for a few days, but then you had your stroke, and I came back to see you."

"That was kind of you."

"I visited a really nice town. It has a lake, and a beach. Lots of wide open spaces. I found you a room at a facility not far from there, and you would have a garden outside your window. You could smell the flowers and sit in the sun. When I visit, we could take walks. We can't walk here. The sidewalks are too crowded."

"Would they have coffee?"

"Yes, Grandma. They would have everything you have now."

Della's expression cleared, and she held her hand. "Is it what you want?"

She nodded, tears filling her eyes. "I would like to move to that little town. I found a job already, and I've made some friends. I would really like to live in Minnesota, Grandma. It's beautiful there, and we'll be happy."

"Then we should go. I like roses, did I ever tell you that? Your grandfather would bring me pink roses when he was courting me . . ."

She melted into her chair and listened to her grandma reminisce. Agreeable to the move, Della sounded as if she might be looking forward to it, but that could change in a heartbeat. She wanted the approval to ease her conscience, but she wouldn't let Della's dementia change her mind.

It would still be a few weeks before she moved Della to Minnesota, and that would give her caregivers more time to determine if there was any permanent damage caused by the stroke. She'd need to start filling out paperwork. One of the brightest spots in all this was the facility's cost. Significantly less expensive, she would have an easier time making up the difference. There might not be a difference at all.

Helen warned her the store didn't bring in much, but she'd do her best to change that. Even if she missed the mark, Marnie had a good idea. She could always go back to headhunting part-time to make ends meet. She'd be driving to Marengo regularly to visit Della anyway. It would work.

"Grandma, I'm going to fly back to Minnesota tonight. I told Marnie I would try my best not to miss her wedding. Will you be okay if I go?"

"I missed my room. Did you know they have good coffee here?"

"Yes, I know they do. I'm having some." She lifted the plain white mug the facility used. "I'm going to go, okay? I'll call and let you and your aide know that I landed safely."

"Goodbye," Della said, flicking her hand, more interested in filling her coffee cup and taking the last cookie on the plate.

Her grandma turned to stare out the window, though it looked to a building across the alley. The large chair dwarfed her small frame, and when she lifted the coffee cup to her mouth, her hand trembled. Normally, Della wasn't aware of the passage of time, but she felt guilty every time she left.

"I love you, Grandma." Her voice cracked.

"I love you, too," Della mumbled, staring out the window.

She held back her tears and said goodbye to the nurses. They smiled sympathetically as they always did. Burying the melancholy under nervous anticipation, she caught a cab to JFK and called the airline during the ride. She didn't care how many layovers she had to sit through to get back to Rocky Point.

She wanted to go home.

Cold and misery settled into Jared's bones somewhere around five that evening after what little sun had been shining disappeared.

His phone remained silent and nothing happened when he tried to make a call or send a text.

Mike would have let his family know he was okay, but his

heart twisted when he thought of Briar worrying about him. He missed his shift at the arena, and someone would have tried calling. He gritted his teeth. He'd changed the names of his emergency contacts to his parents after Rita left, and they weren't in town. They hadn't planned to go to James and Marnie's wedding. If someone from the arena called them when they couldn't reach him, his parents would be upset he missed work without having an explanation as to why. Maybe they'd even drive to Rocky Point to find out what was going on.

None of that mattered if he froze to death.

The plane's insulation didn't make the interior warm enough to sleep through until morning, but the shelter was more than he'd have if he tried to find something else and lost his way in the blizzard.

He shouldn't have waited until now to decide to look for a different place to spend the night. If he couldn't see two inches in front of his face, no one else could either, making a rescue he'd been secretly hoping for despite what Mike said about traveling impossible.

Rescue.

Such a strange word when in the summertime he could have walked or hitched back to the airport. It would've taken him all day, but he wouldn't feel as stranded as he did now.

When he was back in town, he was calling Leah. He was telling her he loved her and that they were going to figure out a life together.

That's what people did when they loved each other. They worked it out.

Rita hadn't loved him.

She left and hadn't looked back.

He'd been in such strong denial because when she left

him, she left Briar behind too, and he hadn't wanted to believe Rita was capable of that.

But she was.

And she had.

Leah's mother left her too, and that was probably a good reason why Briar liked spending time with her. She felt a connection to Leah.

He'd gotten in the way of that.

But, he wasn't dead of hypothermia yet. There was still a chance he could fix things.

He zipped his jacket, put his choppers on, and pushed out of the cockpit. The sharp wind bit into his face. Second thoughts pummeled his brain, but he shoved them aside and jumped into a snowdrift that went up to the middle of his thighs.

Swearing, he struggled to shut the airplane's door. He didn't know how much damage his emergency landing did to the outside and he didn't want blowing snow to destroy the inside. He waded through the snow to the rear of the plane and used the tail to block the wind. Squinting, he tried to look for shining light. Any light.

Car lights, lights from a barn or a house. A snowmobile, though only a lunatic would be out in this.

A murky glow glimmered in the distance, maybe, but there was no way to know for certain if it was real or wishful thinking, or how far he'd have to walk to reach it.

If worse came to worst, he could turn around. If he didn't wait too long to do it, he could follow his tracks back to the plane before the snow covered them.

It wouldn't be that bad out here if it wasn't for the wind. The gusts coming off the plains had nothing to stop them, and they whipped around him in a frenzy trying to knock him off his feet.

He'd never take warmth for granted again. Hot showers. Hot coffee. Spooning Leah, her skin sweaty after a round of hot sex.

He'd never bitch about how cold and boring a task it was to clean the ice.

If he made it to the light and the light belonged to warm shelter, he'd be a better person. He'd be a better dad.

He'd bargain and make promises all night if he could reach a place that would let him keep his fingers and toes, because they sure as hell started to tingle despite the thick socks and the lined mittens he wore.

He trudged over the field, protecting his face the best he could and still see where he was going. His ears burned, and his head ached. He hadn't thought he needed a hat in the plane, and he slogged through the blizzard, his head unprotected and his cheeks stinging as the wind howled past him.

This was one of the worst ideas of his entire life and he should go back before he got lost. He twisted, gauged how far his plane was, then turned again, reluctant to give up. Suddenly, he stopped and blinked, unsure. Was the glimmer stronger now or was he hallucinating? Filled with hope, he pushed himself to keep going, and a faded old barn appeared through the blowing snow, the orange light shining from a pole attached to the side.

Relief hastened his steps, and he was near tears of gratitude when he pulled a heavy, creaky barn door open.

The wind caught it, and he struggled, exhausted, to close the door and latch it against the storm.

He leaned against the splintered wood and sucked in breath after thankful breath, hay, manure, and warmth, oh, God, heat, permeating the air.

"What in holy hell were you doing out there?"

He started, his hands braced above his knees. He

thought he'd be alone or share the space with a shivering animal or two, but he never considered, even for a second, he'd share the barn with another person.

An old man laid in a huge pile of hay, a lantern on the floor and a book straddling his leg. A space heater sat on a cinder block a safe distance away.

"I landed my plane not far from here. Engine failure. I stayed with it for as long as I dared."

"Don't say I blame you none," the man said, pushing his book aside and rising to his feet. "I'm Ryland Anderson, and this is my farm. I was out looking for a lost cow when the snow blew in. Couldn't make it home."

"Jared Hollister. I live in Rocky Point."

"I know who you are," Ryland said, waving off his introduction. "You pulled me out of the ditch a couple winters ago. I had errands in town and some fool dog ran out in front of me. Got me out easy enough, and it saved me from having to wait for a tow. Prolly don't remember."

He *didn't* remember. Some winters were worse than others. Some winters he helped people from the minute he woke up until the minute he went to bed, other winters he didn't need to help anyone do anything. "I'm sorry, I don't."

"That's okay, didn't think you would. Sit down, pull up some hay." Ryland cackled. "I got coffee, but it's lukewarm at best by now. I have a sandwich, bologna, but if you're hungry, you won't be particular."

"Thanks. I tried calling, texting, but there's no service out here."

Ryland scoffed. "The sun could be shining, not a cloud in the sky, and signal out here comes and goes like a case of herpes. You're not getting a hold of nobody until I drive you back. Plane, you say? You'll be needing to get to the airport then."

"Yes, sir." He sat and accepted the Thermos half full of coffee. He hadn't eaten bologna since he was a kid and his mom used to pack him lunches for school, but he dug into the stale bread and cheap lunchmeat like his life depended on it.

A large black cow nosed his shoulder, and he let her lick him.

Disgusting, but not lethal.

The thought should have made him smile, but it made him sad.

"That's Sweet Sally. Didn't like being out there any more than you did," Ryland said, lying in the mound of hay, "but there are worse places to spend the night, if you ask me."

"I'm grateful."

"What were you doin' out in the storm?" Ryland asked.

He finished the sandwich and wished he had five more. "I went out before it started snowing, needed to clear my head."

Clear his head of problems that didn't seem quite so big now.

"Women, huh?"

"Yeah. You married, Ryland?"

"Nope. Almost." He leaned onto a hip and pulled a thick wallet out of the back pocket of his work jeans. "We had one of those fancy rehearsals at her parents' church and dinner at a restaurant after. I was there early the next morning, more nervous and scared than a pig on butchering day. Her ma was driving her over, but a truck couldn't stop at a red light and slid through the intersection, kinda like that semi that hit that bus full of kids a few years ago. Damn shame about those little girls. Anyhow, the light turned green and her ma went ahead. The truck slammed into them."

Ryland handed him the photo and he studied the old black and white. It looked like it was taken at the rehearsal dinner, the clothing straight out of the 1960s.

"Held on in the hospital, gave me enough time to say goodbye and make promises I've kept all my life."

He cleared his throat. "What was her name?"

"Vivian. My Viv. I never liked the winter after that."

He gave the picture back to Ryland and laid in a pile of hay a couple of feet away from the old man. "Why didn't you leave? There're warmer states."

"I bought this farm for her as a wedding gift. She loved animals. Wanted one of each, she said. Like Noah." Ryland laughed. "I got her pa's permission to bury her here. I never woulda left her behind. My heart's here."

"I'm sorry." Though sincere, the words seemed inadequate.

"It was a long time ago."

"But it still hurts like it happened yesterday."

"Only if you do it right. Get some sleep now. We'll get you out of here before sunup, if the weather's cooperatin'. I imagine you got a few people who will sit up tonight wonderin' if you're freezing to death."

Ryland turned out the lantern, and a few moments after that his snores competed with the howling wind outside.

Jared would have people waiting for him.

But he only cared about one.

And she happened to be half a country away.

Leah's layover in Minneapolis dragged on and on. One of the better airports she'd seen, it didn't lessen her agitation. A blizzard had moved into Marengo and Rocky Point, the Weather Channel said, and pilots couldn't land due to low visibility.

At ten to midnight, when she thought she'd have to turn a bench into a bed, an announcement for her flight sounded over the speaker system.

She sat through the hour-long flight anxious to be on the ground, hoping that despite the late hour she'd still be able to rent a car. She hated the thought of spending the night in Marengo, but if she couldn't rent a vehicle, she'd be stuck. Marnie was sweet to drive her, but she wouldn't ask anyone to pick her up, not in the middle of the night.

The thought of driving from Marengo to Rocky Point jangled her already taut nerves. She didn't drive on a regular basis, and never in the winter on snow and ice. It would be smarter to wait until morning, but her anxiety wouldn't let her spend the night in Marengo if she didn't have to. Even though driving there would be dangerous, she wouldn't be able to calm down until she was in Rocky Point.

The bleary-eyed car rental agent urged her to rent a room at a hotel instead of trying to make the drive. "The roads might not even be clear. The plows do what they can, but we've had a lot of snow."

"Then maybe . . . instead of a little car, do you have something bigger?" She had no idea what would drive through the drifts.

"It will cost more," he warned, swapping out keys. "But there's no doubt you need all-wheel drive."

"It doesn't matter."

At almost two o'clock in the morning, she drove an SUV that had all-wheel drive out of the Marengo airport's parking lot. The agent assured her it would get her where she needed to go. "Be careful. It has a full tank, but stop at a gas station and stock up. Buy some snacks, drinks, no booze. You don't have any luggage? Don't tell me, I don't want to know. I was going to suggest getting out an extra sweater or two, in case you need to stop or slide into the ditch, but . . . your jacket looks warm enough. Maybe. Stay with your vehicle at all times."

She nodded, taking his advice seriously. She couldn't let the road conditions scare her. If Rocky Point was going to be her home, she'd have to learn to drive in this. Maybe not in the middle of the night, but all she could think about was making it to town.

She stopped at a convenience store, the neon blue lights looking cheerful and bright, and bought a candy bar, a bag of beef jerky, a container of cashews, a bag of Doritos, and the largest to-go cup of coffee they sold.

If she remembered correctly, there weren't many places to stop to take a break between the two towns, and she hoped she wouldn't have to pee. But on the bright side, if she had to go on the side of the road, she doubted anyone would see her.

She plugged her phone into the charging dock and programmed Autumn's address into the maps app. With any luck, she'd catch her going to the bathroom or getting a glass of water. If anything, she'd pound on her door until it woke her up.

It disconcerted her, being homeless. She'd given up her room at the resort, she didn't have a house. She hadn't priced them, wasn't sure she could afford one. Marnie seemed to think buying a house in Rocky Point would be an inexpensive endeavor, but she depended on her income and her paychecks from Outdoor Wonders would stop two weeks after she stopped working. Maybe before she left she could negotiate a severance package for herself. She'd been a good employee and no one had complaints about her work.

The risk made her stomach burn, but it wasn't anything compared to what she'd lived with in New York.

That alone told her she'd made the right decision.

Snow covered the roads, but the plows had been by creating snowbanks alongside the two-lane highway, and gradually, she relaxed. In the distance, acting as a beacon, the faint lights of Rocky Point glowed in the rich black sky. She sipped her coffee and stared in wonder at the stark beauty.

This was her home now.

She set the cruise control and settled into the seat warming her butt.

An hour out of Marengo, a small furry thing darted into the road. Instinct took over, and she slammed on the brakes. The large truck spun in a circle and she screamed, her hands clutching the steering wheel so tightly her fingers ached.

The SUV shuddered to a stop on the side of the road, its hind wheels wedged into a snowbank, her front facing Marengo, not Rocky Point.

She refused to take that as a sign.

She blew out a shaky breath and shoved the truck into Park. Resting her head on the steering wheel, she urged her pounding heart to calm down.

Little rabbit.

She unbuckled her seatbelt and opened her door, a frozen gust of wind slapping her in the face. Sucking in the crisp air to ease the churning in her stomach, she jumped out of the vehicle to inspect the damage.

Her rear wheels were lodged into the snow, but it didn't look like anything that would keep her from driving away. Still, she kicked the snow away from the tires, hoping it would help.

She climbed behind the wheel, stress tightening her muscles. She sipped her lukewarm coffee, carefully put the to-go cup in the holder, and with a shaking hand, shifted into Drive.

Gently, she pushed the gas pedal.

The tires spun and she let up on the accelerator. Near tears, she tried again, and still, her tires spun.

Shifting into Park, she let out a sob. She was so close to Rocky Point, she couldn't give up now, but she was stuck and had no idea how long it would take for someone to drive by and offer to help her. It was the middle of the night and she hadn't passed anyone the whole time she'd been on the road. She could call a tow, roadside assistance was a part of her rental contract, but God knew how long she'd have to wait. Because of the road conditions, several others could be in her predicament.

She didn't know what else to do. She rifled through the rental paperwork and called the roadside assistance toll-free number.

A bored dispatch transferred her call to the nearest twenty-four hour towing company, which happened to be in Marengo.

She sighed.

"All-Hour Tow," a tired man answered.

"I'm stuck on the side of the road. I didn't want to hit a rabbit." She tried to laugh, but all that came out was a small cry.

"We're scheduling four hours out. No one can stay

home when it storms," the man complained. "How far in the ditch are ya, sweets?"

"I'm not really," she said, trying not to sniffle into the phone. "But my tires spin when I push on the gas. I can't go anywhere."

"Can you take a picture? Send it to my cell?"

Her heartbeat sped up in hope. "Yeah." She scrambled out of the truck, turned on the flash, and took a couple pictures of the SUV and the tires wedged into the snowbank.

She texted them to a number he rattled off.

Her truck didn't look that bad, though she wasn't in any position to know otherwise. She waited as he looked at the photos.

"You look okay, sweets," he said. "Tell ya what, let's see if I can talk you through it. Do you have any kitty litter, or salt? Maybe a shovel?"

She shook her head, then stopped. He couldn't see her. "No. Sorry. I'm in a rental."

"Okay. What you're gonna wanna do is turn the steering wheel, point your tires in a different direction, and then go easy on the gas. Then turn them in the opposite direction and go again. The more you skid on the same patch of ice, the slipperier it will get, do you got me?"

"Yeah," she said, surprised she *did* understand what he was saying. She set her phone on speaker and shoved it onto the dash.

She turned the steering wheel and lightly pressed on the gas, then turned the wheel the other way. Her tires spun, searching for purchase, but a second later they caught. She pushed harder on the gas and the truck shot forward.

She slammed on the brakes, fishtailing on the snowy ice until she stopped in the middle of the road. "I got out," she told the man breathlessly, her heart in her throat. She waited for a response, a yell of victory, maybe, but tinny silence greeted her accomplishment. "Hello?"

Nothing.

He'd hung up on her.

She couldn't do anything but laugh.

She got her truck out of a snowbank! All by herself. Well, with a little help, but she didn't sit behind the wheel and cry. No, she called and asked for help, and she made it.

She made it.

She could do this.

With the radio playing cheerful Christmas music, she hummed all the way to town.

Her phone's GPS warned her that her destination was five minutes away, and at the first red light she stopped at, though she was the only one at the intersection, she texted Autumn. *Surprise! I'll be outside your house in five minutes.*

She choked on the last of her coffee when her phone chimed. Autumn was awake and would unlock the door.

Despite her rabbit-dodging adventures, that still made her sweat when she thought about it, driving through Rocky Point gave her peace. She'd missed the little town in the short time she was gone.

She found Autumn's house without trouble, and she parked her rental in the driveway.

The front porch light greeted her, but she knew to use the side door, and Autumn was already there, waiting for her. "You're crazy," she admonished, opening the storm door, the springs screeching, and giving her a hug.

Autumn wore a terry cloth robe, her blonde hair pulled into a sloppy ponytail. Dark shadows laid beneath her eyes.

"*I'm* crazy? Why are you awake?" she asked.

Autumn looked away. "Come in. I found some pajamas in one of your suitcases. I hope you don't mind I went through your things."

"No. That was nice of you, thanks. After such a long day of traveling, changing into something clean will feel good." She wiggled out of her white parka and kicked off her boots.

"Are you thirsty? Hungry? I cleaned my spare bedroom while you were gone, but be careful walking in the dark. Ty spends the night sometimes, and we keep his crib and toys in there. I tried to pick up, but you never know when you'll step on a stray LEGO. Even the big ones hurt." Avoiding her eyes, Autumn rinsed out a mug and placed it in a white strainer near the sink.

"Are you okay?" She bit her lip. "If you don't want me to stay here—"

"It isn't you."

"Then what is it?" she asked, a ball of dread forming in her stomach. "What is it? Marnie? James?" She wouldn't ask about Jared.

He hadn't contacted her the entire time she was in New York. Not a text asking if she was okay. Not a phone call. Busy with Rita, he didn't have time for her. It hurt, and she hoped he wouldn't think she decided to move to Rocky Point for him.

She let out a shaky breath. In fact, the whole thing seemed stupid now. Move halfway across the country, bringing her grandmother with her, risking her care, having no idea if she'd be able to make ends meet.

What had she gotten herself into?

She gripped the edge of the small kitchen table. Breathe, she ordered herself. Breathe.

"You look like you're going to have a panic attack." Gently, Autumn nudged her into the living room. "Sit down." She sank onto the couch and tucked her hands between her knees. "I was updating the blog when you texted me. Leah, Jared took his plane out yesterday morning. The storm blew in and he had engine trouble. He couldn't make it back to the airport."

"Is he okay?"

"Someone from the airport called Briar. He landed in a field, and he was okay . . . as of yesterday afternoon. But it's cold, and it didn't stop snowing until a few hours ago. We haven't heard anything since."

A scream threatened to rip out of her throat, but she pushed it deep into her chest.

Autumn rubbed her back.

"He's home, then. And he didn't tell anybody. Rita—"

"She hasn't heard from him. She and Briar have been awake all night, waiting. We all have."

"He's at work—" She tried again.

"His plane isn't at the airport. Leah, look at me."

Tears dripped down her cheeks.

She couldn't lose him.

"He's an expert pilot. He landed safely, but we don't know if he found shelter besides his plane. The air traffic controller at the airport says he hasn't been answering his radio, so hopefully he found somewhere to spend the night. There's no cell signal out that way and he can't text anyone to tell us. As soon as it's light enough, people have volunteered to look for him and give him a ride to town."

Her hands shook. "We could look, right now. Why

wait?" she said, standing. "I rented a truck. We should look, drive around. The roads are clear. He's freezing to death."

"Leah—"

"We can search the back roads. Get dressed. We can go."

"Leah—"

"If you won't come with me, I'll go by myself." She rushed into the kitchen and grabbed her jacket hanging off the back of a kitchen chair.

Autumn yanked on her arm. "*Listen* to me. It's dark outside, and the plows are still clearing the rural areas. I talked to someone who works for the city crew, and it takes a long time to move that much snow. They know where he landed, and he's okay. We need to wait. Jared's smart. He'll make it."

She glared at Autumn, her muscles tense, ready to fight, but one look into Autumn's tired eyes and she knew her friend was right. There wasn't anything they could do now. The days shortened in the winter, and at four o'clock in the morning, the sun hadn't even begun to rise. She'd be searching an area she didn't know on roads that were more than likely still drifted over.

"I'm worried about him, too," Autumn said softly, releasing her arm. "We both need rest. Grab a couple hours. You've been traveling all night. When they find him, you can talk to him with your head on straight."

"He's not going to want to see me," she said, sagging onto the chair. She pushed her face into her parka's hood and gritted her teeth against more tears. Finally, she looked at Autumn. "He and Rita . . ."

Autumn shook her head. "I don't know."

She let Autumn lead her into the spare bedroom. A pair

of sweats and a t-shirt were laying on top of the bedspread. "Change your clothes, and we'll get a little sleep."

"Stay with me, please. I don't want to be alone."

Robe and all, Autumn climbed onto the queen-sized bed.

She changed without a thought to modesty, and Autumn wrapped her arms around her. "Get some sleep."

Quaking in Autumn's arms, she prayed until a pink sunrise lit up the sky.

CHAPTER NINE

"Time to rise and shine," Ryland said, kicking Jared's boots.

"Hmmm . . .?"

"Sun's up. Or she's gonna be in about twenty minutes or so. Let's get you into town before they send out the search parties."

His mind swam as he searched for the meaning in Ryland's words. Search parties. Rise and shine.

The emergency landing.

Engine failure.

He rubbed the sleep out of his eyes and sat up.

Groaning, he hefted himself off the floor and brushed hay off his jacket and jeans. "I'm too old for that."

Ryland cackled. "If I can do it, so can you." He pushed the barn door open and the cold morning air rushed in, slapping him further awake. "Let's go see how bad the truck is. Might need your help to dig her out."

They waded through the large snowdrifts, and he sucked in a deep breath, the scent of hay and cow stuck in his nose.

Ryland's half-ton truck sat on the side of the road, the windows frosted over. A ridge of snow hugged the tires, but the plow's driver had been kind and veered away from the vehicle.

"Looks like the plow didn't bother it much. Road's clear," Ryland said, though he could see for himself the plows had come through.

He climbed into the cab, the cushions stiff.

Ryland started the truck, the engine growling to life despite the freezing temperatures. He looked in the rearview mirror at the empty highway and patted the dash in encouragement. Slowly, he eased onto the road, the tires moving reluctantly through the snow. "Where's your plane?"

Pulling his cell out of his jacket pocket, he gestured vaguely out the window. "Over there, I think. The blizzard turned me around."

"Prolly on my property, so no one will bother it. After I drop you off, I'll go find it and flag it. Easier to spot then, when you need to."

"Thanks." He wasn't interested in his plane, waiting impatiently for signal. They were ten minutes from Rocky Point when notifications started pinging his phone.

Several texts scrolled across his screen asking him where he was, if he was okay, each one more frantic than the last.

Over fifty calls and just as many voicemails.

He skimmed through the texts and missed calls searching for Leah's name.

Nothing.

Briar's tearful texts tugged at his heart.

Rita's messages had a reserved but worried tone to them, explaining Mike had called Briar and was he okay? He texted her back. *I'm okay. Spent the night in Ryland Anderson's barn. He's driving me back to town right now.*

Instead of texting a response, Rita called him.

"Hey," he answered, casting a sidelong glance at Ryland who chewed on a toothpick and pretended not to listen.

She babbled and cried, and he didn't understand a word she said. "Put Briar on the phone."

He moved the phone away from his ear and Rita's sobbing filled the truck.

Ryland raised his eyebrows.

"Dad?" Briar's voice cracked.

"Briar, honey. I'm okay, and I'm on the way home. Did your mother understand that?"

"Yeah. We've been up all night waiting for you to message us. Why didn't you? What happened?"

"I didn't have a signal, and there wasn't anything I could do. Caught a ride, and I'll be home in a few minutes, okay? I'm right outside of town. Can you put some coffee on?"

"Yeah. Dad . . ." Briar started crying.

"I'm hanging up, sweetheart. See you soon."

"Got a bunch of crying females on your tail."

"Yeah."

"Makes a man feel good."

"Yeah, it should."

"But?"

He heaved a tired sigh. "Wrong woman."

He gave Ryland his address then closed his eyes, resting his head against the back of the seat.

"Looks like a regular welcoming committee."

Not understanding what Ryland meant, he opened his eyes and blew out a breath. "Jesus Christ."

Cars were jammed in his driveway and overflowed onto the street.

Ryland idled and chewed on his toothpick.

"Thanks for the ride . . . and a place to sleep. I'll be in touch about the plane." He shoved his cell phone into his pocket and released his seatbelt.

"Not in too much of a hurry."

He pushed out of the truck. "Thanks. Careful driving back."

"Hey."

"Yeah?" he asked, pausing before he shut the door.

"Your woman isn't in there waiting for you."

"No. No, she's not." And the reason why broke his heart. It was his fault.

"When my Viv died, I made every bargain I could think of to get her back. Didn't work. If there's a chance, even a small one, that you can fix it, do it. Don't live without her, not if you don't have to."

"She might not forgive me."

Ryland glared. "You know how to beg, boy?"

He huffed a laugh. "Yeah."

"Then I'd advise it."

"I'll keep that in mind. Thanks again." Jared slammed the door and stood in the middle of the street. Ryland's truck turned the corner and out of sight.

He wove his way around the cars in his driveway to the door, but before he could turn the knob, the door flew open and Rita launched herself at him, wrapping her arms around his neck. He let her cling for a moment and then nudged her away. "Rita."

Her bloodshot eyes met his, tears dripping down her cheeks. He shook his head, and she staggered backward.

"Dad!" Briar hurled herself into his arms. This was the kind of hug he wanted, and he gripped her just as tightly.

"Who's here?" he murmured into her ear.

"Everyone."

His heart pounded. "Leah?"

Briar stepped back. "Oh. No. I'm sorry. I thought you meant—"

"Everyone else."

"Yeah." She blushed.

"It's okay."

Whimpering, Rita pushed past him and trotted up the stairs.

He couldn't worry about her bruised ego and hurt feelings now and he let her go. He stepped into the living room, and the number of people who crowded into the small space had him staggering backward.

His mom and dad, Marnie, James. Their parents.

Cole stood in the corner, taking pictures. "Welcome home!" he called.

This broke the spell and everyone converged at once, Marnie getting in the first of the hugs.

"You guys didn't need to—" he started.

"Yes, we did," Marnie said, holding him close. "Yes, we did. You're our friend. We've been here all night waiting for news." She let him go. "Why didn't you call? Or text?"

"I tried to text James but there wasn't service out there. Did you get it?"

James shook his head. "What happened?"

"Engine failure of some kind. I won't know more until a mechanic takes a look. The landing was okay and I'm not hurt. If it was summer, it would've been easier . . . but I found a barn, and . . . you don't need to hear the rest. I wasn't able to call Rita until I was about ten minutes from town. Mom, Dad, it's okay. I'm just tired."

He sank onto the couch and his mother sat next to him, holding his hand in a tight grip.

Briar offered him a mug of coffee, and he sipped it gratefully, wishing everyone would leave. He wanted to go to his room and call Leah, ask about her grandma, but he felt like an asshole for thinking it when so many people cared about him.

"Were you able to sleep?" his mother asked.

"A little. Not much. Hay doesn't make a very soft bed."

"We'll get out of here so you can get some rest." Marnie laughed, relief threaded through the notes of fatigue. "We'll see you later, and I'm glad you're okay."

"Thanks, Marnie. I appreciate you waiting."

"If anyone wants breakfast, come to the resort," she said, shooing everyone out of the living room.

"Go to bed," his mom said, patting his knee. "We'll go have some breakfast and then visit a few of our friends."

"Rita's here," he said, sleep muddling his brain.

"I know. We drove up last night."

He struggled to his feet, and Briar gave him another hug.

"After I get some sleep, I need to talk to you," he said, smoothing his hand over his daughter's hair.

"Yeah."

He didn't see Rita on the way to his bedroom. The one he'd shared with her so many years ago. As time went on and he stopped hoping she'd come back, he'd packed away little knickknacks and things she'd collected but hadn't brought with her. The room became his, and five years after his divorce, there wasn't a trace of female in his room.

He pulled off his clothes and crawled into his soft sheets. With his phone in his hand and the messages app open to text Leah, he fell asleep.

"He's okay."

Leah pushed the comforter away from her face. She hadn't fallen asleep, but she'd laid in bed all morning, thinking the worst and praying for the best. "He is?"

"He came home this morning after spending the night in a barn. Marnie just texted me."

She buried her face in her pillow and let out a sob. Jared was okay. He was okay.

Autumn sat on the edge of the bed and brushed her fingers through he hair. "Shh. Shh. We knew he was going to be all right, didn't we?"

She nodded, but she couldn't stop crying. She hadn't completely believed he would be okay. She'd flown in that plane. She knew how dangerous it felt to be so high in the sky with nothing between them and the ground.

"He's getting some sleep, but everyone's meeting for breakfast at the resort. Are you hungry? Do you want to go?"

She wiped her eyes. She wasn't up to facing all those people. "I don't feel like eating anything. You go."

"Are you sure you don't want me to stay with you?"

"No. Now that I know he's okay, I'll probably get some sleep. I'm worn out."

"Okay." Autumn paused. "I don't know what's going on between Jared and Rita, but I want you to know you've become a good friend and I'm happy you came back. It would've been easy for you to tell Marnie you had to skip her wedding. I'll miss you when you leave."

She sat up. "Thank you. That means a lot to me. I've never let myself get to close to anyone because I was raised to believe I wasn't good enough for people to like me, much less love me. My ex-husband didn't help. I'm glad you're my friend, too, and you won't have to miss me. I'm moving to Rocky Point. I can't live in New York anymore."

Autumn's lips parted in surprise. "Because of Jared?"

"No. Because of me. I feel at peace here. I feel like I have a place here. All my life I looked for a somewhere to belong, and I found it in the wide open spaces of the water, the trees and blue sky, the friendly smiles and Ty's giggles. What little Jared gave me I'll hold close to my heart, but it's this town and the people who gave me a home. It won't be easy, and I'll need your help, but there's time to get into all that. Go eat. I know you want the details of Jared's plane crash for the blog."

Saying the words made her sick to her stomach, but not in the way she'd been feeling while she lived in New York.

"Oh, Leah, that's so great. I need friends too, and I'm happy we'll have each other. I'll do whatever I can, just ask." Autumn kissed her cheek. "Are you sure you don't want to come with me?"

"No. Go. I'll be fine."

"Okay. I'll see you later." Autumn scrambled out of the room.

She leaned against the headboard and grabbed her phone. Since Marnie texted Autumn, maybe Marnie texted her, too.

There wasn't a text from Marnie, but there was one from Briar.

Dad was asking about you. If you heard he was in a plane crash, he's okay. He said his engine failed, but he landed in the snow and wasn't hurt. Why weren't you here this morning with everyone?

She bit her lip. How could she explain she didn't feel

welcome with Rita in their house? How to explain that what she and Jared might have had was gone now that her mother was back in town?

She decided to tell her the truth. *My grandma had a stroke. I had to go back to New York for a few days, but I drove into town early this morning. I'm staying with Autumn. Thanks for telling me about your dad.*

Briar responded with, *I hope your grandma's okay, and I'm glad you came back. TTYL* and a smiley emoji.

She returned the emoji and set her phone on the cluttered nightstand. She'd talk to Jared. Tell him she was moving to Rocky Point and that they could be friends, if he didn't move to New York with Rita. Maybe she hadn't fallen in love with him hard enough that forgetting about him would be difficult. It had only been a few days.

A good, solid plan made her feel better. She'd text him. But first, she needed to get some rest. The past twenty-four hours had taken their toll, and closing her eyes, she burrowed into the bedding.

Jared slept later than he wanted, and he groaned when he read the time on his cell phone. He'd fallen asleep before he could type two words to Leah, and he'd wanted to talk to her sooner than this. Call her. Tell her everything. Confess how he felt and hope she felt the same. Find out when she was coming back to Rocky Point. If she had to miss the wedding.

First, he needed to use the bathroom and find something to eat. Ryland's bologna sandwich was a long time ago, and his stomach rumbled.

He showered, dressed in fresh clothes, and trotted down the creaky stairs wondering how long his parents were going to stay and trying to figure out where in the hell they'd sleep. Every decent room was booked for Marnie and James's wedding. Rita was sleeping in his spare. The best he could do was let his parents have his bed and he'd have to bunk down on the couch. The wedding was still a few days away, but it wouldn't be that bad.

Rita sat in the kitchen, flipping through one of Briar's magazines and sipping a cup of coffee.

He poured a mug of coffee and prepared for a talk he didn't want to have. Though tired, relieved to be home, and worried about Leah, when he pushed Rita away, he hadn't missed the look of hurt and betrayal.

He opened the fridge and asked, "Where is everyone? Mom and Dad?"

"Your parents went to the resort to have breakfast, then to Linda and Roy's. Briar's in her room on the phone talking to Skylar. You're letting her see too much of him."

He bristled and empty-handed, slammed the fridge door shut. "It's not like you've been around to help. And I've had the talk with her. She's not going to do anything foolish."

"She's going to end up like us."

He sat at the table and held her hand. "Were we that bad?"

She sagged in her chair and squeezed his fingers. "No. We weren't that bad, but if we would have waited, we wouldn't have had to live in that shitty apartment. You would have a college degree. We could've bought a better house than this."

"I like this house, and I can always go to school. I was even thinking about taking night classes, or doing something online. The only thing that would've changed had we waited is that Briar would've been younger when you left. You never liked it here. I wasn't enough to keep you in this little town, and I came to terms with that a long time ago." Or tried to.

She pushed the magazine across the table and stood, wrapping her arms around herself. "It wasn't you. Not all of it. I hate this town. I hate how everyone has their noses in everyone else's business. I hate the cold. I hate that there's nothing to do."

"And in the end, you hated me because I was here, because I represented everything you hated about Rocky Point. But you came back for Marnie's wedding, hoping what?"

She settled in his lap, and he let her, one last time. "Hoping that we could try again. In New York. I'm a different person there, happier. We would have things to do, places to go. Briar could graduate in a better high school. New York has some of the best."

She skimmed her lips over his jaw, down his neck.

He nudged her away. "Rita."

"You pushed me away this morning, too. You really hate me for leaving, don't you?"

"What if we didn't work? You know jobs here are hard to find. Briar and I are comfortable on my salary. If I up and moved us to New York, for you, and we didn't work . . . I might not be able to even come back. There wouldn't be a way to make a living."

"See? There's nothing here. Come to New York. Unlike here, there are jobs there, and you could find something you like more than driving a stupid Zamboni all day."

"That's the difference between us, Rita. I never hated it

here. I don't hate my job. I like the people I work with, and I have friends here. Briar has friends here."

"*Briar* is going to leave, just like everyone else who has a brain, and you're going to be all by yourself because you're holding on to something that has no meaning. This stupid little town. What has this godforsaken town given you?"

He shoved Rita off his lap, and she leaned against the kitchen sink where, before she left, she'd done dishes hundreds of times. This old house didn't have a dishwasher and he never got around to installing one.

"More than you've given me. This town, this place . . . when you left, I spent a lot of time on the water. I would cry, wondering what in the hell I did so wrong I couldn't keep you here. Couldn't keep our family together. The water, the woods . . . they healed something inside me."

Her features softened. "I didn't mean to hurt you."

"Maybe you didn't mean to hurt Briar, but you wanted to hurt me. And you did. For the past five years I've missed you, missed what we had together. Love. And not emotional love, but physical. I missed that, and I haven't been with anyone until—"

She stiffened. "Who? You haven't been with anyone until who?"

"No one."

"This is about Leah."

"No, it's not. It's about you and me. Seeing you made me realize that I loved you for a long time, but when you left, I got on with my life and I don't love you anymore."

She narrowed her eyes. "I hope you didn't fall in love with her. You'll end up in the same situation you were in with me. Do you think a woman from New York is going to move to this shit town? I feel sorry for you. Never moving forward, stuck in the same rut day after day, until years have passed and you have nothing to show for it."

"That's where you're wrong. I do have something to show for it. I have a steady job and work with people I respect, in a community that looks out for each other. Briar's a strong, independent young woman. I did that. Here, in Rocky Point. I did that without you. When she leaves to go to college and she makes something of herself, I'll be proud of her because that's what I raised her to do."

"Well, you better get a dog. After she graduates, you aren't going to have anything left."

She hurried out of the kitchen and shortly after the side door slammed shut.

He hoped she had a ride or took Briar's keys. It was too cold to walk far. But maybe that was a good thing. She needed to cool off.

So did he.

He pried the cap off a bottle of beer and took a deep drink. He leaned against the counter and looked out the window into his backyard. Small, fenced in. Briar had played on a swing set when she was little. Now it was a patch of grass covered in snow.

"Dad?"

"Hey, sweetheart. Are you hungry?"

"No." She sank into a chair at the table. "I heard you and mom fighting."

"I'm sorry."

"She hated this town more than she loved me."

He sighed and sat in the seat he'd vacated moments

before. "That's not true. She hates this town, but she loves you very much. She left you with me because deep down, she knew growing up here was better for you. We had fun, when we were kids. Going to the beach, fishing. Skiing at the resort. She knew you'd have the same kind of childhood we had." At least, that's what he hoped Rita thought when she'd told him she was leaving and wasn't going to take Briar with her.

"Do you love her?"

"Your mom?"

"No, Leah."

He rubbed his eyes. If Briar heard his and Rita's whole conversation, there wasn't any point trying to hide it. "Yeah. I do."

"Then we should go."

"Go where?"

"To New York."

"Briar—"

"No, listen. Mom left us behind because we wouldn't go with her, but she's right. I'm going to graduate, then I'm going to college. What will you do by yourself? I don't want you to be alone because you're stubborn. New York doesn't mean living in a gross apartment that has a meth lab across the hall. New York doesn't mean billions of people and dirty air. Mom lives in a nice apartment, and she goes to Central Park all the time. It's not Rocky Point, but it wouldn't be as bad as you think."

"Briar—" He stopped and sighed.

She was right. Even Rita had a point. If he wanted Leah, he was going to have to bend.

"You'd move there and give Leah and me a chance to figure things out?"

"Yeah. I'd get to see Mom more. You'd have Leah. I like her. She's really nice, and I don't want you to blow it."

"What if it didn't work? I'd give up my job, you'd leave your school, we'd lose this house. You heard me talking to your mom. Jobs aren't easy to come by here, not one that has a living wage. There would be a really good chance that if Leah and I didn't work out, we wouldn't be able to come back. We'd have to live in Marengo or Decatur. Maybe near your grandma and grandpa."

Briar tilted her head. "Is that bad?"

"I don't like the thought of dragging you all over the United States."

"You have to take risks. Isn't that what you told me? When I was scared to try out for the cheerleading squad. Or when I was afraid to ask Skylar out on a date. You told me to always try so if I failed at least I knew I took a chance. If you don't try with Leah, how will you know?"

"I've only known her for a few days."

"And you've been happier. Why do I feel like the adult right now?"

"Because I'm scared. I haven't talked to her since she saw us with your mom at Marnie's dinner. Her grandma had a stroke and she went back to New York. I don't know when she'll be back."

"She heard about your plane crash, Dad. Autumn told her. I bet she's really, really worried about you, and she probably thinks you and Mom got back together. That's not very nice."

"I know. That's why I'm scared to talk to her. I've been screwed up since we met, and I've been taking it out on her."

"Then you need to explain that to her and apologize."

"She's in New York. I have to wait until she gets back. This isn't a conversation I want to have over the phone."

"She's here. She flew back last night and she's staying with Autumn."

His mouth dried. Leah came back. She hadn't come back for him, he knew that, but she didn't let her grandma's health give her an excuse to stay in the city.

That had to be an omen. A sign he needed to take this last chance.

"Are you sure, Briar? I don't want to get Leah's hopes up and then have to change my mind because you suddenly don't want to go. That wouldn't be fair."

"I'm sure."

"What about your mom?"

"Mom's been fine without us." She kicked his ankle. "And we've been fine without her."

He smiled. "We have, haven't we?"

"Yeah. Maybe you and Leah could give me a brother or a sister."

"That would be a long ways down the road, honey. I don't know if she'll even talk to me right now."

"Let's find out." Briar pulled her phone out of the back pocket of her jeans.

"What are you doing?"

"I'm texting Leah. How do you think I knew she was back in town?"

"You're nosy."

"Yeah, but this time it's okay."

He laughed and finished his beer while they waited for Leah to respond. He never did have anything to eat. Rita ruined his appetite.

Briar's phone chimed, and his heart pounded.

"She's at the Supply Company."

"Okay. I'm going to go talk to her."

"Bring her some flowers or something. And you might have to grovel."

"Right." That was two people today who told him to beg, and he'd drop to his knees if it meant Leah would give him five minutes of her time.

Driving down the residential street that hadn't been cleared by the town's snowplow yet, he kept an eye out for Rita but didn't see her. Briar's car was still parked outside their house. He shrugged it off. She wasn't his responsibility anymore, and while that sounded cold, it had been her choice, not his.

He followed Briar's advice and bought Leah a large bouquet of pink and red roses. The woman who rang him up threw in a free stuffed teddy bear, and he hoped the dopey bear's eyes and the flowers would persuade Leah to let him explain why he'd been so stupid.

Parked in front of the store, he tried to steady his hands. He didn't want an audience, but it's what he deserved for waiting to speak to her. This wouldn't feel like such a big deal if he wouldn't have been such an asshole and called her when she was in New York instead of waiting like a coward.

When he stepped inside the warm store, Christmas music greeted him, and an old woman standing at the register smiled at the flowers he held in his hands.

"Jared! I bet you're bringing those to Leah. To congratulate her?" Helen asked, handing a receipt to the woman.

"Yeah. No. Congratulate her for what? I was hoping to speak to her for a few minutes."

"She's in the back. A truck came in, packed tight with holiday stuff. She's picking through it now. Alone," Helen added, wiggling her eyebrows.

"Thanks."

"Good luck, young man," the woman said. "A bouquet that big, you're going to need it."

He shook his head, pressing his lips together, thinking about what Rita said. He'd always known the people in town were busybodies, but it hadn't bothered him to the point he'd ever wanted to leave because of it.

He pushed the heavy, hinged doors open and stepped into the back room.

Leah sat on the floor wiping her eyes.

He tried to swallow past the lump in his throat. "Hey."

She glanced at him then looked away. "Hey."

Shit.

CHAPTER TEN

He brought her flowers. And a sad bear, if his big brown eyes were any indication of how it felt. Leah could commiserate.

Nerves prickled her skin.

Jared shifted on his feet, his boots dripping water onto the scuffed tile. "Can I sit?" he finally asked.

"Umm. Yeah. Let me . . ." She pushed a large cardboard box out of the way. Instead of moping about Jared, what he was doing, how he was doing, what, if anything, he felt for her, she'd called Helen and asked if she could work for a few hours. In her blunt way, Helen told her the store was hers now and she could do whatever the heck she wanted.

She'd wanted to do a full inventory of the store, but then a truck came in and threw her plans out the window.

All afternoon she'd tried to convince herself she wasn't in a good place to be in a relationship. Divorced barely a year, time alone wouldn't be a bad thing. She'd be busy anyway, with the store, finding a place to live, and settling her grandma into her new facility. They were all true, even if the excuses were just a bandage she'd have to rip off later.

She was in the middle of unpacking thick, cable-knit sweaters when Jared pushed through the door, looking confused, hurt, and resigned. He'd come by to let her down easy, and that was all right, brave of him, actually, after ignoring her for the past few days.

He lowered onto the floor and handed her the large bouquet and teddy bear. She sniffed at the roses and set them aside, but she let the bear sit in her lap and dug her fingers into his fur.

"How's your grandma doing?" he asked, his voice gravelly, and the timbre made shivers run up and down her back.

Don't think about how he sounded, whispering in the dark after making love. Don't think about it.

He looked tired, and he needed a shave. She itched to scrub her fingers along his jaw, but there wouldn't be any more touching him. He belonged to Rita, and tears filled her eyes. All the time she tried to convince herself she didn't love him, that she would be okay without him, had been for nothing. When he broke it off, it would hurt, and it would hurt bad.

"The stroke wasn't as serious as it could have been. The doctors have been very careful to warn me side effects could surface, but for now, she seems okay."

"That's good. I'm glad."

"Yeah."

They sat in silence, and tension hung heavy in the air.

"Look," she finally said, "you don't have to do this. I know what you're going to say."

"You do?"

"I'm not stupid. We haven't spoken since Marnie's dinner. Actually, we didn't talk then, either, so never mind. You never texted or called, and I know why. It's okay. I expected it. When I saw you and Rita together, I knew this would happen. It's fine."

He looked down at his hands. He wouldn't deny it. Okay.

"How are you?" she asked, hugging the bear, hoping it would keep all her broken pieces inside her. "I stayed at Autumn's last night and she told me about the crash. I was worried."

"I'm fine. I found a barn and spent the night with a cow."

She tried to smile, but she couldn't quite manage it.

"The whole time I couldn't stop thinking about you and how relieved I was you weren't with me. You never would have flown with me again."

She wouldn't be flying with him again, anyway. "I'm glad you're not hurt. If that's all . . ." She couldn't do this anymore, couldn't let him sit there, couldn't look at him knowing he and Rita were starting over.

"It's not."

"Then what is it?"

"I'm trying to get there. This is hard."

She spoke to the top of the bear's head. "It's not that hard to say you and Rita are going to give it another try. I already know that, and I think it's great. Briar must be excited to have her parents back together. I know you came here to finally tell me the truth."

"That's not why I'm here." He gripped her chin. "Will you look at me?"

She met his gaze, and his damp eyes stunned her. Tentatively, she reached to wipe the tears off his cheeks but dropped her hand.

"I talked to Briar before I drove here, but not about Rita and me giving our marriage another shot."

"About what, then?"

"I told her I love you. And I told her that Rita and I are done. There's no point in us trying again. She wanted to, I can't lie to you about that, but I don't love her anymore, Leah. Maybe I'm slow, maybe I didn't realize it until she tried to pick up where we left off like nothing happened, but I look at her and see Briar's mom. I don't see the woman I love. I see her when I look at you."

For the first time since Marnie's dinner, hope flickered in her heart. "But—"

"I didn't call while you were in New York . . . I was going to say because I didn't want to bother you, but that's not true. I felt like an asshole knowing Rita slept down the hall and how unfair that was to you. But she's Briar's mother and I'm always going to have to make room for her. I hope you would never hold that against me."

"No," she whispered. "I never would."

He nodded, one quick jerk of his head. "Good. Then the only thing we have left to talk about is where we're going to live."

"Live?" she asked faintly. He was a million miles ahead of her, and she was still stuck at the part where he said he loved her.

"That's mostly what I talked to Briar about. After Marnie's wedding. When you go back to New York, I want to go with you. Briar said she'd be willing to finish high school there, but maybe, if we can compromise, we can do the long-distance thing until she graduates. It'd only be for a year and a half, and I'd try to visit you as often as I could."

She blinked. "You're willing to move to New York? You'd hate it there. And what about your house? Your job? Jared, you love Rocky Point."

"Not more than I love you. That's what Briar said this

afternoon. Rita loved the city more than she loved her own daughter. I tried to smooth over it, but Briar knew. I can't be like that or I'll lose you. I love you more than I love this town, and if moving to New York is what it takes to keep you in my life, then I will."

There'd been a lot she'd learned about her family since she spoke with him last. If he was willing to give up his life in Rocky Point, she'd have to be honest and let him decide if he wanted to take on the baggage that came with being with her.

"I've kept a few things from you, too. I don't want you to go to New York."

His stomach dipped, and he stood, his hands fisted at his sides. "I knew this would happen. I *knew* it. The minute I saw you in the airport, I knew you'd wiggle your way into my heart, into this town, and then you'd leave mass destruction behind you. I tried to keep it from happening, but I was stupid and let myself fall in love with you." He kicked at a box, but it barely moved. She flinched, and he tried to rein in the hurt. "Whatever. I'll let you get back to what you were doing."

"Wait. Can I tell you a couple things first?"

It didn't make any difference what she had to say, she'd already said enough, but he nodded tersely and sat on a flimsy plastic chair.

"Before my grandma had her stroke, she asked me to find my mom. She never asked before, and I didn't want to. I was scared of what I'd find." She played with the bear's ears.

He tried to calm down. He didn't see how her mother

had anything to do with him, but he forced himself to listen. She hadn't said she didn't love him, only that she didn't want him to go to New York with her. He had to give her time, or once again, he'd push her away, and he had a feeling he'd used up his quota of second chances. Apologies only went so far.

"Did you find her? Has she passed away?"

"Worse."

"What do you mean? How can anything be worse than someone dying?"

"I asked Autumn to help me. I thought maybe since she's a reporter she'd have resources if we got stuck. It turned out all we needed to do was a social media search. She didn't even bother to change her name, and I could have found her years ago. What's worse than someone dying? How about them living a happy life without you? She remarried. I have brothers and sisters I've never met. Nieces and nephews I'll never meet. She built a whole new life without me. Without reaching out to us. For over thirty years. She works in a dental office somewhere in Iowa. How *normal* is that?"

"I'm sorry, Leah." The words didn't seem like enough.

"Thanks. When I was in New York, I got rid all the keepsakes I moved out of my grandma's apartment. This was the one thing I saved." She slid a piece of paper and photo out of the back pocket of her jeans and handed them to him.

He scanned the letter and studied the young, tired woman holding a baby in the black and white picture.

"Can you see it on her face?" she asked. "Can you see she didn't love me? Her note said she did, but she didn't."

He *could* see it, but he would never say it out loud. He wouldn't do that to her.

"She left me behind. Just like Max. I saw him, too, by the way. I didn't change the emergency contact information on my grandma's forms, and they called him. He said my pacs were ugly."

"You look beautiful in your winter clothes," he said. "I'm sorry I wasn't there. I should have been."

"Thanks." She paused. "I . . . didn't tell my grandma I found her daughter. I told her I tried my best, but knowing my mom was out there and didn't get in touch, it would have hurt her, maybe more than it hurt me. My grandma didn't take it well and she told me I was stupid and that nothing I did was good enough. I've never been good enough, Jared. For my mom. For my grandma. For Max."

You're good enough for me, he wanted to say. But he couldn't. He couldn't because the whole time she'd been in Rocky Point he'd treated her like she wasn't.

"While I was in New York, I decided to be good enough for *me*. If I couldn't make anyone happy, I was going to at least make myself happy. I like my job okay, but I hate New York. You know when I came here, my stomach felt better? Then when I went back to New York, my ulcer flared up again. I've never felt more at peace than when I'm here, in Rocky Point . . . with you."

"Leah."

"I have friends here. I have a place here."

"I don't understand," he said, standing from the wobbly chair. He wanted to believe what she was saying, wanted to believe it with all his heart, but until she spelled it out for him, he couldn't.

She got off the floor and set the stuffed bear on a cardboard box. "Before I flew back to Rocky Point, I called Helen and asked her how much she wanted for the store. You know what she said?"

He shook his head.

"Free. She said I could have it. That means the debt that goes along with it, like stock and rent for the space, but she didn't want anything for the displays, racks, or the registers. On a twenty-minute phone call, she gave the store to me."

He couldn't wrap his mind around what she was telling him, and his tongue felt thick in his mouth when he asked, "The Supply Company's yours?"

"Yeah. Helen said she still wants to work here, part-time, but all the decisions will be mine. Scheduling the employees, paying taxes." She wrinkled her nose. "Repairs. There are few things she let slide for too long, like the flooring, but the store's mine."

"And you decided to move to Rocky Point even when you thought I was giving Rita a second chance?"

"It took a lot of soul-searching, but in the end, it was almost better we weren't speaking. Then I knew for certain the decision was mine. It will take some work, because there's one other thing I haven't told you."

He cuddled her to his chest. After what she said, anything else she had to say would be a small hurdle. "Whatever it is, we can handle it together."

She smiled and brushed her fingers across his cheek. Her touch gave him goosebumps, and anticipation for a future he wasn't sure he'd have after the way he treated her sparked in his heart.

"I hope so." She sighed. "My grandma has dementia. It's part of the reason she's cruel to me. Not all of it, she treated me with dislike and disdain my whole life, but it means she can't live on her own. It's not safe for her to be by herself, and she's been living in an assisted living facility for the last year. When Max left me, it pushed her over the edge. Maybe it was too close to how my dad left my mom, I don't know, but since then, I've been struggling to make ends meet."

"Money—"

"Isn't everything, I know. But I need you to understand what you're going to be dealing with if we try to build a life together."

He frowned. "I'm not going to let money determine how we live our lives. There are a lot of things we can do—"

"I've been thinking about that." She pulled away, and Jared let his arms drop to his sides. Without her close, he felt empty, but he let her pace the floor as she spoke aloud her thoughts. "Helen's been able to eke out a small living owning the store, but she made it clear her Social Security payments have helped her pay her bills. I know I need a way to make extra money, too."

"Leah, I can—"

"Please, let me finish. This is really important, and I need you to listen to everything before you say anything else, okay?"

He nodded, but at this point, nothing she could say would change his mind, or his heart. He could tell her for the rest of his life, but she would never fully understand how much it meant to him she decided to live in Rocky Point for herself and not for him. He'd never have to be afraid of her leaving because she loved it here as much as he did.

"Marnie gave me the idea, actually, when we were at the resort to feed the chipmunks."

"You've been thinking about moving here for that long?"

Leah shrugged and smiled ruefully. "Maybe back then I was thinking of what it could do for us, more than me, because . . . you told me, but I haven't told you. I love you.

I'm not sure when it happened. The first time we made love? When I fell though the ice and you did everything you could to make sure I wasn't hurt? Snowshoeing, maybe. Kissing under the northern lights. I don't know. But when Marnie and I went to the bathroom, the Supply Company wasn't on my radar yet and she told me I could always go back to headhunting. She's right. It's something I'm good at, and I made a good living doing it. I could work part-time out of Marengo, and that suits because I'm going to have to move my grandma, Jared. I can't leave her in New York and the small nursing home here doesn't have room."

He stepped forward. "I would never, ever, ask you to do that."

"I appreciate you saying it, but her care . . . moving her . . . the facility in Marengo is a lot cheaper than where she's at now, but it balances out because I won't have my salary from Outdoor Wonders. Paying for good care has been really hard."

"You've given this a lot of thought."

"I've had to. And it will be a while before I can completely move here. My grandma's only a part of it. I'll need to put a notice in at my job and sublet my apartment until my lease runs out." She laughed. "I don't know where I'm going to live. I'm staying at Autumn's right now."

"Come here." He held her in his arms and brushed his lips over hers. "I want to make love to you," he growled, frustrated, "but there's nowhere to go. Rita's at the house, and you're staying with Autumn. All the rooms in Rocky Point are booked."

"How about we at least get out of here?" she asked, wrapping her arms around his neck. "Helen can close the store. She said she hadn't planned on me being in."

"Sounds good. I know exactly where to go."

Leah clutched Jared's arm as he led her out of the store.

Helen beamed at them, and she waved.

Rocky Point was becoming familiar enough to her now she knew as he drove out of town they were heading toward the water tower.

Light snow started falling, creating a winter wonderland she knew she would never get tired of. He parked, opened her door, and brushed a kiss over her lips, a warm hand to her cheek. She could feel it in his touch, his love for her, but looking back, she always could, no matter the nasty things he said out of fear. Actions speak louder than words, and she forgot that in the abusive ways her grandma and Max treated her.

She paused on the stairs of the tower and lifted her face to the sky.

"You're so beautiful," he said, his warm breath whispering over her skin.

"You make me feel that way," she said, placing her mittened hands on his shoulders. "I've never felt the way I feel when I'm with you. My relationship with Max was all hard lines and sharp edges. I mistook it for adventure, excitement. He wasn't who I thought he was, and his moods were dangerous. I wasn't who he thought I was, either. He decided he didn't like me, and after a while, he let me know it."

He brushed a snowflake off her cheek. Sparks lit his eyes, and happiness radiated from him. It gave her so much joy she could make him feel like that after what they'd been through.

"I know this has been fast. It feels like I met you and *boom,* you were all I could think about. But we don't have to . . . I mean . . . we can take our time. We should, so you know this is right. I love you, Leah, and I can say I'll never hurt you, but you won't believe that yet because it's all I've done."

She rested her forehead against his, her palms suddenly damp inside her choppers. "You have, but it's how I knew this was real. Max didn't hurt me, only tore at scabs I already had. What happened between you and me, it was different somehow. The pain was different somehow, deeper, maybe. Newer."

"Leah—"

"No. I don't want to hurt you by telling you this. I want you to understand that these past few days, they were difficult, but they meant something. They're the start of something good, and I'm sure, Jared, I'm sure. I want to get married. You want to get married, don't you?"

Laughing, he nudged her up the stairs, a hand to the small of her back to steady her. She'd never felt more steady, Jared there to support her.

The sun was beginning to set, casting a pink glow over the white horizon, and they looked across the frozen lake.

"I think that's supposed to be my question for you," he said, cuddling her to him and tucking her head under his chin. "I don't want to rush you, but, yeah, eventually I would like to get married. You said you didn't want to be a mom, but maybe . . . maybe someday we can talk about kids?"

"I'm not sure. My childhood, how my mother left me. I'll need time to get used to this life, this life with you. We have time to think about it, don't we?" She didn't know how to be a good mother, but Jared was an excellent father. She knew that by how he'd raised Briar to be a sweet, caring young woman. He'd teach her, show her how to love a child who would love her, too.

"Yeah, we do. We have a lot of time, but there's something else I wanted to talk to you about."

She stiffened. She thought they'd covered everything. "What?"

He kissed her. A long, slow kiss before answering, her lips trembling. He leaned away and she whimpered in protest. He chuckled. Things were going to be okay. "I think I should sell my house. We could buy something new, start our lives in a house we pick out together."

She stared over the water. "You don't have to . . . I mean, if we're going to date a while . . . but I'll have to figure out something. I can't impose on Autumn forever, even if she says I can."

"We'll work it out. I want to share a bed with you, Leah. Wake up to you, bring you coffee in the morning. A lot of time has already gone by, too much, for both of us. But things move slowly here, and it could be months before my house sells. We'll hurry up and wait, but it feels right. It will give us what we need. Time to get to know each other, but security knowing we're moving forward."

"Okay. I've hurried all my life, chasing what? I don't know. Happiness? Someone who would love me? I found those things, here, and moving slow now is fine. I need to be able to breathe."

"Good. Always tell me if there's something you need, Leah. You're not alone and I want you to always be happy here. Happy with me. Rita wanted more and that's not my fault, but please, give me time to fix something if it breaks. She hid how she felt, never said anything until she was packing, and I won't know if you don't tell me."

"I promise, if you promise the same. I don't have much, I never have, but all that I do have, you're welcome to."

"That you're here and you love me is enough. Maybe it hasn't been for other people in your life, but it is for me." He hugged the woman he'd fallen in love with, her lithe body molding to his perfectly, despite their bulky jackets.

For the first time in five years, he could see a bright future, for him and his family.

"My mom and dad are in town. Someone at the arena called them when I didn't show up for work. Do you want to go over to the house and meet them?"

"The crash . . . Jared." She turned in his arms and buried her face against his chest. "I was so scared."

"I was stupid, the way I treated you. I was afraid of my own feelings, and I took them out on you. The crash wasn't serious, sweetheart, and all I could think about was getting back to you. It made me see I was making things harder than they had to be. If you love someone, you make it work, simple as that."

"Is Briar okay with this?"

"She told me where you were. She's very much okay with this and said not to blow it."

"That's why she asked me where I was." She laughed.

"Yeah. So she could tell me. I think you'll have plenty of help with the store. She's looking forward to spending time with you."

"I'm looking forward to it, too." She paused. "I wasn't trying to be her mother."

"I know, and I'm sorry I said that. I was scared. I could

see you in our lives so easily and I had no idea how I was going to make that happen. If I even could. But you're part of my family now, and she'll look up to you like I do. I love you very much." He kissed her again, covering her cold lips with his. "Are you ready to go?"

She blew out a breath. "Your mom and dad, huh?"

"They'll love you as much as I do. I promise."

"Okay. I trust you."

"Then let's go ho—" He almost said home, and he sighed.

"Hey," she said softly, and he looked into her silver eyes. "It doesn't matter if we don't have a place to live yet. My home is in your arms, and I'm already there."

"Then let's sit for a little longer."

He sat on the grated platform and snuggled her between his legs. Rocky Point was spread out before them, a little town on a lake that gave him everything he needed. She rested her head on his shoulder and he tangled his fingers in her hair. They'd make this sleepy little town theirs, and he knew, without a doubt, that because she chose to stay, she'd make all his frozen dreams come true.

Logan and Ivy's story is now available! *Her Frozen Memories* is available on Kindle, in Kindle Unlimited, and Paperback.

Do you like billionaire romance? Sign up for my newsletter and receive a free standalone novel, an ugly-duckling billionaire romance, *My Biggest Mistake*. There you'll be the first to know of sales, new releases, and what I'm working on. Don't miss out! Go to www.vmrheault.com/subscribe.

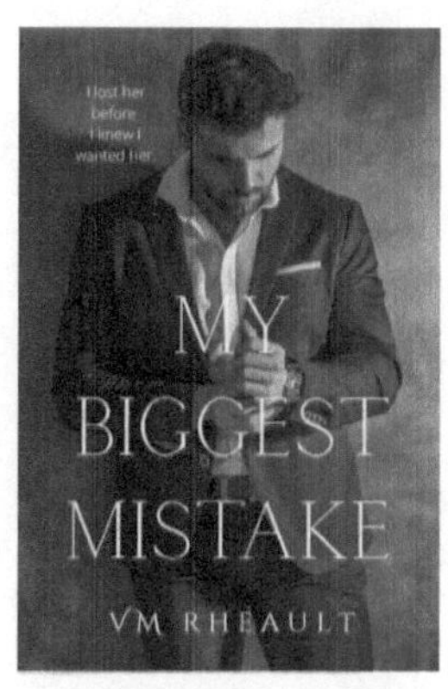

ALSO BY VANIA RHEAULT

Don't Run Away

(Tower City Romance Trilogy Book One)

Chasing You

(Tower City Romance Trilogy Book Two)

Running Scared

(Tower City Romance Trilogy Book Three)

The Finish Line

(Tower City Romance Trilogy Book Four,

Bonus Novella)

Wherever He Goes

(A Steamy Forced Proximity Standalone)

The Years Between Us

(A Steamy Age-Gap Standalone)

All of Nothing

(A Steamy Enemies to Lovers Standalone)

His Frozen Heart

(A Rocky Point Wedding Book One)

His Frozen Dreams

(A Rocky Point Wedding Book Two)

Her Frozen Memories

(A Rocky Point Wedding Book Three)

Her Frozen Promises

(A Rocky Point Wedding Book Four)

As VM Rheault

Captivated by Her (Cedar Hill Duet Book One)

Addicted to Her (Cedar Hill Duet Book Two)

Rescue Me

Give & Take (The Lost & Found Trilogy Book One)

Lost & Found (The Lost & Found Trilogy Book Two)

Safe & Sound (The Lost & Found Trilogy Book Three)

Faking Forever

Twisted Alibis (Ghost Town Trilogy Book One)

Twisted Lullabies (Ghost Town Trilogy Book Two)

Twisted Lies (Ghost Town Trilogy Book Three)

A Heartache for Christmas

Cruel Fate (King's Crossing Book One)

Cruel Hearts (King's Crossing Book Two)

Cruel Dreams (King's Crossing Book Three)

Shattered Fate (King's Crossing Book Four)

Shattered Hearts (King's Crossing Book Five)

Shattered Dreams (King's Crossing Book Six)

ABOUT THE AUTHOR

Vania Rheault has lived in Minnesota all her life. In 2003, she graduated with a BA in English with a concentration in creative writing from Minnesota State University, Moorhead. When she's not writing, she's sleeping, working her day job, or going to movie night with her sister.
Find her at vmrheault.com